SLIPPING
THE CABLE

By Bill Schweigart

Martin Sisters Publishing

Published by
Ivy House Books, a division of Martin Sisters Publishing, LLC
www. martinsisterspublishing. com
Copyright © 2012 Bill Schweigart
ISBN: 978-1-937273-71-2
Fiction/Thriller
Cover design by Scott Trolan
Printed in the United States of America
Martin Sisters Publishing, LLC

DEDICATION

For Dad and Pop – none of this would have been possible without both of you. And for the men and women of the U.S. Coast Guard, who always go out but don't always come back.

ACKNOWLEGEMENTS

Many people were responsible for this novel, from helping it embark on its voyage years ago to guiding it to its new homeport, in your hands. The danger of making a list is that you inevitably forget someone, so forgive me if I accidentally left you off. Please accept this blanket, heartfelt thank you and I apologize doubly if I inflicted an early draft upon you.

To my professors, Jordon Pecile, Janet Peery, and Sheri Reynolds, thank you for introducing me to the world of writing, and for providing me the writer's equivalent of a nautical chart, clearly marking the ways to transit safely as well as the rocks. Before you can break the rules, you have to learn them, and I learned from the best. If this novel is effective at all, credit them and I'll take responsibility for the rest.

Similarly, credit for any heroics and high adventure found within these pages belongs to the men and women of the United States Coast Guard. With Coasties as your characters, you're already halfway to telling an interesting story. And I had the excellent fortune to know, and be inspired by, many Coasties. Thank you to my classmates at the U.S. Coast Guard Academy ('95!) and my shipmates aboard the Coast Guard Cutter BEAR. You have no idea how proud I am to be associated with you. And special thanks to two Coasties in particular: Jorge Martinez, who I've been in awe of since we first met and who I consider to be the consummate Coast Guardsman, and George Bamford, who has provided me with every manner of support over the years, none more valuable than his steadfast friendship and counsel.

Then there are the alchemists who turned a pipe dream into reality, and reality into a handsome product. Thank you to Denise Melton and Melissa Newman of Martin Sisters Publishing for taking a chance on me and for smoothing over the rough edges. And to Scott Trolan, who provided the striking cover design.

Finally, thank you to my family, whose support of me passed unwavering long ago to border mania. To my incandescent Kate and my ray of sunshine Sidney, to my loving mother Linda, to my stalwart sister Jaclin – to further strain the nautical metaphor, for years you've filled my sails with the wind I needed during my doldrums. And thank you to my grandmother Marion, my Gilligans, my Hansens, my Schweigarts, my friends far and wide – cheerleaders all. And finally, to my grandfather Jack Sensor and my father Bill Schweigart, gone but not forgotten. Pop, you're all over this book in the most obvious way possible – thank you for serving as the story's true north. Less obvious but no less important, Dad, thank you for the steel in my spine. You don't get anywhere without first having the guts to cast off, and you're still the sturdy deck under my feet.

An imprint of Martin Sisters Publishing, LLC

PROLOGUE

From the *Ocean City Gazette*, dated July 20, 1996:

Memorial services to be held for local Coastie lost in hurricane

Memorial services will be held for Ensign Kelly Sensor, one of the sailors presumed dead in the July 13 Potomac River collision between the Coast Guard Cutter Sentinel *and the fishing boat* Gloria May. *Divers spent the weekend on scene attempting to salvage the sunken fishing vessel, while Coast Guard boats and aircraft searched the river and Chesapeake Bay for survivors. Several bodies of Coast Guardsmen were recovered by divers belowdecks before* Sentinel *was towed to Baltimore, but earlier this week, Coast Guard Commander of Atlantic Area Operations, Admiral Roger Stokes, downgraded the ongoing search from "rescue to recovery." To date, the body of Ensign Sensor has yet to be recovered, but the hope of recovering any more bodies, let alone survivors, is "highly unlikely," according to Stokes. The cutter and fishing boat collided while trying to evade Hurricane Bertha, the storm that raked Ocean City and much of the Northeast last week with high winds and rain. Sensor, 22, who had been serving aboard* Sentinel *since June of last year, was a long-time resident of Ocean City until his appointment to the Coast Guard Academy in 1991. Memorial services will be held at the Trinity Methodist Church in Marmora tomorrow at 3:00 p.m.*

Chapter 1

Equilibrium, the word bounced on Ensign Kelly Sensor's tongue as his ship, the Coast Guard Cutter *Sentinel*, pitched and rolled on the heaving March waters of the Caribbean Sea. He repeated the word, hoping to invoke it. Instead, he retched once more into the toilet of his stateroom's head.

The sea was rough and Kelly had been vomiting since reveille with little relief. It was only mid-day, but he had already voided all of the food and water in his system and was now coughing up yellow bile. What little he had urinated today burned.

Kelly had heard tales of men so delirious from seasickness they had jumped overboard, to be washed every which way, to be a part of the ocean rather than battling above it. They didn't seem so crazy now.

Kelly was finishing another volley when "Now Ensign Sensor, lay to the bridge" boomed from the loudspeaker outside, echoing through the passageways of *Sentinel*. Custom dictated that when an officer is needed, the standard announcement is Your presence is requested; the pipe Lay to was reserved for the enlisted. Though a minor indignity, it meant the captain was on the bridge, and that greater humiliations were forthcoming.

"You hear that?" a voice called from the other side of the door.

"Got it," said Kelly.

"If something hairy comes up, swallow. It's your balls."

Kelly swept his fingers through his dirty blond hair, now matted with perspiration to his forehead. He rose, swaying, then tucked in his shirt, smoothed his rumpled uniform, and emerged from the head. Jorge Vargas lay on his rack with his fingers interlaced behind his head and a tight grin on his narrow, aquiline face. Pound for pound, Kelly believed the diminutive Cuban to be the strongest son of a bitch to ever walk the halls of the U.S. Coast Guard Academy. He was built like a prizefighter and upperclassmen hoping to discipline him with pushups had only exhausted themselves. Better, Jorge made the unbearable laughable, a knack Kelly appreciated since their first day of Swab Summer four years earlier.

"I grow up at the Jersey shore and puke. You grow up in Newark," said Kelly, splashing cold water on his face at the basin, "and nothing."

Jorge smiled. Even when he smiled, Kelly thought, he had the look of a predator. "You got 'laid' again. The captain must be up."

"Here we go."

Kelly walked past Vargas and out of the stateroom. He swayed through the narrow passageways of Officer's Country as the ship jerked randomly. The corridors smelled of sweat and cleanser and mop water, of corners that never stayed clean. He stopped at the foot of the bridge and took a small sip of water from the scuttlebutt at the bottom of the ladder. He listened. The only other sound from the bridge was the hiss of ocean spray against the windows. It never fails, Kelly thought. No matter how interesting a conversation was between the bridge watchstanders—and the livelier the weather, the livelier the sea stories—it trailed off within seconds of the captain's arrival. Kelly took a deep breath and mounted the steps.

He saluted as soon as he set foot on the bridge. To his right, he saw Commander Aregood in his captain's chair, staring out to sea. He slowly twirled the blade of his marlinspike, a nautical pocketknife with a point metal spike, on his palm. After a few moments frozen in salute, Kelly cleared his throat.

"Good afternoon, captain."

Aregood returned the salute but continued to face front, toward the windows of the bridge, out to sea.

"Have your celestial navigation qualifications been signed off yet?"

Celestial navigation—driving the ship by the stars—was one of the many areas Officers of the Deck were to master aboard *Sentinel*. It required "shooting" the horizon with a sextant, an instrument resembling equal parts gun, compass, and telescope. With it, and a level horizon, a sailor could determine the angle to a celestial body and with further calculations his latitude and longitude. Kelly looked at the imposing seas.

"Yes, sir."

"Well, it can never hurt to practice."

Kelly looked through the windows again. Twenty-foot waves rocked their blunt-nosed, 270-foot cutter. The sky was gray, the sun missing.

"Captain, the horizon…there isn't one."

"Just think how well you'll be able to shoot one when there is. Harmon, give Sensor a sextant."

The Quartermaster of the Watch, Petty Officer Second Class Sean Harmon, opened a drawer beneath his chart table, removed the sextant, and handed it to Kelly. Harmon's movements were slow and his face yellowish green, and Kelly noticed a small white trash bag looped into his belt. The petty officer must have had a similar morning, and for a moment, Kelly regarded the quartermaster with empathy.

"You break it, you buy it."

New junior officers, the "boot" ensigns, were never particularly popular aboard ship, and clearly Harmon was not about to risk the ire of the captain with courtesy toward him. But to go out of your way in the other direction.... Before he could finish his thought, a glint caught his eye. The captain, eased back in his chair, crossed his legs and revealed a small silver tab affixed to the sole of his shoe. Made for military drill teams, not shipboard life, they sent out rattling reports that preceded Aregood wherever he went. For no purpose whatsoever, thought Kelly, unless you're in love with the sound of your own footfalls.

The ensign stepped out onto the bridgewing and faced the sea. It was dangerous to be topside with the waves pitching the cutter so. He made his way to the mounted compass and alidade, which rested atop a sturdy, four-foot stand. When the conning officers swiveled the alidade toward a passing ship, it indicated the true and relative bearing of the other vessel. Today, Kelly used it solely for balance. He wedged himself into the small space between it and the chest-high bulkhead as he adjusted the knobs on the sextant and pretended to fix on the absent horizon of the Windward Passage, the channel between Cuba and Haiti. The weather decks should be secured, he thought.

What am I doing here?

It was Jack's certificate. It always had been.

Since he was eight years old. Since the day he found it in his grandfather's old cigar box the summer he adopted him. The paper was thin, but Kelly handled it as if it were ancient parchment. He unfolded it gently and was surprised by its detail. A fiery sun broke over crests of waves thick with sea-life. Mighty King Neptune rode a skiff pulled by sharks and dolphins and porpoises. His trident and crown gleamed, reflected in the full breasts of the mermaids found in each corner of the certificate. It was a photocopy, in black and white, but Kelly saw the colors. An inscription had Jack's name;

his ship, the USS *Burns*; the exact position of the crossing; and the reason for the transit. For action against the enemy.

No matter how many times Jack described what he had to endure to get it, it never fazed Kelly. Not the gauntlet of shellbacks wielding their sun-dried canvas bats stuffed with rags. Not the cook who rammed dough and grease into his Jack's mouth and dunked him in a shallow pool until he threw up. Not the one who prodded an electric wand to Jack's testicles while he stood naked and wet on a steel deck. And not all of them, who swung their canvas shillelaghs in high, wide arcs down on his grandfather's back as he crawled through a tunnel filled with coffee grounds, egg shells, and cigarette butts. All Kelly ever saw was the colors. Not even tales of Jack's first ship, USS *Donnell*, the one that got torpedoed, would dissuade Kelly from joining the service, and someday getting his own certificate. And he had. For a price.

"It was just a silly tradition," Jack had said once.

"It's not silly, Pop. It means something."

"Whatever it means, you can't get away with that kind of baloney these days."

Sentinel slid down the face of a twenty-five foot wave and Kelly, lost in the colors, went weightless. The cutter landed in the trough with a jolt. The impact knocked Kelly off the alidade and into the bulkhead. He felt it in his kidneys. The next lurch of the ship caught him off balance and pitched him headfirst back into the alidade. He went down. A strange heat flowed down his right cheek. On his hands and knees, he wiped his forehead in the crook of the arm still clutching the sextant. It came back red.

A vague sensation nagged at him. Something hiding behind the pain. Too late, he realized his mistake—he had spent too much time collecting himself. His concentration had been siphoned to things like his head and his back and his balance, and away from maintaining his tenuous equilibrium. His body began to buckle. Train's coming, he thought.

With a final burst of energy, he scrambled to the open section of the bridgewing, a small platform that hung over the water, barely large enough for two people. The sea, on a calm day, was thirty feet below. All Kelly could see now were whitecaps.

Suddenly, there was a terminal lurch in his abdomen and a roaring in his ears. His throat distended. Everything came up in a hot rush. Kelly was amazed by the reservoir of sickness he had tapped into; things he barely remembered eating now revealed themselves. Chunks of half-digested Saltines shot forth like doughy bullets. Soda burned as if its original can was forcing its way back up his esophagus. God, I'll never eat clam chowder again, he thought.

Kelly vowed to get drunk as soon as he reached land again. The next time he puked, he swore it would be on his own terms, at least the result of something fun. And no sooner had he made his pledge, it was over. The relief was immediate. From his vantage on the bridgewing, he could see the side of the bow with its wide, familiar red stripe and a thinner blue one just aft of that. The cutter bit into another swell and a startled school of flying fish freed itself from the bow wave and skittered away on the surface. The seas were still as rough as before, but the nausea was gone. For now.

"That will cost you."

Kelly spun around on all fours and saw a pair of knees. He looked up and saw his captain, standing five and a half feet and topped with a shock of red hair, smiling down at him. His own noisy retching must have drowned out the normal clacking of Aregood's approach. Kelly hauled his drained and shaky body to its feet, making sure to look the captain in the eye as he rose. This was not the first time Aregood had summoned him to the bridge for sport, but this must have been the most satisfying. Blood flowed from the gash on his head. His head rung and his back ached. He looked down at the sextant in his hand and saw the crack in its eyepiece.

"You can make a check out to the quartermasters' division," said the captain.

Kelly gripped the gun-like handle tightly. He turned it over in his hand, palm up.

Aregood smiled with no warmth and held out his hand. "Here."

Kelly held onto the post with one hand, and curling his other arm, lifted the sextant to his hip. Pointing it in the direction of his captain, the ensign held it out for him. Before Aregood grabbed it, Kelly looked him in the eye and triggered his forefinger slightly. Aregood saw. Both men swayed in tandem as the cutter buffeted the next wave, their eyes locked. Aregood's smile curdled. He snatched the instrument and turned his back on the ensign.

Kelly followed his captain into the pilothouse. Without breaking stride, Aregood dropped the sextant on Harmon's chart table, who looked at the ensign spitefully. In an exaggerated motion, Kelly flung his hands down, shaking the ocean spray from his windbreaker and spattering the quartermaster's chart.

Kelly started toward the ladder below, but stopped short. He took a deep breath and faced the captain's chair. Rankled and bleeding, he fought to sound even, but monotonous was as close as he could come. "Permission to go below, sir?"

"Permission granted."

Kelly started down the steps.

"Clean yourself up, ensign," Kelly heard over his shoulder, "you're breaking in next watch."

Chapter 2

Ensign Jorge Vargas entered the stateroom holding purloined food in one hand while the other searched for the light switch. As their stateroom was inboard, with no porthole or access to sunlight, when the lights were out the darkness was total, and his roommate liked the lights out when he slept. This made Jorge uncomfortable, reminded him of his father's prison stories. He found the switch, turned it halfway, and the room was bathed in a sanguine glow. The red light illuminated the stateroom enough to see, but not enough to spoil his night vision.

He passed the racks quickly and walked to his desk. He glanced at Kelly's desk. Among his roommate's effects – papers, nautical manuals, a picture of his grandfather fishing by their house at the Jersey shore – Jorge spied a bottle of hydrogen peroxide and a bag of cotton balls. He peered in the wastebasket by the desk and saw several more of the white balls, compacted and wet with blood.

Jorge walked back to the bunks. The only souvenir Jorge could see from the afternoon was a Band-Aid above Kelly's left eye, and the dark line that rimmed it where the blood had dried and crusted black. The red light hid everything else. Jorge shook his head and returned to his desk.

Kelly Sensor had been the most conscientious cadet Jorge had ever met. So much so, that from their first summer together Jorge felt compelled to loosen him up. And for the next four years in New London, Jorge took great pride in that whenever Sensor had gotten into trouble, he was usually behind it. Jorge had looked forward to continuing that tradition when he learned they were assigned to the same ship. Once aboard though, Kelly found trouble all by himself.

During their first patrol, *Sentinel* had completed a joint exercise with the Colombian Navy in the Pacific when the captain ordered they steam the sixty nautical miles to the Equator and induct all of the pollywogs onboard, including he and Kelly, into the Ancient Order of Shellbacks. The crew was in high spirits. Even when Gaskey, the large gunner's mate, commenced the ceremony by lining all the pollywogs on the fantail and showering them with frigid water from the fire house. It was overcast on the day of the crossing and before long, Jorge was freezing. Kelly stood next to him, but all chatter had stopped and there were no distractions from the chill. Jorge thought of Cuba. Of hot summer days, throwing seashells at the banana rats with his brother and eating mangoes. Of torrid nights, the soothing hum of cicadas. Of warmth.

After forty-five minutes, Jorge sat with his knees drawn to his chin. The hose was biting. He was prepared to think about the sloop, the hottest he had ever been, when Everline lost it. Secure those fucking hoses...we've had enough.... Everline may have been a pollywog, but he was still an officer, and the party seemed over until Kelly piped up....

"How was dinner?" asked the ensign.

Jorge opened his eyes and stretched. "Uncomfortable silence broken by bursts of shameless ass-kissing. The usual. No one mentioned your little training session today."

"Good."

"Here." He threw the fruit cup at Kelly.

"You're a king."

"Still puking?"

"Not since the bridge. Dry heaved a bit though." He fished a peach wedge out of the cup and popped it into his mouth. "You get nothing for your work."

"It's getting out of hand up there."

"The seas are lying down."

"Not what I mean. You should have the corpsman look at that gash."

Kelly stopped eating. "Would you have?"

Jorge grinned. "You could've gone over the fucking side."

"And whose fault would that have been then?"

"You did call Everline a pussy in front of the whole crew."

"No I didn't."

"Sorry. A fucking pussy."

"Credit where credit's due, thank you very much."

"That fucking pussy is still a lieutenant."

"Lieutenant junior grade." Kelly laughed, winced. "I think we're even."

"I've got the twenty to twenty-four hundred watch." Jorge rose. "You want to take a header into the drink, I get the stateroom to myself."

"A bona fide, qualified officer of the deck."

"You want I shouldn't have qualified?"

"Don't listen to me. I'm just pissed."

"It'll happen soon enough."

Jorge grabbed his blue ball cap with the golden ensign's bar pinned to its forehead and "*Sentinel*" stitched in yellow lettering above it, and headed for the stateroom door. As he pulled it on, his roommate lay back down.

"Fade to black, Jorge. And thanks for the grub."

Jorge passed through Officer's Country, past the captain's cabin, to the ladder. Before assuming a watch, an officer of the deck was required to complete a "round" of the cutter for safety, so instead of climbing to the bridge Jorge descended to the main deck, then down further into the bowels of the ship, to the engine room. After getting the status of the ship's main engines, Jorge ascended to the main deck again. He walked to the forecastle, as far forward on the cutter as one could go. He then walked aft down the main passageway, which ran the length of the entire ship, passing berthing areas for the crew, the ship's office, the wardroom where the officers dined, and the mess deck, where crewmembers were playing cards and watching a movie. Aft, he descended another ladder to the small arms locker, where the weapons and gear for the boarding teams were kept. Jorge climbed the ladder back up to the passageway, which had reached its end. As far aft as he could walk on the inside the ship, he stepped outside.

Jorge was greeted by complete darkness. Below, the propellers hummed and the ocean hissed. Above him, one by one, the stars revealed themselves as his vision adjusted. Off the port side, to the south, laid Cuba. He could not see it, but he felt it.

When Castro purged his jails in 1980 and opened Mariel to the world, it was to these very waters where his family fled. His father, a journalist during Batista and thrown in prison under Fidel, did not hesitate. He traded all the family owned for their spots on a sloop, for the chance to escape. The ocean would deliver them to America and a new life. The ocean always delivered, he promised. On the fourth night, the ocean did not deliver the sloop to America but it delivered America to them. Jorge awoke, dehydrated and raging with fever, to the sounds of yelling. Their craft was awash with light. The sweeping light came from another, larger vessel, the largest Jorge had ever seen. In the moonlight, it was as white as fresh laundry but for a thick red stripe next to a thinner blue one on the bow. Through cracked lips, he asked his father what it was.

"*Son los angeles, mijito.* Angels."

With his vision fully adjusted to the night, Jorge inspected the ready boat on the fantail, then climbed the ladder to the flight deck. He crossed that wide, open area to the second ready boat, gave it a look, then continued toward the helicopter hangar. At the far end of the hangar, he passed through the watertight door right back into Officers Country. With his circuit of *Sentinel* complete after twenty minutes, Jorge headed past his and Kelly's stateroom once more to the ladder that led to the bridge.

This time, he paused outside the captain's cabin and listened. Typing. It was the same every night, sometimes for hours. "War and fucking Peace," he said under his breath. He climbed the ladder.

Next Jorge made a circuit of the bridge itself. He read *Sentinel*'s latitude and longitude on GPS, logged the coordinates, then plotted them on the chart. He read the previous watch's log, checked the weather entries, then asked the helmsman, a skinny kid named Irving, for their course and their speed. He moved to the radar. No contacts.

Finally, he approached the officer of the deck, Everline. "Got anything?"

"Nothing to be scared of, Var-gas," replied the lieutenant. "We're out of that squall system."

"*Mar de leva.*"

"What'd you call me, boot?"

"It's a *mar de leva*. A Caribbean wind storm. It lasts for a couple of days. The wind picks up, the sea swells. Kind of like a nor'easter, but without the rain. It's common this time of year."

Everline looked quickly over his shoulder at the rest of the bridge team. "Whatever. It's quiet tonight. Don't fuck it up, boot."

"Well, I'll be sure to avoid those squalls," said Jorge. He saluted.

Everline returned the salute half-heartedly. "On the bridge, this is Mr. Everline. Mr. Var-gaaas has the deck and the conn."

The bridge team shouted, "Aye!"

The next three hours passed quietly. Every hour, the helmsman and the lookout switched positions to stay alert, reporting their information to Jorge as they assumed the other's position. He barely listened. He roamed the pilothouse. He checked the radar incessantly. He stalked the bridgewings, scanning the horizon for contacts, but they were alone in their small sector of ocean, steaming toward the Gulf of Mexico and Key West. Cuba passed below them.

"Mr. Vargas, is that true about the wind storm, the mar de lever?" asked Harmon.

"*De leva*. Yeah. Surfers dig it. Sailors, not so much."

"Looking forward to mid-patrol break?"

"Hell yes."

"Some pretty crazy shit up here today, huh, sir?"

"A few days in Key West will do us all some good."

The skinny helmsman chimed in. "Yeah, what was that all about, Mr. Vargas?"

"Don't worry about it, Irving."

"That guy's trouble, sir. Why do you hang out with him?"

Jorge glared at the helmsman. Irving slowly closed his mouth.

Jorge looked at the quartermaster next.

"Don't look at me, sir. I didn't say a word."

"You think it though."

"He did bust the sextant today. The good one."

"Like he had a fucking choice...." Jorge paused. He had to choose his words carefully. He did not want to undermine the command, even if the command was a prick. It was the principle of it.

"It was pretty funny though," said Irving.

Jorge spun on the helmsman. "One more word out you, Seaman Irving, and they'll be pulling that helm out of your ass." The green light thrown off by the radar swept across their faces. With each pass, Irving's expression fell further, until he was staring at his shoes. Suddenly, Jorge felt very tired. It was nearing midnight, the end of his watch and a very long day. Jorge walked out to the bridgewing. The wind cooled his face. He exhaled loudly.

A few moments later, Harmon stepped outside. "Sign the logs please, Mr. Vargas?"

"Sure."

"With all due respect sir, he is kind of jinxed."

"I might give you that, Sean."

Jorge was quiet for a while. Harmon looked over the bow and into the night.

"I don't know," said Jorge. "The captain, the crew, even the ocean kicks his ass. And he's still into all of this."

"Aren't you?" asked Harmon.

"Yeah." Jorge thought about his father, the sloop, and the great white boat. He then thought about his friend's halcyon home by the sea. "But he doesn't have to be."

Chapter 3

Commander Kevin Aregood sat at the head of the wardroom's table, presiding over another silent meal. He looked to his right. The executive officer, Lieutenant Commander Richard Tyndale sat poised for the slightest command. The man never missed a meal. The paunchy, balding man was a bootlick, but there were worse examples to set for the rest of his crew.

To the captain's left sat *Sentinel*'s operations officer, Lieutenant Keith Griffin, who stared at his plate as if it held a secret. Aregood considered LT Griffin to be one of the cutter's milder disappointments, a lanky, bookish man who, though he never really disobeyed orders, carried them out with such a complete lack of vigor that he may as well have.

Aregood surveyed the length of the wardroom's table. At the other end, among the dining officers, he noticed Vargas, and was pleased to note Sensor's absence from the meal. The boy had nearly broken on the bridgewing today, but when he handed over the sextant... He took a deep breath and concentrated on loosening his jaw.

The clink of a glass brought him back to his surroundings, to his officers and their silence. Kevin Aregood did not mind the silence. Still, he had to promote some conversation if only for the training of the junior officers. He turned again to his right.

"Two more days, XO."

"Key West is one of the crew's favorite ports, sir," answered Tyndale. "Excellent choice, captain."

"Speaking of Key West, who has the port brief?"

Griffin looked up from his plate. "Everline, sir. I think."

"Steve's been here almost two years now. What do you say to using one of our new ensigns? I'm sure they could use the experience."

"Aye, captain...."

"Good." He put his elbows on the table and interlaced his fingers. Resting his chin on his knuckles, he closed his eyes. Giving it to Sensor would be too obvious, especially after today. When he opened his eyes, his second-in-command was waiting. Aregood lifted his little finger toward the sole ensign at the other end of the table.

"Vargas," said Tyndale, "you're up."

Vargas looked up from his plate. He stared at the XO with a grave expression. "Is it because I'm Hispanic, sir?"

Aregood glanced quickly at his second-in-command to gauge his reaction. Tyndale was aghast. He tried to respond, but could not find the words and looked to his captain for guidance. Aregood offered none.

As Tyndale began to stammer, Vargas exploded into laughter. The free sound of it rang out in the wardroom, and the other officers squirmed. Aregood smiled tightly while his executive officer flushed. As quickly as the laughter burst forth, the walls of the wardroom absorbed it. Silence returned to the table once more.

"My apologies, sir. Just having some fun," said Vargas. "Excuse me please, captain?" He leaned forward, hands on the arms of his chair, ready to leave. He looked pleased with himself.

The captain responded with a jovial wave of his hand. "Leave at will, everyone," he said. Vargas rose and walked quickly toward the door. Aregood noticed he was concealing food behind him.

"Mr. Vargas?"

"Yes, sir?"

"Will this be your first time in Key West?"

The ensign stopped short. Aregood and Vargas regarded each other until all traces of the ensign's smile had vanished. "No," he said. "Sir."

Ah, thought Aregood. The last laugh.

After dinner, Aregood's strolled the main passageway, his footsteps echoing ahead of him. Loitering crewmembers scurried into their berthing areas. He contemplated Vargas. Everything the boy said had an edge to it. If anyone ought to show respect....

He was familiar with Vargas' history, of Mariel, and his boat ride to America. Sixteen years ago, Aregood himself had been involved in the massive exodus of 1980, when over 100 Coast Guard cutters and small boats were deployed to rescue the fleeing Cubans in the Straits of Florida. Aregood was a lieutenant junior grade at the time, just one rank higher than Vargas was now, and in command a 95-foot patrol boat, CGC *Cape Hatteras*. Though he despised overcrowding his pristine boat with filthy Cubans, he realized the potential in such a high-profile mission. When refugees were spotted, rather than remain on the bridge, Aregood left one of his crew to drive the cutter, while he waited on the boat deck with the enlisted. He equipped one of his men with a camera, and whenever children were brought aboard, Aregood ordered that it was he, with his muscular arms, who plucked his little neighbors from the south from their rickety crafts. During the rescue of a dilapidated fishing boat, Aregood was photographed leaning over the rail with his arms outstretched, grasping a baby a hopeful mother passed to him. The picture landed on the cover of Newsweek. He had been on the fast track ever since. When he entered his cabin, he was greeted by the very same picture, framed and hung alongside a feature on the dashing young skipper from The *St. Petersburg Times* entitled "Coast Guard Saviors."

Despite the ensign's smart mouth, Vargas was untouchable. Mostly. Any obvious poor treatment of him could be perceived as discrimination. Aregood feared those "soft" career killers more than running *Sentinel* hard aground. He had even used his detailer contacts to ensure that no women were sent to *Sentinel*—one less potential for scandal—so he was not about to risk twenty unblemished years on one cocky wetback. Even if Vargas suspected it, it was better to treat him with kid gloves.

And there was an upside. Once again, Cubans could prove to be his good luck charm. A former migrant rescued by the Coast Guard, now himself a Coast Guard officer and serving aboard a cutter commanded by one of the Mariel Boatlift's biggest heroes.... The first chance he had, the very first vital evolution Vargas participated in, he would call Public Affairs in Washington, maybe even some local newspapers. Making captain was already a lock, but Vargas might take him all the way to admiral.

That left him Sensor, *Sentinel*'s greatest disappointment.

It was during the shellback festivities last summer when Aregood overheard Seaman Irving tell a crewmember about one of the new ensigns mouthing off to Everline. Lieutenant Junior Grade Everline was a buffoon, but he outranked ensigns, pure and simple. He summoned Irving to his cabin to relate the story in full.

"Tell me exactly what Vargas said," ordered Aregood.

"Vargas? No, sir. It was Sensor."

The captain was dumbstruck. Ensign Sensor had been squared away, respectful. He had only been aboard for a month, fresh out of the Academy, but he showed promise. Aregood felt as if his hand, offering a bright future, had been slapped away.

Irving smiled as he told the story. He may as well have been laughing at him. He had been laughing about it before on the mess deck, and now he was laughing about it in the cabin. At attention, laughing. Aregood slammed his fist on the desk. Irving recoiled, lost his balance, and fell into the cabin door. He jumped back to attention.

Aregood's face burned. He took several deep breaths until his pulse slowed. This was not about the seaman.

"Irving, I'm sorry. Sit, please. Carry on."

Irving took a seat, slowly, watching his captain.

"What's sad is that you're the victim here."

"Me?"

"We have a chain of command for a reason, son. On one end is you, doing all of your fine work for this ship. On the other end is me, making sure that you – and the crew – are taken care of, but when there's a disruption in the chain like this, I have to spend all of my time and energy on the weak links and not the strong ones like you. If I had some help from the crew, I could spend more time promoting those strong links, calling their detailers to put in a good word. Follow?"

Irving leaned back in his chair. "How can I help?"

"First, this conversation never happened."

"And second?"

"The crew." Aregood smiled. "Tell them about the chain. And about Sensor."

"What'll I tell them, sir?"

"Whatever I tell you to."

Two hours after dinner, the captain stared at his computer screen and frowned. He scratched his tight, red hair, then typed:

Conducted impromptu celestial navigation training session with junior officer to enhance professional development and general seamanship skills.

"Perfect." He saved his work and shut the computer down. Leaning back in his chair, he surveyed his captain's cabin and smiled, content at the end of another good day at sea. At home, total chaos. Fat wife, shiftless son. But at sea...total control.

Aboard *Sentinel*, his command was absolute. And, as always, the events of his day were captured in his brag sheet, which he would soon send off to the promotion board in Washington. His promotion to the rank of captain was imminent. Barring any unforeseen circumstances, it would be announced this summer – a full two years ahead of his commander peers. He attributed this to his belief that there were no unforeseen circumstances. He anticipated obstacles, and when necessary, eliminated them, quietly, in house, in his own way.

Aregood's thoughts were interrupted by a knock at his cabin door. It was Sensor.

"Daily SITREP, captain," said the ensign.

Aregood waved him in without looking at him. He removed his pen and began slashing passages of the situation report with red ink. Preparing the daily message that informed those same superiors in Washington of every aspect of that day's operations, then routing it through every officer in the wardroom, was a tedious and thankless task which is why he assigned it to Sensor, a daily reminder of the chain and his place in it.

"Where is yesterday's message?" asked the captain.

"Sir? I didn't think you…."

Aregood flung his hand outward, slapping the ensign in the face with the folder. "Bring it."

Aregood leaned back in his chair, now waiting for his officer's return. It was his standing order than Sensor reroute the message through everyone again with his changes. The record for a single SITREP was eight hours. In half an hour, Sensor returned. The captain looked at his watch, then at the ensign.

The captain read the corrected message and frowned. He uncapped his red pen and changed the text back to its original wording. He handed it back to Sensor.

"How's your head?"

"Fine, sir."

"Wonderful."

"Permission to shove off, sir?"

"Not so fast, Sensor." Aregood drew a deep breath and exhaled it. "What do you want to do in the Coast Guard, son? I want to know. Do you have a plan?"

"Of course, sir."

"Do tell."

"My own cutter, sir." The ensign paused. "Commanding officer."

The captain smiled. He spread his hands. "Just like me."

Aregood noticed the ensign's nostrils flare, just slightly.

"Permission to shove off, sir."

"Don't forget those corrections. I'll need to see it one last time."

"Aye, sir."

"Shove."

As the door closed behind the ensign, the captain reclined in his chair and shut his eyes. After a moment, he turned on the computer again and began typing.

BILL SCHWEIGART

Chapter 4

The first thing Kelly noticed about Key West was sky. As *Sentinel* slowly passed through the main ship channel to the west of the island, the ensign watched massive cumulonimbus clouds barrel across the sky. The mar de leva had caused powerful winds to blow into the Florida Keys, the clouds to stack and roll overhead. The little Key looked isolated and vulnerable.

In helping Jorge prepare his port brief for the crew, Kelly educated himself on the harbor. He recognized that the ship now approached Mallory Square, where people congregated to watch the sunset every evening. The square was a big tourist draw. Since none of the waterfront buildings were more than a few stories high by law, any weather felt more immediate, majestic, and the crowd erupted into cheers every night a visible sun dipped below the horizon. Only today was different. People clutched their bags and hustled into the wind, heads cocked slightly toward the imposing white sky. The water was still placid, but from his position on the starboard bridgewing, Kelly thought the island itself looked nervous.

Harmon cut Kelly's observations short with a sequence of bearings as they steamed past the square. Kelly prepared to make an entry in his green logbook as the quartermaster dictated, "076...077...078. India, 078!" When the appointed bearing was called, Kelly recorded the time and turn bearing and simultaneously heard a rudder command from inside the bridge proper. A moment later, he felt the ship list beneath his feet, and he shifted his weight to steady himself. The landscape swung. As the cutter turned, both men stopped their tasks.

"So, Harmon, ever been to Key West?"

"Yes, sir."

"How'd you like it?"

"Fine, sir."

"Is it possible to get any more than two words out of you at a time, or is that heresy?"

Harmon chuckled.

"Holy shit, I made him laugh."

Suddenly, Kelly heard a commotion coming from inside the bridge. Both he and Harmon turned toward the open window. The entire Special Sea Detail was on the bridge: the captain, executive officer, operations officer, quartermasters, phone talkers, bearing takers, and more. Jorge, as conning officer, was chastising the helmsman.

"Irving, I said right fifteen degrees rudder not five!"

"Sorry, sir."

"I don't want sorry, I want you to mind your helm or you'll put us on the rocks!"

"Easy, Mr. Vargas," the captain said. "He'll get the hang of it."

Jorge regarded the captain with utter bewilderment then turned to face forward. "Aye, sir."

Kelly looked at Harmon, who also appeared stunned. When Harmon saw the ensign watching him, he shrugged his shoulders and turned back toward the water.

Kelly shook his head. He leaned in, so as not to be heard within the pilothouse, and said, "'He'll get the hang of it?' Is it opposite day and no one told me? Up is down, black is white...."

Harmon concentrated on scratching some salt film off the glass face of the alidade.

"I'm filling a seaman's Special Sea Detail billet. I'm not even shooting the fucking bearings, I'm writing them down for you. And Irving as master helmsman? Fucking Irving? And the captain doesn't even mind when he screws up? This isn't Key West, we've sailed into the Twilight Zone."

"What's wrong with Irving as master helmsman?"

Kelly looked at him.

Harmon laughed. "All right."

Kelly counted on his fingers. "Leahy or Gray or Cilinski, good guys who are infinitely more qualified, got passed over for that job. Come on...."

Kelly blew out a long breath. He had said his piece, too much of it, he thought and to Harmon, no less. Twilight Zone indeed. Mallory Square was now off their quarter. The piers of the Coast Guard base were visible off the starboard bow. Kelly studied them.

"I'll replace the sextant. I know it was the good one."

Harmon turned to the alidade again. "We have another one." He peered through the eyepiece and aligned it with the piers. Get ready, Juliet coming up," he said, then resumed calling out bearings.

Within the hour, *Sentinel* was moored at Integrated Support Command Key West. In their stateroom, Kelly and Jorge sat with their feet kicked up on their desks, waiting for liberty to be piped.

"What's first on our agenda?" asked Jorge.

"Drink. Repeat."

"Bearing recorder stress?"

"Now liberty, liberty, liberty. Liberty to all hands not in Duty Section One," came the pipe from the loudspeaker.

Both men cheered. Jorge sprang up and punted the metal waist basket across the room, cracking Kelly up. They were changing into their civilian clothes when there was a knock at the door. Before they could answer, Lieutenant Commander Tyndale stuck his head inside. He looked at the overturned wastebasket, the litter on the floor, and the half-dressed men.

Jorge pointed at Kelly. "He did it."

"Clean it up."

As the ensigns stooped to pick up, Tyndale cleared his throat. "Not you, Sensor. Captain needs you to draft our position report."

Kelly smiled. "Already wrote it, sir. *Semper Paratus*. Always Ready."

Jorge looked up. "Go get it signed. I'll wait."

"Don't bother, Vargas," said the XO, "Sensor has the duty, too."

"I'm not in Section One, sir. Chief Norris has in-port OOD today."

"Not any more. I sent him on a supply run. Last minute thing."

"I'll bet," muttered Jorge.

"Watch it, Vargas, or I'll find work for you too."

"It's all right, Jorge," said Kelly.

"Good man, Sensor." Tyndale leered. "Be on deck in two minutes." His head disappeared and the stateroom door slammed behind him.

"That little fuck," said Jorge.

"It's not coming from him." Kelly offered a weak smile. "Just give Nancy my best and have a few beers on me. I'll call Pop tonight, and I'll catch up with you tomorrow when I get relieved. You can get drink two nights in a row, can't you?"

"An alcoholic is someone who wants to quit. Stay out of trouble, man."

"I'm not the one going out."

"Like that matters."

The quarterdeck was set up on the fantail where crewmembers checked out before crossing the brow to the pier. Kelly watched them file by, hustling from *Sentinel* to pier, pier to dry land. He gazed at the small, uninhabited islands across the ship channel. On the nearest one, between the clear blue of the water and deep green of the trees was a thin lip of yellow beach. He imagined ripping off the uniform, leaping overboard and swimming for it, each gratifying stroke pulling him through the cool water until he was on the other side, barefoot in warm sand.

After making a round of the ship, Kelly entered the wardroom. It was deserted. Tourist pamphlets of Key West and the day's newspapers littered the large table. Kelly grunted and walked over to the phone. He dialed the quarterdeck's extension. "Outside line, please," he told the watchstander.

When Kelly heard the dial tone, he called his grandfather's house. A woman's voice answered.

"I'm sorry," said Kelly. "I must have the wrong number."

"Is that you, Kelly? It's Ms. Thompson."

"Hi, Ms. Thompson. Where's Pop?"

"Hold on, honey, I'll get him."

Several moments later, Jack Sensor's voice filled the line. Kelly instantly felt buoyed. "Hey, it's Ensign Charlie Brown! How are the high seas treating my boy?"

Kelly recalled his bouts with nausea, his recent "counseling session" with Aregood. "You know me, Pop, kicking ass, taking names."

"You don't sound too swift. You sure?"

"Couldn't be better." He closed his eyes. "Just around the corner from qualifying as underway OOD. But enough about me, why is the next door neighbor answering the phone? You know she has a crush on you, Pop."

"Well, we had a little to-do here last week...I had a little heart attack, is all."

"What?"

"Don't get excited, Kelly, it's all right. I'm fine, really."

"What the hell's a little heart attack?" Kelly suddenly felt nauseated again, like twenty-foot waves were still battering the boat. He grasped for a chair at the long table and collapsed into it. "What happened?"

"You know how it is, fending off all these young girls...."

"I'm serious!"

"It's nothing to worry about. I felt a little shaky. Off. So I called the hospital and they came and got me right away. Turns out, an artery was partially blocked." His voice lilted, as if singing a beach song. "Little surgery...it's cleared now and I'm home. In and out within the week. That's that."

"That is not that. Why didn't you call the ship's ombudsman?"

"What good would spinning you up at sea have done? Besides, there were no fireworks at all. And I'm taking no chances. Ms. Thompson's here looking after me just in case. I'm already walking around, and the doc says I'll be fishing in no time."

"I'm coming home."

"Baloney. I'm not going anywhere and neither are you. You'll be back in a few weeks anyway. Take some leave then. We'll celebrate your qualification."

Kelly winced.

"You sure everything's okay down there?"

He's asking how I'm doing. Kelly swallowed. His throat felt thick. "Living the dream, Pop."

"I'm proud of you, Charlie Brown. You know that, right?"

"Just promise me, if anything else happens, anything at all, you'll call the ombudsman. Give Ms. Thompson the number, too, and explain that it's the families' point of contact for the ship. Promise?"

"Sure," he sang.

"Swear. On Mom and Dad."

"Okay, Charlie Brown. I swear."

When he hung up, Kelly placed his hands on the table in front of him, trying to steady himself. He pressed his palms hard, and his class ring glinted in the wardroom's fluorescent light. The stone inside was a Cape May diamond. In South Jersey, they called it a "goodie." One afternoon, during Kelly's third summer at the shore, walking along the pebbly beach of Cape May Point, Jack had discovered the modest white stone peering out of the surrounding marl. Standing ankle-deep in the alluvion, his grandfather explained that only a jeweler could tell the difference between a regular, opaque rock and a goodie. "Or trained beachcombers like us," said Jack with a wink. It had gone into the old cigar box that day, but during Kelly's junior year at the Academy, Jack presented the stone to him, cut and polished, clear and shining like a real diamond.

Kelly stared at the stone in his ring now and concentrated on his breathing. He refused to cry inside the skin of *Sentinel*. Never though, had he felt so claustrophobic, so powerless, not in any storm, natural or manmade. He called the quarterdeck watchstander again. "It's Sensor. Get me the operations officer."

"He's already departed on liberty, sir."

"Page him."

I'm getting off this ship tonight, he vowed.

Chapter 5

Sentinel moored at the same base, the very same pier, where he had landed sixteen years ago, wracked with fever and first degree burns after setting off from Mariel. As Jorge exited the gates of the Coast Guard base, the Trumbo Point Naval Air Station came into view, and though military housing now stood in its place, visions of the aircraft hangar that served as his first home during those first few days in the United States flooded his memory. His family and the rest of the boat people, *los balseros*, were processed there. While the crowd bristled and jostled one another in the heat of the packed hangar, his father, Rolando's spirits soared. He collected any keepsakes he could find. Stones, shells. Inspirational leaflets left by Cuban-Americans. *Mementos americanos*.

When Jorge was a teen, his father had given him one of these souvenirs, a bleached, inch-long scallop shell. Rolando had bored a hole in its hinge, and presented it to his son as a necklace. He never wore it. He carried it in his pocket and stroked the shell there now, running his fingers along its sharp, fanned ridges as he wandered down Trumbo Road, toward the waterfront area called Lands End Village. Even on a windy March afternoon, the sun had warmed the Key to seventy degrees, and tourists gathered at the Village to eat, drink, and shop at the restaurants and markets by the shrimp boat docks. The air smelled fertile with fresh catch and the atmosphere was festive, but Jorge realized that on an island only two miles wide by three-and-a-half miles long, there was nowhere he could go to avoid reminders of his previous visit. He wished Kelly was around. He wanted a drink, but decided to call Nancy first.

Jorge had met Nancy Myers two years before at the Academy ring dance. On the afternoon of the ball, he had just finished a week's restriction for mouthing off to an upperclassman, and was dateless, but decided to go anyway. Just for the piss of it.

Once at the ball, he felt stupid. The ceremony of the ring dance called for each date to wear her cadet's ring on a ribbon around her neck, then each couple passed through a giant model of the ring for pictures. Tradition dictated that each cadet cut the ribbon and kiss his or her date in exchange for their ring. Jorge felt stupid. Alone, conspicuous in his full dress uniform, he brooded by the punchbowl and watched couples file by.

He spotted a pretty blonde in a blue cocktail dress, on the on the arm of a cadet, approach the giant ring. Before passing through, the cadet swooped down for a greedy kiss. Demurely, the girl bowed her head to the side, looking over her shoulder. The kiss landed harmlessly on her cheek. She saw Jorge.

The room pivoted like a ship that had just changed course. He glanced at the crest emblazoned on the ring that encircled her—*Audentes Fortuna Iuvat.* "Fortune favors the brave," he said. He dumped his punch in the bowl and walked toward her.

Jorge found a payphone near the wharf. Despite himself, a smile cracked his face when he heard her voice.

"Jorge! I knew you'd call today. How's the patrol?" she asked.

"Miserable," he said, "but I don't want to talk about that now. I just want to talk about marrying you."

"You're lucky I said yes. 'Come on, you're not going to make me say it, are you?' That's how you ask a girl to marry you?"

Jorge laughed. "I thought the diamond was all that mattered."

"Damn right." she said. "Actually, I've been thinking about the honeymoon. I have an idea."

"That's more like it."

"You're there right now. Key West."

Jorge felt a sharp pain behind his right eye.

"What do you think?" she asked.

"Are you serious?"

"Of course I'm serious. It'll be fantastic."

"No, I mean are you fucking serious? You're kidding me, right?"

"Baby?"

"You think this place makes me happy?"

"Jorge...I just thought seeing your roots would be neat, and since—."

"My roots? This place ain't my roots."

"You didn't let me finish. I was going to say that since Cuba is out of the question—."

"Fuck, why don't we check out your roots? We could honeymoon in Connecticut, go yachting, or to the country club."

"What's wrong with you?"

"What's wrong with me is that I want to go on a honeymoon, not some fucking field trip to *Jorge de los balseros*' past!"

Jorge heard her voice quaver. He felt miserable as soon as he realized he had lashed out. "Baby—."

"Fuck you, Jorge. Fuck you and your temper. I only suggested it to feel closer to you." Her voice quavered. "Like family."

She began to cry. His anger ebbed instantly. "Nancy, wait."

Jorge heard a click followed by dial tone followed.

Nice job, asshole, he thought. He slammed the phone into the cradle.

Ten minutes later, Jorge sat in Turtle Kraals, drinking. Everywhere he looked, memories rose like sea smoke from the tiny, dense island. His father picking through Key West dirt in search of his *mementos americanos*. Is this your first time in Key West? Fuck you, captain. Fuck you all.

"You look like a guy who needs a few laughs."

A few stools away, a tanned, athletic girl sat alone. A ball cap covered her hair, but a lone, dark lock spilled and curled around her eye. Despite the fact she appeared to have spent the morning working aboard one of the shrimp boats outside, she was striking. She turned to him and offered a warm, wide smile. Her skin reminded him of sweet things. Caramels and canela, the color of the raw cane sugar. *Cubana*, Jorge thought.

"Not allowed, engaged." Jorge shrugged. "I hope," he added.

The girl offered an amiable laugh. She continued to laugh as she picked up her beer and walked to the outside deck. As she passed, Jorge spied a tiny dolphin, arced in a leap, tattooed on the small of her back. As Jorge watched her go, the waitress sidled up to his spot.

"Can I get you something else, honey?"

"Conch fritters. What else do you have on tap?"

"A deal," she said, handing him a hot pink card. It was a checklist. "Drink these twenty microbrews in the next year and you get a free Turtle Kraals tee-shirt."

He studied the card for a moment then slapped it down on the bar. "And here I was about to drink all that for nothing."

Chapter 6

Aregood sat in the Hog's Breath Saloon & Raw Bar, cheerful and surrounded by most of *Sentinel*'s chief petty officers. They commandeered most of the tall, wooden stools at one end of the bar for several rounds and cheerfully defended them from locals and the tourists from the cruise liners. A live band played blues. He was amazed the bar was so crowded on a weeknight in March. With an older crowd, too, he noticed. That was a relief. It meant the youngest members of his crew would be sure to avoid the place.

He had come to the bar with Tyndale and Griffin, but running into members of the chief's mess had been pure luck. Everyone understood that the day-to-day leadership and true knowledge of any ship resided with the chiefs. No one challenged them outright, not even Aregood; they were indispensable. A few drinks, he figured, was always a solid investment.

He ordered them another round and left Tyndale at the bar. Aregood decided not to leave the chiefs in his company any longer than necessary. His XO may be loyal, he thought, but he was also a one-man morale killer. As he hastened to the bathroom, he spied Chief Norris heading toward the bar.

"Chief, good to see you out tonight."

"Good to be seen, captain, though I'm not sure how. I had the duty until this morning."

"Well," Aregood said, placing his arm around the chief's shoulders. "Let's just say I put the bug in XO's ear. It seemed like every time I turned my head, you had the duty."

"Much appreciated, sir, but I don't have it any worse than anyone else."

Aregood waved away the protest. "Old sea dogs have to look out for one another. Now post to the bar. I heard the Old Man's got the next round."

Norris laughed and offered a drunken salute. "Aye, aye, skipper!"

Aregood snapped to attention and returned the salute. Turning back toward the bathroom, he noticed a group of women sitting at a bench inside of the Hog's Breath, watching the scene intently. He smiled, tapped his brow, and continued on.

In the men's room, he scanned the flyers tacked to the wall. Para-sailing, jet-ski rentals, booze cruises… Despite the variety of advertisements, nearly every one featured bikini-clad women, tanned and toned. After weeks at sea, he thought he had better stop looking, lest he battle an erection just trying to piss. Then he remembered to call home.

Lisa had not looked good in a bikini for years. The first year of their marriage seemed like a lifetime ago, when it would not be a crime to wear one. Before Scott was born, she had a trim, athletic build. It was what had first caught his eye on the beach in St. Petersburg years ago. After Scott, ten pounds of shit stuffed into an eight-pound bag. Since when did a thyroid keep you from exercising? Jog, aerobics? Something.

Just as she slowed down, his career had begun to accelerate, and he found himself relieved to take those jobs that would further it. Operational jobs that required lots of sea time.

One year ago, he was serving a staff tour at Coast Guard Headquarters in Washington, D.C. when the detailer offered him command of *Sentinel*. "It's in Portsmouth, Virginia," the detailer said. Aregood had just purchased a new home in Arlington and it was becoming clear that Scott was going to need to "see someone" as his wife put it. "Get me out here," he told the detailer.

As he exited the men's room, he caught his operations officer heading toward the exit. "Not having enough fun, OPS?"

"Oh, no," said Griffin, startled. "I just have to go."

"The boat?"

"Yes, sir."

"It's the OOD. It's Sensor, isn't it?"

Griffin paused for a moment. "It's nothing I can't handle, sir."

"Tell you what. I'm in a good mood tonight, Keith. Leave at will."

"Aye, sir."

Griffin moved past. Aregood called after him. "OPS!"

Griffin halted. "Sir?"

"Smile, man. You're in Key West."

Griffin complied and hurried from the bar. Aregood sighed, then found a phone. He dialed Arlington.

"Hello?"

"Hello, Lisa."

"Kevin, hi! Where are you?"

"Key West. Mid-patrol break. How's Scotty?"

Aregood's wife groaned. "We haven't had a real conversation in weeks, unless you include grunts and requests for food. When are you getting back?"

"Couple of weeks."

"Tell me what day and maybe I could get off from work. Maybe Scotty and I could drive down to meet the ship."

"Oh, Lisa, I don't know. Schedule's up in the air right now."

"Oh. I understand."

"I'll let you know as soon as I can."

"It's just that the sooner Scotty sees you, the better. Dr. Lenox thinks he'll be better once you're around more. You know, on a regular basis."

"I'm not having this talk now, Lisa."

"I'm not saying you're—."

"Put Scott on."

"He's at a friend's."

"Wonderful! He has friends. It can't be that bad then."

"Kevin—."

"I've got to run. I'll call you again before we pull out. Tell Scotty he's my number one swab."

"I miss you."

He looked around, saw another flyer for a scuba trip. This one featured a boatful of buxom blondes modeling snorkeling gear. He remembered the first, torrid year of his marriage when she could have given any one of them a run for their money. In the bed of their first apartment in St. Petersburg, Lisa's legs hooked around him, her heels digging into the backs of his thighs as she gripped him with her entire body. He looked over the bar at the tee shirts for sale. They read "Hogs Breath is better than no breath at all." He frowned.

"You too," he said and hung up.

When he returned to the bar, the chief's corner was deserted. No doubt fleeing from XO, he thought. Even Tyndale had vanished. Ingrates. Aregood decided he could use the peace. He was tired. He ordered a rum and Coke.

"Where'd all your little friends go?"

Aregood turned to see one of the women he had saluted earlier. Her hair was blonde and cropped very short. She wore a blue, flowered sarong, with a tight, white blouse that was complimented by a deep tan. As she bent forward to summon the bartender, he noticed her bare midriff. Exposed, he could see her toned abdomen, the muscles outlined and firm. His glance drifted from her stomach to her chest pressing against the edge of the wooden bar.

"They must've deserted me," he said, smiling. "Yours?"

"All gone. Rookies." She pulled a pack of cigarettes from her purse. "Light?" she asked.

"Sorry."

She laughed. "I didn't think so," she said, and turned toward the bartender, who held out a flame for her unlit cigarette. "Stoli," she said.

"What's that supposed to mean?"

"You just look the straight-laced type, is all."

He shrugged. "It's in the job description."

"Navy?"

"Coast Guard."

"Stationed here or port call?"

"Port call. And you? Local?"

"A genuine conch."

"Kevin." He offered his hand. "Genuine shellback, I guess."

The woman shook it and smiled. "Evelyn Exmore. Those men earlier," she said, exhaling a plume of blue smoke, "you outranked them."

"How'd you know?"

"Military men are pretty easy to figure out."

"That so?" Aregood swiveled on his stool and propped his elbow on the bar. "What else can you figure out?"

"Well, you're their boss. Probably the captain?"

"And?"

"And you looked pretty blue, until I decided to rescue you, that is. Left all alone. Probably brooding about the 'burdens of command.'"

"Hardly."

"No?"

"No," he grinned. "I love being in command."

"Really?"

"Really." Their eyes locked. After a moment, Evelyn glanced at his hand.

"Fifteen years," he said.

She picked up his hand and twirled the ring, inspecting it with a studious look. Her play with his fingers caused a warm ripple to travel up his arm. She laid his hand back on the bar.

"Happily?" she asked.

Evelyn chose side streets to get to Higg's Beach. "This way is faster. You can see the sights later." They rode the rest of the short drive in silence, heading south. Evelyn parked, and led him down to the sand. Aregood noticed the clouds were breaking up, revealing a crescent moon. An occasional cloud blew past it, sending shadows racing down the strand.

As he walked behind her, staring at the sway of her hips, thoughts of his wife tried to intervene, but like the lines that held *Sentinel* to the pier, they were cast off. As she stopped short of the water, he smoothed his hands along her waist and brushed his lips against her exposed shoulder.

They went at each other. They collapsed in a heap, rolling around, groping and kissing and seeking traction in the sand, until she released him suddenly and stood. "I'm in charge here," she said. She walked toward the dark water, looking up and down the beach, untying her sarong as she went. As it slipped to the beach with a whisper, revealing her firm, bare bottom, she looked over her shoulder at Aregood, sitting in the sand, leaning on one arm. He could hear her laughing voice over the gentle waves.

"On your feet, skipper."

Aregood obeyed.

Chapter 7

Duval Street, the most famous thoroughfare in Key West, bisected the western half of the island. Beginning on the northern tip at Old Mallory Square, where the cruise liners docked, Duval continued to the southern tip of the island. Kelly walked south along Duval, stopping in nearly every bar he passed. It was just after nine o'clock, an hour-and-a-half since Griffin relieved him, and Kelly did not feel nearly drunk enough.

At Duval and Greene, he walked into Sloppy Joe's, attracted by its buzzing red neon sign, but the band was too loud and the place too crowded. After one beer, he moved on. The din and density of people on the sidewalk was no better, so Kelly continued south along Duval and stopped in front of Rick's. From upstairs he heard, then felt deep in his gut, the loud thumping of bass. He looked ahead, through an archway next to Rick's, toward the wide entrance of Durty Harry's, and a platinum haired singer with piercings in his face screamed in time with a raucous band behind him. Kelly made an unsteady about-face and continued south.

Kelly passed people leaning out the windows of the saloon-like façade of Rumrunner's, and thought of his OPS Boss. The man never really exhibited enough of a personality to love or hate, or get any sort of bearing off of at all, but he was easily the most human of what Jorge called "The Big Three." And to his credit, it was Griffin himself who entered the wardroom tonight, lifting his hand in salute as custom dictated for the oncoming officer of the deck.

"Just go," he said, "before he comes back."

Soon, the horde of revelers thinned. The noise of crowd trailed off. It was as if Kelly had passed some invisible demarcation. He exhaled and looked around. Cheerful rainbow flags hung in the storefronts. Finally, he thought, quiet.

He glanced down a side street and noticed what appeared to be a bar nestled among some banana trees. The fact that he almost missed it entirely was enough to entice him. Drawing closer, he found the entrance flanked by white lattice and festooned with purple blooms of bougainvillea. He stepped through and crossed a small courtyard to get to the door of the bar, passing several wrought iron tables. The tables were empty save for a lone white candle burning on each. Above the door, a sign read The Wayfarer.

Chimes rang as Kelly stepped inside. He noticed a marked difference from the courtyard. To the left were more tables, only these were of a deep red wood. To the right, a mahogany bar ran the full length of the room. At its corner, a well-dressed, white-haired man made notes in what appeared to be a ledger. Beyond him was a darkened hallway. The tavern suited him. He settled into a seat at the bar.

Behind the counter, a large, bald man with a goatee said, "What can I get you, sport?"

"Dark and Stormy."

"ID?"

"Right." Kelly fished out his wallet and produced his green military identification card. The bartender studied the front of it, then glanced toward the old man at the corner of the bar. The old man looked up.

"The date's on the back," Kelly said.

"I know," the bartender said, still looking at the old man. When the old man nodded, the bartender handed the card back. "Puddle pirate, eh?"

"I've heard them all."

"Bet you have," the man said, and walked away.

Kelly watched the bartender snatch a bottle of dark rum off the shelf. He poured a shot into a highball, then twisted the cap off a bottle of ginger beer and added that next. The black liquor swirled upward as the reddish beer splashed into the tall glass.

"Thanks," said Kelly. The first taste felt thick. It fizzed on his tongue and burned flowing down his throat. It was not an unpleasant sensation. He quaffed half of it.

"One of those days?"

Kelly took another swig, nodded.

"Another day, another kick in the peaches," the man laughed. He winked at the patron to Kelly's left, then moved on to serve another customer.

"Right," said Kelly. He was unsure whether he was privy to the joke or the butt of it.

Kelly looked into a long mirror on the wall behind the bar. Mounted above it was an eight-foot white marlin, candle lights reflecting in its glossy hide. He stared at the fish for a moment, at its thin pointed snout and sleek lines. He surveyed the rest of the bar and noticed nets and harpoons and sundry seafaring items adorned the saloon. Kelly felt at ease. It reminded him of those restaurants in Cape May where his grandfather had taken him as a boy. The two would always go during the winter, when the town was mostly deserted and closed down, except for a few social beacons for the locals. It was always better to visit on the coldest, most miserable nights when everyone felt a quiet kinship; the restaurants seemed much warmer, cozier for the men and women who linked their livelihoods to a lonely ocean. For a brief moment though, he wondered if it had been a career at sea he had truly wished for, or just that warm sense of camaraderie on a cold night.

The Wayfarer did not seem so different. The place was sparsely populated, but not entirely deserted. The drinks were catching up and he took comfort in that too. It felt as if a woman's fingers were caressing the inside of his head.

"First time in Key West?"

Kelly swiveled his head toward the young man next to him. It took a moment for his vision to follow.

"Yeah."

"Like it?"

"Only really seen Duval."

The fellow patron laughed. "It's the longest street in the world."

"Yeah?"

"One end of the street touches the Gulf of Mexico, the other end, the Atlantic."

The man introduced himself as David. He told Kelly of all the landmarks he should see: the homes of Ernest Hemingway and Tennessee Williams, the historic cemetery with its statue of Cuba's revolutionary leader José Marti, the Key West Lighthouse, and Fort Taylor, now an island state park. After a few minutes, the conversation meandered back to Duval.

"They say it takes about twenty minutes to walk from one end of Duval to the other," said David. "Three weeks if you stop in all the bars. By that math, it looks like you've been here a week."

"Yeah, well…another day, another kick in the peaches, right?"

David's eyes widened. "Want to talk about it?"

"How much time you got?" Kelly laughed. He looked at the marlin and lifted his drink to his mouth.

Kelly felt a hand on his thigh. "All night," said David.

Kelly stopped mid-swallow, coughed. It took his mind a moment to process what was happening. He slammed the highball down, firing Dark and Stormy onto the bar, and shoved David, but with no leverage except the high barstool he lost his balance. Both men toppled backward. Kelly stood, wobbled, and grabbed the bar for balance. "The fuck?" he yelled.

In the corner of his vision, Kelly noticed a blur of movement in the mirror—a man's broad back lunging—then focused on the foreground in time to see a fist loom from behind the bar. Knuckles eclipsed his field of vision and his face snapped back suddenly. He did not feel the punch. Vaguely aware that he was on the floor, Kelly felt a dull pain now pulsing beneath his temple. He tried to rise, but the room was spinning, and he only rose to his knees before falling over again. The floorboards whined, and Kelly looked up to see the bartender striding toward him. Had he been this big when I walked in, he thought. He reminded him of a professional wrestler Kelly had once seen in Atlantic City. He stared in awe, as if this was happening to someone else.

"Ah shit," said Kelly.

The bartender hauled him up by the front of his shirt. Kelly's head lolled, and he looked at his dangling feet. They appeared to be gliding over the hardwood floor. He giggled. He heard the pretty jingling of bells as the man kicked open the front door, then felt a sense of slow weightlessness.

Suddenly he was fishing the beaches of Ocean City again, hauling back his pole and whipping it forward, the lead sinker soaring into the air, the line streaming out behind it, whizzing off its reel. A grainy strip of squid bounced in the air, inches behind the graceful arcing of the sinker. Kelly numbered a good cast as one of the most satisfying sensations he had ever experienced, the tiny lead weight piercing the air for a few pregnant moments before it plunged into the ocean with a plunk! Kelly continued to float as he heard the door's chimes' tinkling fade and a voice saying "'Anchors Aweigh,' sailor," until everything shattered in a cacophony.

Kelly sailed into an iron table ten feet from the door. He bounced off its top and rolled across it, toppling to the concrete below. A wrought-iron chair landed on top of him. He shook his head. He pushed off the ground to get to his feet, but his legs got tangled in the chair, and he fell onto his back again. Reeling, and unable to extricate himself, he raised his fists in front of him in an attempt to ward off an impending attack.

He was alone.

He groaned. He kicked the chair away from him and sat up. He cradled his head in his hands. "'Anchors Aweigh' is the navy, asshole." He stumbled out of the courtyard. Remembering a promise, he vomited in the bougainvillea then wove to the street, toward one of the many taxicabs that prowled Duval for drunken, late-night fares.

The next morning, he awoke in red light. Jorge, he thought. He flopped down from the top rack and the jolt of his feet on the deck sent an electric shock up his spine. He stifled a shout. As he limped to the head, he looked over his shoulder. Jorge was asleep in his clothes, wearing a tee shirt over the collared shirt he had worn yesterday that read "I Drank My Way Around The World." Kelly began to smile, then winced.

As he relieved himself, he tried to organize the patches of memory from the previous night into a cohesive narrative. He left the head and walked to the sink in the stateroom, switching on the fluorescent light above medicine cabinet. Kelly nearly mistook the purplish bruise by his eye for a shadow. Damn, he thought. First the alidade and now this.

"For the love of God, turn off that fucking light," Jorge muttered from his rack. He propped himself on one elbow. "What happened to you?"

"A very large fist happened to me." Kelly turned back toward the mirror and traced a ginger finger down the side of his face. He remembered enough to know that he did not want to talk about it. "Details are sketchy."

"Wait. You had duty last night."

"I got relieved. And now I wish I hadn't."

"Oh." Jorge lay down again. "I feel like I've been shot at and missed, shit at and hit."

"What happened to you?"

Jorge gave Kelly an even stare. "Details are sketchy."

"Fair enough." Kelly climbed up to his rack. "You degenerate drunk."

"At least I got a tee-shirt, Rocky."

Kelly awoke an hour later. After his first week on board, he had learned to tune out the everyday noises, but not today, not with this hangover. He lay awake, listening to *Sentinel* breathe in the red light. The steady drone emanating from the engine room was punctuated by the whine of hydraulic doors opening and closing. It reminded him of indigestion. He followed voices as people traveled through Officer's Country and around the passageways like the lifeblood of the cutter. When he listened closely, he could even hear outside the skin of the ship, the duty boatswain's mates on deck, chipping, painting, and cursing.

Kelly climbed from the rack carefully and showered. He hungered for breakfast, coffee — off the ship. He thought about shaving, but decided against it. He took three pain relievers instead. He looked closer at the lower rack, could barely make out his friend's breathing. Let him sleep, he thought.

Kelly knew there had to be other places on the island to eat, but Duval Street was the only area he had visited, and he was in no condition for exploring. He thought the walk to Duval would do him good, but Kelly's eyes teared as soon as he stepped outside. It felt as if the sun's rays were trying to pry open his skull like a clam. He walked to the gate of the base and hailed the first cab he saw. "Anywhere on Duval," he said, "on the northern end."

The taxi drove along the Gulf. Kelly spotted clusters of mangrove roots in the shallows, arching from the topaz waters. His headache began to recede. The partygoers from the night before had surrendered Duval at this hour. Families and elderly couples walked the strip, stopping in the art galleries and tee-shirt shops, eating breakfast in the many restaurants. In a courtyard at the intersection of Duval and Caroline, exotic birds and snakes were on display, as well as paintings from local artists and trinkets from vendors. He settled on a nearby café and found a seat outside in the shade of an odd-looking tree. He ordered scrambled eggs, sausage, toast, and coffee and devoured them all in silence.

He decided to stay a while. The sun was shining, the sky was pastel, and the only remnant of the mar de leva was a slight breeze through the small courtyard. He had nowhere he needed to be. He ordered a café con leche, added several sugars, and watched the people pass by. After a few minutes, he looked upward at the tree that offered him shade.

"Banyan," said an old man from the next table, dressed in khakis and a pressed white shirt. A straw hat shielded his eyes from the sun, but Kelly could tell the man was deeply tanned.

"Excuse me?"

"It's called a banyan tree."

"Yeah?"

"They're quite fascinating." The man paused for a moment. When Kelly did not interrupt him, he smiled and continued. "Most banyans have their roots in the air. They grow downward, and finding purchase in the ground, continue to spread. The tree can populate an entire area that way."

Kelly craned his head back for another look. His aching body reminded him to be suspicious of locals and he was in no mood for conversation. Still, Kelly estimated his age to be around sixty, ten years younger than his grandfather, so he offered a polite smile as he glanced up into the tree again. It was interesting. Its branches looked poured, like wax, onto the other tree.

"It looks like an octopus sunning itself," he said.

"That's a very apt description."

Kelly stared into the tangle of roots.

"Little birds take the seeds, and deposit them in the crowns of other trees. Especially the palm, just like this one here. When the seeds sprout, they send their roots cascading down."

Kelly turned his vision from the tree back to the table. Something in the old man's tone chilled him suddenly, and though his voice had not altogether lost its breezy tone, Kelly now watched the man instead of the tree.

"After some time, the roots embrace our friend the palm here, and begin to constrict." He clasped his hands together for emphasis. "The banyan invades, constricts its prey and crowds out the other trees. Very much like an octopus, in fact. Eventually, all that's left is the banyan. It has those broad, beautiful leaves and that pretty scarlet fruit, but make no mistake, that tree next to you never would have gotten to where it is without the strong back of another tree. And it choked that tree to death."

Kelly suddenly wanted to slide away from the tree. He studied the man. "Do I know you?"

"What's choking you, Mr. Sensor?" asked the man.

Kelly sat upright. "How do you know my name?"

The old man raised the brim of his straw hat, revealing his face. "I'm the owner of The Wayfarer. You were in my establishment last night, and I might add, caused quite a to-do."

To-do, Kelly thought. "Sorry, I don't take too well to being grabbed by you guys."

"'You guys?' Charming."

"Look, if this is about damages, I'm sure there were more done to my face than your table."

"I'm just here for a chat. You looked very distressed when you came in. Just as you seemed to be enjoying yourself, there seemed to be an unfortunate misunderstanding."

"Misunderstanding?" he said, louder than he meant. He looked around then leaned closer to the man's table. "I'm not gay."

"Neither am I," laughed the man. "What does that have to do with anything?"

"Look. Sir. I'm very sore. And very tired. And very hungover. I don't know why you care to ask me all of these questions. I know what this is all about, but I'm very sorry for fighting in your bar. I can guarantee it won't happen again. So if that's all, I'll be on my way."

"That won't be necessary. I have to be going myself." The old man stood. "May I share just one final thought?"

Kelly pinched the bridge of his nose with his thumb and forefinger.

"Thank you. Like I said," the man continued, "I was in the military once myself and I was miserable, as well. Last night, you looked to me like...like a fellow traveler. I just wanted to inform you there are always options." The man turned for the street. Over his shoulder, he said, "The Keys are a wonderful place to get lost."

Kelly leaned forward in his chair. "Wait, what options? What do you mean, 'get lost'?"

The man stopped, gestured toward the street. "Let's just say there are the laws of the United States, and then there are the laws of the Conch Republic. One of the laws is 'anything goes.' Another is 'questions are not appreciated.' This place keeps its secrets, Mr. Sensor. That's all."

"Hold it." Kelly stared at the man. "Are you suggesting I desert?" He nearly spat the word.

"I've made a mistake." He tipped his hat. "I won't waste any more of our time."

Kelly sat back and laughed. He looked around for Jorge; this was his best practical joke yet. Then he remembered he had told Jorge nothing about the night before. The old man smiled patiently. He stopped laughing. "You're serious."

The old man bent forward and lowered his voice.

"I'm merely saying that I was in your shoes once. A long time ago. Then I came here and now I'm not. On occasion, I've helped several others relocate."

"You're telling me you run…an Underground Railroad," Kelly asked, "for deserters?"

"Ha! I've never heard it put quite like that. But close enough. I've helped a few friends start over, yes. And I would appreciate it if you kept this to yourself."

"Who'd believe me?"

"Please. I didn't have to come see you, but I did so as a gentleman. Can I assume you'll be a gentleman as well, Mr. Sensor?" The old man extended his hand.

Kelly shook it. "How did you find out my name, anyway?"

"Your military identification. Fritz has standing orders to memorize all green IDs."

"Why?"

"Well, in the event you decided not to be a gentleman, my very large and very homosexual bartender would go to your ship and lodge a complaint with your supervisors about your visit. Fritz's version would be considerably more lurid."

"Clever."

"*Semper Paratus*," said the man, grinning.

Kelly laughed despite himself. "Sir, this is without a doubt the craziest conversation I've ever had, but you have my word. It'll never leave this table."

"In case you ever change your mind." He handed Kelly a teal business card for The Wayfarer. On the front, "Do you know the Way?" was printed in white type. Kelly turned it over and the word "Chaplain" was written in blue ink. There was no telephone number.

"What's this?" Kelly asked, holding up the back of the card.

"People I've helped sometimes call me that. If by some chance you do happen to find yourself in my bar again, present that card. First, it will be the only thing that keeps Fritz from ripping off your arms and handing them to you. Second, I will help you. Provided you do not leave a trail. I can't stress that enough."

"I won't. Need this, I mean. But thank you."

"You remind me a lot of myself," said the old man. He tipped his hat again. "Before I was happy."

The old man strolled in the direction of a car parked across the street, which Kelly now realized had been there all along. And like the man, it had also been nondescript: small, blue, tropical, like everything else on the island. Another old man sat behind the wheel, tall and thin with a prominent Adam's apple.

As the owner of The Wayfarer entered the car, he held his hand up in a final wave, but his face was lost in the shadow of the brim of his hat. The car pulled into traffic and Kelly quickly lost it in the growing, late morning tourist bustle. He stood and craned his neck in the car's direction. He peered down both ends of the thoroughfare, past rows of boutiques and fleets of mopeds, aware that the waters of both the Gulf and the Atlantic teemed just beyond his vision, converging on this tiny key where he now stood. His chest swelled as he drew a deep breath. He smelled a whisper of salt on the air. Moments later, he thought he spotted the car briefly before it disappeared down a side street.

Chapter 8

Aregood looked down at the returning members of his tattered crew. It was the morning of their departure from Key West, and from his vantage on the bridgewing, he surveyed their sad and painful shuffling up the brow—some alone, some in groups—with a generous smile. He felt refreshed and vibrant, as if he had taken his first bracing plunge into the ocean on a sweltering day.

Sometime during their carnivorous sex, Aregood realized he was in trouble. They had coupled to exhaustion and after lay nestled in the sand. She draped her naked body over his while he traced his fingers down her moon-dappled back.

"You're not bolting." Aregood could not tell whether it was a question or an announcement.

"No, I'm not," he said, kissing her neck. "You're my ride."

She jumped up and grabbed his hands, the cool night air filling the void she left. He shivered and protested, but she pulled him to his feet. "Come on," she said, "let's go get some sleep."

They drove north toward the center of the island, then east, past Key West Cemetery. Evelyn parked on Petronia, a small avenue in a tight residential neighborhood. Aregood noticed that the few yards in the neighborhood were tiny as he passed through a wooden gate, then followed her down a walkway thick with palm trees toward the entrance of her condominium.

Evelyn led him to the bathroom, where they showered together to wash away the sand, then toppled into bed. Aregood fell into a deep, dreamless sleep that lasted until late afternoon. He awoke to her. When he lifted his head from the pillow, he saw her cropped blonde head bobbing in sensual rhythm.

They spent all day in bed. That night, Evelyn lived up to her promise of showing him the attractions she had sped past the previous night. He thought of reciprocating with a tour of *Sentinel*, but thought better of it, of appearances. And she showed no interest in the ship. Surprised, he found her lack of curiosity not unpleasant.

He spent that night, the last night of mid-patrol break, at her place again. The next morning, as she dropped him at the gate to the base, her eyes brimmed with tears. He murmured warm pledges to her and meant them. When he watched her drive out of sight, he felt his chest tighten, as if he had been underwater too long.

"Captain?"

Aregood turned to see Tyndale in the doorway to the bridge. "Everyone onboard?"

"Missing one, but we still have ten minutes, sir."

"Very well."

"You seem in good spirits, sir. What was her name?"

Aregood glared at his executive officer, then remembered Tyndale had already left the bar before he met Evelyn. A lucky guess. He said nothing, glanced at the blue folder in his XO's hand.

Tyndale cleared his throat and looked down. "I almost forgot. This was on desk this morning."

The captain took it but continued to stare at Tyndale without a word.

"By your leave, sir?"

"Of course, XO."

Aregood watched Tyndale duck back inside the bridge. When he disappeared belowdecks, Aregood opened the folder. It was stamped "CONFIDENTIAL." Inside was an official memorandum from the operations officer. A special request on behalf of Ensign Sensor, which if approved, would allow him to depart on emergency leave for his grandfather's recent hospitalization. Griffin's memo further explained that since the ensign was not yet a fully qualified officer of the deck, his absence would not disrupt the watch schedule. It was also noted that the grandfather was Sensor's only living relative. The captain knew all of this; Sensor's file had been committed to memory since the shellback incident. Aregood scratched his chin, looked toward the gate, then out to the main ship channel. He tapped the sole of his shoe against the steel post of the bridgewing—clack clack clack.

Just then, Aregood saw Irving dashing down the pier. Slipping the cable, he thought. Aregood was reminded of the phrase whenever he saw crewmembers running for the ship. It meant the death of a shipmate, but the phrase originated when a vessel left its anchorage in a hurry, leaving its anchor and chain on the seafloor, never to return to that port. Running from trouble. But the only real trouble, the only real emergencies were to be found at sea.

Sailors are a superstitious lot, thought Aregood, and he was no different. Meeting Evelyn had been a sign, a validation, a reward from King Neptune himself. No, he would stay the course. Below, Irving clambered across the brow and disappeared inside the ship. That was everyone. Aregood uncapped his red pen and wrote "Denied" in bold, block letters.

Chapter 9

Like a seabird fanning a wing, the trail of the sun unraveled itself upon the water. Not a wave broke the surface, and from the starboard bridgewing, Jorge stared through the alidade at the spot on the ocean where the sun should have met the horizon, but did not. It was hidden in the haze. The sea and the sky were the same mercury, pooling into one another, and somewhere in the middle floated a few golden sparkles.

From the Keys, *Sentinel* had steamed eastward, north of Cuba, then down into the Windward Passage to patrol for a few days, boarding any suspicious vessels they encountered. Today, the crew's primary job was to prepare for, then conduct a gun exercise later that afternoon. As for Jorge's watch, the morning had been uneventful. He had but to simply continue their course and conn the cutter southeast, out of the confining Pass and into more open waters to fire their 76-millimeter.

Jorge breathed in the salty, glittering silence. Because of one phone call, his mid-patrol "break" was a bust. Kelly's was even worse. Right now though, the scenery was sublime, as peaceful as a church. The ensign stooped to peer through the alidade again.

Feeling that it was alive, Jorge did not want to disturb the water at play, just bring it into his line of sight and the soft light of day.

From inside the bridge: "Zero six thirty-five—sunrise!"

Straightening, Jorge gazed at the gleaming scene without the aid of the alidade—still no horizon, just the silver curtain all around him, broken only by the brush of fire from a bashful sun. The sun itself would soon enough burn off the morning cool. He turned and entered the bridge, picked up the starboard phone. It rang once, followed by a jostling on the other end of the line. "Cabin."

"Morning, captain. This is Mr. Vargas on the bridge. The time is 0635, sunrise. We're on a base course of 225 degrees True, speed twelve knots. No contacts, visible or otherwise. Visibility is about six nautical miles. Closest point of land is Navassa Island, 35 nautical miles off our port quarter. Nearest shoal water is the same. All's quiet, sir. Weather-wise, it looks like it's going to be a hot one."

"Barometer?"

"30.25 millibars, holding steady throughout my watch."

A pause. "Direction of waves and swells."

"F.A.S. sir."

"Winds."

"None."

"Engine and generator status."

"We're on the number one main diesel engine and the number two ship's service diesel generator, as per your night orders." He hoped he hadn't stressed your too much. It was Aregood's boat, Jorge knew this. The captain was ultimately responsible for everything, good and bad. He was also the one responsible for qualifying me, thought Jorge.

On a morning like this, if Jorge did not distract himself with the natural marvels of the sea, he would have been downright bored. This was open ocean. The sea was "flat ass calm." There were no visible contacts, so there was little chance of collision, and with the nearest shoal over thirty miles away, even less chance of running aground and the captain knew this.

"I'm coming up."

Jorge shook his head. "Yes sir."

He hung up and turned to address the bridge team. "Alright, look alive. He'll be up any minute."

"See if we wiped properly?" a seaman named Hosea mumbled from the helm.

With his face obscured as he peered through the visor of the radar's daytime hood, he smiled to himself at Hosea's crack. The young men tucked in their shirts and replaced their ball caps, and set to straightening up their workstations. Jorge watched his tired bridge team shuffle around and said, "Come on guys, you know you love the dogwatch?"

The 0400-0800 watch, or "dogwatch," was generally the crew's least favorite watch and since all watches aboard *Sentinel* required a relief by at least thirty minutes prior to the appointed time, in this case 0400, this meant the oncoming section actually took over at 0330. In order to properly relieve however, each watchstander had to ensure that his eyes were fully adjusted to the darkness, then gather all of the information from his predecessor and workstation. This process required that most of the oncoming bridge team be on deck between 0310 and 0315, which in turn meant waking up well before. Most watchstanders slept until the last possible moment. Jorge, as officer of the deck, responsible for not only the off-going OOD's information, but that of the entire bridge team, was on deck, showered, with coffee in hand, at 0250.

"This blows," said Hosea. "Zero to four is where its at. It's cool, it's quiet. Everyone's in the rack. Moon's out... The dogwatch starts that way, but then it gets lighter and lighter, and people start waking up, bugging you." He glanced at Jorge, broke into smile. "Grilling you about the barometer and shit."

Jorge laughed. "Fuck off, Hosea."

"Seriously, this watch reminds me of when my dad would kick open my bedroom door and yank up the blinds on a Saturday morning, telling me to mow the lawn or something."

"No way, the mids are boring. Sensor's a mids fan too and I just don't get it. If you're going to be on watch—."

Hosea looked away as if he had caught a whiff of something foul.

"Not you too. What'd he ever do to you?"

Hosea's mouth made an even line before he opened it to speak. "Sir, how would you like it if I said all officers were assholes?"

"What?"

"Right. So why should I like it when Sensor calls us deck apes? Says he can train a monkey to do what we do?"

Jorge was shocked. It was so ridiculous he started to laugh, but stopped himself. "He never said that."

"Not what I heard."

"From who?"

"Around the deck plates."

"You're serious?"

Hosea said nothing.

Jorge grew agitated. "That's horseshit. His only family was enlisted for fuck's sake. Seriously, put that out on the deck plates. Who told you that?"

"Sir..."

"A name, Hosea."

"Well, I heard Ir—."

"Captain on the bridge!" the quartermaster yelled.

As Aregood made a slow lap of the bridge, Jorge flashed Hosea a stern glance. Commander Aregood strolled over to Vargas to collect a salute. After a slow sip from a mug emblazoned with *Sentinel*'s crest and the letters "CO" in gilded script, Aregood asked, "What have you got?"

Jorge saluted, then faced the bow.

"No changes, captain."

"Changes?" asked Aregood, feigning naivete. Then his face tensed so quickly that it stunned Jorge. "From what."

A corner of Jorge's mouth ticked upward in the hint of a smile. Very well, he thought. "Base course 225 degrees True, ordered course 230..." Jorge repeated his report, ticking the facts off quickly and word for word from his previous report in his staccato delivery, just slow enough so as not to sound disrespectful. He slowed to a close. "No contacts. No wind, no waves, no swells." He grinned his shark-like grin. "No problems."

"I'll determine that, Mr. Vargas."

The captain brushed past him to get to the radar. He bent over and peered inside the visor. "When was the last time you checked this?"

"About three minutes ago. Just before you came up, sir."

"Well," he said, adjusting some knobs on the console, "looks to me like you've got a contact." The captain stood up suddenly and gestured toward the radar. "Maybe you'd like to see for yourself."

Jorge peered inside. A small yellow block had just come into view on the fringe of the screen, corresponding to a point off their port bow. He slipped his hands through two holes in the side of the hood and with a yellow grease pencil and knowledge of geometry, began calculating the contact's closest point of approach. He forgot about the captain hovering over him and became lost in the alternating blackness and sweeping yellow inside the hood, the small block whose course and speed he was calculating. The captain's own standing orders stated that only those contacts that approached *Sentinel* within three nautical miles or less, six thousand yards, required informing him, unless of course the contact appeared to be a TOI, a target of interest. The radar signature of this contact was small but defined even though it was over twenty miles out. Jorge finished and stood, trying not to smirk.

"Sir, the contact's heading 045 degrees True, speed 10 knots. Closest point of approach is off our port beam, at ten thousand yards. It's looks too small for a cruise liner or tanker but too big for a fishing boat. My guess is a coastal freighter. Unless you want to investigate, I recommend maintaining course and speed."

"Come left and calculate an intercept." The captain turned for the ladder to the rest of the ship below. "I'm going to eat breakfast. Call me in the wardroom when you get a visual." He stopped at the top of the ladder and faced Vargas, and loud enough for everyone on the bridge to hear said, "And Mr. Vargas, next time you report there are no contacts, make sure. That is a problem."

Jorge watched his captain recede down the steps, and when he could no longer hear the sharp clatter of his footsteps, glanced at Hosea. The seaman met his eyes for a second, then looked down.

Jorge turned and stared hard at the radar. "Thanks a lot," he said.

Chapter 10

Aregood sat at the long wardroom table poring over the watch schedule. The rotation was fairly fat for his Officers of the Deck. It had been a one-in-three rotation, but he had recently qualified Vargas, throwing him into the pool of certified ship-drivers so it was now a one-in-four rotation, meaning an OOD stood a four-hour watch, then had off for three shifts, twelve hours, to work or sleep. Of course, the captain, the executive officer, and the operations officer were also qualified officers of the deck however, of those three, only OPS stood watches if the rotation became too lean. The XO had administrative duties to contend with and as captain, it was only appropriate for Aregood to take the conn whenever absolutely necessary, or in cases of emergency. He ran the ship, others drove it. As he swallowed his last slice of sausage, Tyndale entered the wardroom.

"Looks like it's shaping up to be a scorcher, XO. Do we have anything of interest on the Plan of the Day today?"

"The 76-millimeter GUNEX after quarters. After that, the executive Steering Committee meeting at 1530. That's it, sir."

The phone rang. Aregood answered it, and received a brief status report from Ensign Vargas. Aregood ordered him to continue the intercept, then covered the mouthpiece and craned toward his executive officer. "What boarding team is on deck?"

"Alpha, sir."

"No. No, make it Bravo."

"Vargas is on that team. Isn't he on watch right now?"

"Just coming off," the captain said. Tyndale nodded. Aregood spoke into the receiver again. "Alert Bravo, Mr. Vargas. Yes, I realize Alpha is up. "A coastal freighter will be a good experience for you." He hung up.

"Coastal freighter, captain?" Tyndale asked.

"Vargas just got a visual, says it looks to be between 175 and 200 feet. Can't tell its flag yet, but it's heading northeast, probably toward the Pass. How about this morning, anything of import?"

"Just some engineering drills that can be rescheduled. Sir, with a freighter that size, will the normal four-man team be enough?"

"What did you have in mind?"

"Well sir, just thinking, but wouldn't this be an equally valuable experience for Ensign Sensor as well?"

Aregood consulted the watch schedule; Sensor just had the midwatch earlier that morning. In fact, he had the mids every night, and the 1200-1600 every day, putting him in a one-in-three status. Aregood would have had him stand "port and starboard," every other watch, but some onboard were beginning to question why he was not already qualified. Word in the Chief's Mess was that he was a decent ship-driver who ran a tight watch. But being a responsible OOD, and a good officer, was more than merely driving the ship from Port A to Port B. He looked at his watch: 0700. He would still be in the rack.

"Roust him."

When the captain stepped onto the bridge for the second time that morning, with Tyndale now in tow, there was no trace of the haze from just thirty minutes before. He could clearly see the contact six nautical miles away, off *Sentinel*'s starboard bow. He grabbed the "big eyes" marked CO, his personal set of binoculars, and stepped out onto the starboard bridgewing. As soon as he left the shelter of the pilothouse, he could feel the sun on his face. The air was still. Bravo's in for a hot one, he thought.

Through the big eyes, he had a perfect view of the freighter's beam. The ship appeared to be 175 feet in length, with the pilothouse forward, close to the bow. Amidships was a wide, clear area that swept all the way back to the stern, whose transom Aregood could not see enough to make out a name. The gunwales were roughly fifteen feet above the water. The freighter would have to throw a rope ladder down, if they consented to a boarding at all. Most did, though. A foreign-flagged vessel in international waters was not bound by U.S. maritime law and did not have to comply with a request for a U.S. Coast Guard boarding; Aregood imagined the 76-millimeter gun on the bow of his big white ship appeared quite compelling.

Aregood turned around and spoke to Vargas through the open window. "Who else is on Bravo?"

"Everline, Harmon, and Locklair. Chief Norris is on his way up to relieve me."

"No good. With the First Lieutenant on the boarding, Norris has to run the boat deck. Get Dane up here for the conn. Did you call OPS?"

"On his way, sir."

"Very well, continue your intercept. Hail them at five miles and begin 'Right of Approach' questions until Dane relieves you."

"Aye aye, sir."

"And get Irving up here on the helm."

Vargas hesitated. "Aye, sir."

"Something the matter, Mr. Vargas?"

"No sir."

"Well, don't just stand there gawking at me. Move!"

Aregood turned back toward the water and took a deep breath as he heard Vargas hurry away. He tasted the salt air and felt the sun's warmth bathe his face, ears, and neck. He closed his eyes and listened to the sounds of increasing activity inside the bridge. This was their business. There were one hundred men aboard *Sentinel*, and each man had his own area of expertise. It was times like these that their skills were harnessed, coalescing in to one smooth, safe evolution. The members of the Operations Department stood the bridge watch, keeping *Sentinel* on station and processing navigation information. The Deck Department lowered the ready boat to the water's edge, ensured the boarding team embarked safely, and piloted the boat once it was ready. The engineers ensured both of the cutter's engines were running without fail, and that the shafts could be disengaged at a moment's notice in case of emergency. The Support Department, comprised of storekeepers and yeoman, served as vital communication links throughout the ship, manning sound-powered phones and augmenting the bridge watch, who in turn kept *Sentinel* on station. It was *Sentinel*'s cycle of life. And at the center of it all, Aregood's hand guided their efforts.

A boarding was just another evolution performed by the symbiotic entities of his cutter, one of hundreds the crew would perform during any given patrol, which included Search and Rescue cases, flight operations, a variety of drills and exercises. Still, the very nature of their work, on the sea as they were, was inherently dangerous. All it took was one stray swell, one lost grip, a parted line or someone not paying attention, "losing the bubble" for just a second, for a limb or life to be lost. Even the simplest of evolutions was never to be taken lightly.

He smiled though. His boys were falling into place before him. He watched the quickened precision of his bridge team. Structure in action, the chain of command manifest. He smiled.

"Captain." Vargas appeared at the window. "Ready, sir?"

"Pipe it."

Chapter 11

"Now set the Law Enforcement Bill, set the LE Bill. Boarding Team Bravo on deck. This will be a hard-soled shoe boarding!" boomed from the loudspeaker outside Kelly's stateroom, louder than usual. Kelly grinned in the darkness and rolled over. A moment later, the stateroom telephone rang. Kelly groaned and reached for the wall-mounted receiver next to his rack. "Ensign Sensor."

"Kelly," Jorge said, "you're on deck for this boarding."

"I'm Alpha."

"I know, but the captain wants you on this one," then whispered, "coastal freighter. Says it'll be a good experience for both of us."

"All right, I'm up."

"I'll meet you on the fantail."

Kelly jumped from the rack and replaced the receiver in one motion. He flicked a nearby switch and pale fluorescent light flooded the stateroom as he stepped to the sink. He splashed some water onto his face. Peering into the mirror, he noticed that the black eye had faded once they put out to sea from Key West.

To become an underway officer of the deck, this was the singular reason an Academy graduate was sent to the fleet, their primary job aboard a cutter. Kelly and Jorge had both qualified as in port OOD's, running the watch section while in port, but underway was the showstopper. Once someone had all of their qualifications signed off, stood enough watches, and gained enough experience, the captain convened a board, comprised of himself, the XO, OPS, first lieutenant, and engineering officer to grill the break-in OOD on every aspect of *Sentinel*. If the candidate answered everything to their satisfaction, and earned the confidence of the captain, Aregood would deign the break-in "OOD qualified." He would then place a letter into their professional record, which is the first thing the promotion board for lieutenant junior grade looked for in an ensign's file. Without this underway qualification letter, a giant polished shoe descended to slam the brakes on the ensign's career, just eighteen months after it began.

Jorge had his underway qualification letter, allowing him the opportunity to pursue other qualifications, such as assistant boarding officer. His friend was speeding past him. Kelly tried to console himself with the knowledge that he was ready for qualification; the qualified officers who he broke in under, either out of confidence in him or their own laziness, always left him alone to run the watch his way. He knew all of the necessary nautical facts and then some, and he handled the ship just as well as any of the junior officers, except Jorge, he thought, whose instinct for the movement of the cutter seemed to border on the preternatural. But Kelly had developed his own "feel" for *Sentinel*. After eight months, he thought, I know my shit. He also knew, however, that it did not matter. Aregood would never grant him a board, and if he did, too late for the promotion round for lieutenant junior grade. Kelly peered into the future of his Coast Guard career. He could not see very far.

"Concentrate on the task at hand," he said to his reflection.

The farther Kelly peered into his Coast Guard career, the bleaker it seemed, because he could not, in fact, peer very far at all. Only the terminally incompetent, those who ran cutters aground or slept with another crewmember, got passed over. If you could fog a mirror and kept your nose clean you were promoted to LTJG. But if an officer did manage to get passed over once, chances are they would not rebound at the next promotion board, and those who were passed over twice were separated from the service and sent home with a severance check, a joke among their peers. There was no way around it. He was terminal. And all because he couldn't keep his mouth shut.

Kelly addressed his reflection in the mirror above the sink. "Concentrate on the task at hand."

He pulled his boarding gear from his locker. First, the bulletproof vest. He lifted it over his head and onto his shoulders where it hung like a heavy sandwich board. He jerked on the Velcro strips along the torso until the vest fit snug over his tee shirt. Then, he pulled on his dark blue coveralls with U.S. COAST GUARD stenciled in white on the back. Next he grabbed his marlinspike, a tool most of the crew carried, from the boatswain's mates who actually used to them to splice strands of rope, to the captain, who only played with his. Finally, he pulled on his boots, grabbed his ball cap, his orange life vest, and an empty black gunbelt and left the stateroom.

As he brushed past shipmates down the tight, bustling corridors of *Sentinel*, he heard quick footfalls throughout the rest of the cutter as people rushed to get to their appointed LE Bill stations. Within a minute, he reached the stern and the small arms locker belowdecks. Gaskey, the huge gunner's mate, sat cross-legged in the small space, waiting to sign over custody of his weapons. "You're the last one, sir."

"Sorry. Late rack."

"Uh huh," Gaskey answered, looking at his clipboard. "All right, got your cuffs?"

Kelly felt along the small of his back to be sure. His handcuffs, cool to his touch, sat in their pouch on his gunbelt. "Yep."

Gaskey continued, "One nine-millimeter, two clips." He handed Kelly a hollow pistol with the slide back and two fifteen round clips. Kelly held the pistol for a moment, felt the teeth of the grip bite into his hand. He then fit the gun into its holster on the right side of his belt, and one clip in a pouch just behind it. The other clip he placed in a pocket of his coveralls.

"Pepper spray," Gaskey read, then handed him a small, innocuous-looking canister. Kelly knew better. In order to be certified to carry pepper spray, one had to first be sprayed with it. For a brief, deceptive moment, Kelly had felt nothing, then his vision exploded in red flares and his eyes clamped shut against his will. He dropped to his knees. His throat burned as he tried to breathe and torrents of mucous gushed from his nose and obscenities from his mouth. Next to him he could hear Jorge shouting curses as well. Suddenly, the instructors attacked, trying to steal the ensigns' prop sidearms from their gunbelts. After a brief struggle, the ensigns were then told to identify how many fingers the instructors held up. Kelly pried an eye open, but could not see for the tearing.

By this time, his entire body was weak and shaking, and he and Jorge were led to buckets to dunk their burning heads and a garden hose to irrigate their eyes. The instructors told them to be careful when taking a shower when they got home. The next morning, Jorge cracked up the crew with a story of how, in the shower, the spray had washed out from his hair and dripped onto his privates.

"Something funny?" asked Gaskey.

"Nothing." Kelly slipped the spray into the left side of the gunbelt, gingerly.

"Sign here." Gaskey handed him a clipboard and Kelly scrawled his initials next to each of the items Gaskey had relinquished. As Kelly turned to walk away, Gaskey stopped him. "You forgot this." He tossed him a small but heavy rod, covered with a foam grip, the expandable baton. With one flick of the wrist, the six-inch steel rod telescoped to a full two-feet, with a small, shiny ball at the tip. The baton, like the pepper spray, was to be used as an intermediate step, a last resort before going for the nine-millimeter. It was not considered a "deadly force" weapon, but when wielded with enough force, it could crack bones with ease.

"Thanks, Gaskey."

"Break a leg."

Kelly ascended the stairs to the main passageway then exited the watertight door that led to the fantail. The air-conditioning and muted illumination inside *Sentinel* gave no indication of the tropical morning outside the skin. He squinted. The humidity was stifling, like walking into a wall. Immediately, he felt beads of sweat soaking the undershirt beneath his bulletproof vest and coveralls. When his vision cleared, he could see the deckies lowering the port ready boat, the rigid hull inflatable dubbed SENT-2, to the water's edge. Beyond them, at the end of the fantail, he saw Bravo team gathered.

Before joining them, Kelly walked over to starboard railing. He could see the freighter. *Sentinel* had taken station behind it and to the left, off the freighter's port quarter, about two miles away. The freighter's deck was high off the water. They would have to climb to get onboard. He slammed a clip into the grip of the gun with his palm then released the slide, careful to keep the muzzle pointed over the cutter's side. He flicked the safety on, then snapped the nine millimeter into his holster. Locked and loaded, he joined the rest of the team: LTJG Everline, Jorge, Harmon, and Locklair, an electronics technician from Georgia.

"Nice of you to join us, Sensor," Everline said, pulling a small notebook from the front pocket of his coveralls. "Mind if I start?"

Kelly ignored him, returned a nod from Jorge.

Everline, the boarding officer, began. "All right girls, we've got a 180-foot Panamanian-flagged coastal freighter, name of *Doña Maria*. The master is Panamanian, but the crew's a mixed bag.

Last port of call was Balboa, Panama, on their way to Port-au-Prince. The master says there's no weapons onboard and the cargo is miscellaneous. Sugar, thermoses, toys, you name it. You all know the deal. It's a consensual boarding, but we're checking to see if there's any intel on it. All we have so far is that it's on a course that could potentially take it to the southeast U.S., and the skipper wants another boarding for the books. Once we get over, Sensor, Harmon, and Locklair, you three fan out for the Initial Safety Inspection. Vargas and I will question the master and crew. Any questions?"

When no questions followed, Everline spoke into the team's portable radio. "*Sentinel*, Bravo. Manned and ready."

A second later, the operations officer's voice crackled back, "Roger. Man the boat."

The boat's coxswain, Hosea, and an engineer named Turner were waiting for them. One by one, the members of Bravo dropped aboard, rocking the boat with each new member. Standing over the precipice, Kelly felt his adrenaline really begin to rush. Soon, the boat would whisk them to another ship, where they could encounter anything. "Anything" usually meant in a lot of crawling in the grimy holds of foul-smelling freighters or getting seasick on tiny, bobbing sailboats, but still... He scurried down the rope ladder and at the last rung, leapt onto the boat.

The sea was serene, like a mirror, and Kelly was always amazed to see the passage of the water up close. The small boat was still lashed to *Sentinel*, and little rivulets of water curled around it. Kelly stared down at the blue, then back up at the white side of the cutter, running his hand over the cool hull.

When the last boarding team member embarked, the deckies above dropped the lines into SENT-2 that had held it fast to *Sentinel*. Kelly and Jorge, sitting in the rear of the boat, dutifully coiled them. When the final line, the sea painter, was disconnected from the bow of the small boat, Hosea, at the wheel, spoke into his radio. "SENT-2 away."

Suddenly, the seaman gunned the engine. The boat picked up speed like a gunshot, then planed above the water as it diverged from the cutter. Though Kelly had been on dozens of boardings, the sight of *Sentinel* shrinking away from them still amazed him. *Sentinel* was his home on the sea, but he relished the boat ride away, those few moments after leaving but before the real work of the boarding began. With no waves to slow the boat, SENT-2 skimmed across the pond-like water, the breeze a cool blessing on Kelly's skin.

"Look alive, girls!" barked Everline.

The ready boat closed on the freighter, then matched its speed. Only inches from *Doña Maria*, Kelly was surprised at how large the freighter appeared up close, and how filthy. The pasty smell of algae and iron assaulted him. The elements had taken their toll: running rust everywhere, strings of seaweed hanging from every outcropping, a hull encased in barnacles and sorely in need of a fresh coat of paint.

SENT-2 advanced alongside until it reached a thick rope ladder hung amidships. Staring up, Kelly guessed the climb to be about twenty feet. He was never wild about this part, being at the mercy of a freighter full of strangers. And though he had never heard of such a thing, what if those strangers decided to cut that ladder, their lifeline, as the team dangled alongside the crusty hull? They would all end up in the drink, bouncing along the waterline of the freighter until they were sucked into its enormous propellers. Even with the freighter traveling at just five knots, it would take only seconds. There wouldn't even be a chance to surface, to scream and claw along the hull. One minute you're climbing, a young Coast Guard officer with a belt full of weapons; the next, chum.

It was time to dismiss those thoughts now. He was poised to climb. First Jorge, then Everline. When it was his turn, he caught the swinging ladder with both hands and propelled himself off the pontoon with one foot, hooking a rung with the other. It was slippery, but he clambered up the ladder as fast as he could without climbing onto the back of the man ahead of him. He made it over the rail in seconds, and when he was firmly on his feet, he noticed that Jorge and Everline had already fanned out, taking positions to ensure the safety of the teammates still climbing aboard. Moments later, Harmon and Locklair came over the gunwale.

A small, plump man with bronze skin stood several feet away. He wore ratty shorts and a torn tee shirt and offered a wide smile. Behind the fat man stood a wiry young man who looked no older than Kelly, wearing a Chicago Bulls jersey. The younger man paid no attention to the boarding team, scraping the rubber toe of a high-topped sneaker across the metal deck.

Everline addressed the cheerful fat man. "Good morning sir, I'm Officer Everline with the U.S. Coast Guard. We're here to check your compliance with applicable federal laws and regulations. Now sir, without reaching for or touching them, do you have any weapons onboard?"

The man held up his hands and laughed. It sounded like a grunt. "No, señor. No, no."

"Very well. Are you the master of this vessel?" Everline asked. When the man nodded, he continued the standard speech. "Please muster your crew on the fantail while my teammates check this ship for your safety and ours."

"Sí, of course."

Everline circled the air with his finger. "Alright you three, begin the ISI." The Initial Safety Inspection meant sweeping the entire boat to ensure that the platform was safe enough for the boarding team to even be there. It also gave them their bearings, and a chance to spot any clues or contraband in plain view. With that came "articulable suspicion of wrongdoing," and by the standards of maritime law, cause for an extended search.

Each man took off his life jacket and left it along the bulkhead. Everline and Jorge headed aft to the fantail.

"Alright, old man," said Harmon to Locklair, "you're the boarding guru. How do you want to do this?"

"Start low," Locklair said, "do a quick sweep of the holds. Then we'll work our way up, check out the main deck, berthing areas, bridge, etc. That fine by you, sir?"

"You're the guru."

Locklair smiled. "Good answer."

The three men started forward and found a hatch leading to the holds below. Kelly followed Locklair and Harmon down a ladder into the darkness. Even out of the sun, the heat and humidity in the hold was stifling. Renewed perspiration rolled into his eyes. When he reached bottom, Kelly wiped his brow and pulled a pen light from his boarding belt. Pallets stretched as far as the eye could see.

"Fan out," Locklair said.

The men walked abreast of each other, walking from fore to aft, sweeping their lights along the decks to look for standing water or other safety hazards, and also along each pallet to look for any signs of smuggling. Kelly could only make out rust, filth, and sundry stacks wrapped in cellophane: plastic thermoses, roach motels, Kewpie dolls. After thirty minutes, the men congregated at the ladder. "Anything of interest?" Locklair asked.

"Nothing," Kelly said.

"Not unless we want to break open some of these pallets," Harmon said.

"Normally, I think we could get away with a random sampling," Locklair said, "but we've got no real cause at this point."

Locklair led the way back up the ladder. The heat was still intense, but once topside, Kelly was relieved to discover the hint of a breeze. The trio walked back to fantail where five crewmen lounged around the metal decks like lizards on a hot rock. The man in the basketball jersey stood alone. Locklair did not interrupt as Everline and Vargas questioned the master, but gave the boarding officer a thumbs-up to indicate the hold checked out. Everline returned it and the trio filed past the lolling crew to an open door that led inside the ship.

Before them was a long passageway, and to Kelly's immediate left another ladder descended to the deck below. Locklair spoke up. "No air-conditioning? Fuck!"

"Even we have that," Harmon said.

"All right, check out the berthing areas. Sean, you take this deck. Sir, you've got the one below. Grab each other when you're through, then rendezvous on the fantail so we can get off this steambox."

Harmon disappeared into a stateroom and Kelly went below. At the base of the ladder, he stood before a nearly identical passageway to the one above, lined with doors on both sides. Situated halfway to the end of the main passageway, another smaller corridor ran perpendicular.

Kelly opened the first few doors and discovered staterooms for the crew. He scanned the rooms looking for any hazards or signs of contraband. All of the rooms on either side of the passageway were the same: scattered laundry, small bunkbeds, posters of naked women adorning the bulkheads. Near the intersection of corridors, he entered a cramped stateroom and bashed his right hand on a metal leg of one of the double racks. It resounded with a loud clang, the impact jolting Kelly's arm up to his elbow. He gritted his teeth and squeezed his wrist. Looking down, he discovered his Academy ring was now hollow, the goodie missing.

"Shit!" In the small compartment, the curse sounded like a rocket launching.

He spun around, searching the floor. He saw nothing but heaps of dirty clothes. He looked at the closed door leading back to the passageway, then dropped to his knees and inspected each piece of clothing before flinging it over his shoulder. While on his hands and knees, he noticed two tiny eyes glittering at him from beneath the bunk. Kelly flinched. The eyes remained motionless as Kelly pulled his penlight from his boarding belt. He shone it under the rack, but could not discern exactly what looked back at him. It did not look alive. He grasped the object and pulled it out, a small wooden totem with a garish mouth and two black, stone eyes.

Voodoo, thought Kelly. From his port briefs and boarding team training, he knew it was a popular religion in parts of the Caribbean. Smugglers who practiced it often placed charms around their contraband to ward off bad luck, and potential discoverers. Conversely, it helped Coasties zero in on the goods. Of course, Kelly reasoned, not all voodooists were smugglers. It seemed unlikely to him that anyone would hide contraband in a stateroom, especially with a nice, dark hold crammed with endless pallets and nondescript containers. Still, he straightened and scanned the walls and shelves again, just to be sure. Nothing out of the ordinary.

As he bent down again to find the goodie, something caught his attention in the corner, another totem. Slowly, he looked behind him. A small totem stood in every corner. They all glared at Kelly.

Chapter 12

Vargas and Everline had been roasting on the fantail for nearly an hour. The sun glared at them like the eye of an angry god, causing the air above the deck plates to shimmer. Everyone had soaked through their uniforms.

"My God," said Everline, "these guys smell like a bucket of dicks."

They had finished questioning the master twenty minutes before. It had not gone quickly; the man's broken English slowed proceedings. Jorge had offered to translate in Spanish, but Everline sent him away. He knew the boarding officer enjoyed making the master fumble with his words. When he finished with his questions, Everline leaned against the gunwale at the stern and completed the boarding report.

Jorge scanned the fantail...the crew lounging without a care. They had been through the drill before and despite the sluggish heat, the boarding gave them a respite from their labors. They joked among themselves quietly, and every so often, would burst into quick, raucous laughter, then quiet down and doze again as if the effort proved too much in this weather. The wiry man in the basketball gear stood alone by the starboard rail, facing the sea. Every few seconds, he glanced at Everline.

Skirting past the dozing men, Jorge approached him from the side. He placed his palms on the railing and was standing in place beside the man like he had been there all along. "Jordan fan?"

Startled, the young man swung his head away from Everline to Jorge. He had seemed anxious to Jorge from the moment the ensign set foot on *Doña Maria*. That was the case for some boardings though. A team of armed men coming over the railing was never an experience free of anxiety for anyone, even if crews had nothing to hide, but on coastal freighters, the crews became accustomed to a certain amount of U.S. Coast Guard presence.

The young man's features and complexion made it difficult to discern his nationality at a glance. Could be from any of the islands, Jorge thought, Central or South America too. Jorge decided to stick with English. "I asked if you were a Michael Jordan fan."

"Jordan, yes. Yes." Jorge detected a coastal accent.

"Yeah, he's something. I'm a Knicks fan myself." If he recognized the team, it did not register on the young man's face. "What's your name?"

"Silvio."

"It's hot as balls out here, Silvio."

Silvio smirked, gave a stuttered breath through his nose.

"Where're you from, Silvio?"

"Venezuela."

"Whereabouts?"

"La Guirra."

Jorge brightened. "Our boat was there last summer! I'll tell you, there's some damn fine looking women down there." He held two imaginary melons in front of his chest, "*Tetas grandes*, no?"

Silvio laughed, freely this time, but he soon craned his neck toward Everline again, then back toward the ocean in front of him. "What's he doing over there?"

"Oh him? Standard operating procedure. Hell, we must do a hundred of these a patrol."

Silvio's eyebrows arched. "Yeah?"

"Sure. We'll be out of your hair soon enough. Anyway, nice talking to you, Silvio."

"Yeah, man." His hand darted up in a quick wave, then back down again.

Jorge walked past him, then stopped. "Oh, just so we can wrap up and get out of this heat—where did you say your last port of call was again?"

"Oh, Barranquilla."

"Right. Thanks, Silvio."

Jorge walked past the dozing men once again, this time with no regard for stealth. Some of the men awoke, scrunching their eyebrows and looking at one another, as if they had forgotten where they were. A few looked toward Silvio. Jorge leaned up against the gunwale next to Everline, watching the group of men stir.

Everline acknowledged Jorge's presence by glancing at the ensign's boots and sniffing once. "What were you doing over there, asking him out?"

"Have you ever heard of rapport?"

"I am filling out the report, boot."

Jorge lifted his head toward the sun and gave it a tiny shake. Without opening his eyes, he said, "Just humor me and tell me *Doña Maria*'s last port of call."

"Balboa, Panama."

Jorge folded his arms and grinned.

"What?"

"My boy over there just told me it was Barranquilla. Colombia."

Everline pressed his behind into the railing, bouncing himself to a standing position. He pivoted to face Jorge, all smiles. "Really now...."

Chapter 13

The ensign's hands had been deep in a pile of clothes when he realized he was surrounded by a troop of voodoo icons. Each wore a hideous grin, rimmed with fangs and eyes that bored into him, accusatory. Though he wore a bulletproof vest and a belt lined with formidable weaponry, the idols gave him a chill. Kelly ran his fingers across the carpet, moving a bundle of clothes aside and staring at them staring at him when his forefinger snagged on something.

Kelly swept the clothes into a corner, on top of the nearest doll, and stared at the stateroom's carpet, gently running the palm of his hand back and forth. In the center of the room, a section of carpet roughly two square feet was slightly raised. He pulled his expandable baton from its slot and tapped the butt in various spots along the deck, inside and outside of the square. Despite the dulling quality of the thin, gray carpeting, a faint hollowness could be heard from the raised section of the deck.

He stood and surveyed the room once more, trying to remember the legal standards of a search, but the heat, and the gallop of his own heart made it difficult to concentrate on the tenets of maritime law. He wiped his brow with his forearm and remembered. Articulable suspicion of wrongdoing.

But what did he have so far, really? A few voodoo dolls and a raised, maybe hollow deck. Of course the decks were uneven. It was an old Panamanian rustbucket for God's sake, not exactly the apex of of marine design and shipbuilding. Was it articulable? Would he look like a fool to the rest of the team? Did he really need to give them another excuse?

"Do your damn job, Sensor," he muttered.

Suddenly, he spied a faint line in the carpet by his feet. The line formed a large, squared U, its three sides flanking the raised square of deck. Kelly walked over to the door and locked it, deciding he would investigate on the spot. If it turned out to be nothing, he'd be back on *Sentinel* within the hour, with no one the wiser.

He crouched along the outside of the U, tugging at its base. It came up neatly. He continued to lift, rolling back a five square foot swatch of carpeting, revealing the dark deckplates below. The plates appeared normal enough, but he noticed a small hole in one of them and inserted his thumb to lift it, moving slowly so as not to bang the steel plate and alert anyone. With a small shing, the thin plate came up with ease. Kelly peered inside the small space. He spied a temperature gauge and nestled alongside it, a single, transparent bag of snow-white powder. It gleamed against the black plates and the drab tones of the cramped stateroom.

"Oh."

His heart slammed in his chest and a wave of heat, beginning in the base of his neck swelled up the back of his head to his brow. He thought it was difficult to think before, his concentration was now shattered. He tried to think, but every cop show he had watched flooded his head: the stoic detective raising his little finger to his mouth, the fingernail coated with the questionable powder, the outcome unsure until he rolls his tongue around his perfect white teeth for a few dramatic moments. A knowing smile. The partner nods, the handcuffed suspect sags. Jackpot, punk.

He replaced the deck plate, and rolled the carpet back into place. In two steps, he was back at the door, quietly unlocking it. He stuck his head into the passageway, looking up and down the corridor. As loudly as he dared, he whispered, "Harmon." Again, louder, "Harmon!"

Finally, giving a raspy yell, "Sean!"

To his left, from the stairwell at the end of the passageway, he heard footsteps. It was the quartermaster. Annoyed, he crossed the distance to Kelly. "What's taking you so long? Let's go."

"Come in here."

Once Harmon stepped inside the stateroom, Kelly locked the door behind him. "What?" Harmon asked, but Kelly did not bother to answer, just rolled the carpet back and stepped aside. He gestured toward the deck plate. "Go on."

Harmon looked at him, then bent down and stuck his thumb into the hole, removing the plate. He stared inside for a few, speechless moments.

"Oh."

"Good, you see it too. I thought I was hallucinating."

Harmon looked up at Kelly, his irritation replaced by an enormous, goofy grin. His eyes gleamed. "I've been on a hundred boardings and all I've ever found was some swordfish below the legal limit, but this…this…"

"This is articulable suspicion?"

"This is beyond a reasonable fucking doubt."

This was not business as usual for anyone; Harmon's reverie snapped Kelly out of his own. "First thing, we need to coordinate with the rest of the team. Where's Locklair?"

"Still on the bridge, I guess."

Kelly considered it for a moment. "Alright then, go tell Everline. And Jorge. I'll wait right here."

Harmon sprung to his feet. He unlocked the door, but turned around before stepping into the passageway again. He looked at Kelly once more, as excited as the ensign had ever seen him. He struggled with forming an appropriate word. Kelly felt his own smile beginning to cramp his cheeks. "Go on, before I piss myself," he said. He replaced the plate as soon as Harmon disappeared.

"Wait, Sean!"

Harmon's head reappeared in the doorway. "What?" He was already breathless.

"We don't want the crew getting frisky. Remember to use the password."

"Right." Then the quartermaster disappeared, leaving Kelly to the idols once more.

Chapter 14

Within minutes, the demeanor on deck had changed. Jorge stood in the starboard quarter of the ship, his back to the sea. From his station, he watched the rousing men with mounting unease. Most of them were still sitting, but they were all alert now. Several of the men glanced over their shoulders, at Silvio, and the young man seemed to wither under their stares. He looked nauseated. The heat helped no one's disposition.

Everline was either unaware of or unconcerned with the escalating level of activity on the fantail and acted as if all it took to quell any dubious inclinations of a boatload of men was the swelling of his own chest. He renewed his questioning of the master. Once the conflicting reports of *Doña Maria*'s previous port of call had been detected, other tiny fissures became apparent in the crew's pretense. Coming over the rail, Jorge had noticed a welding rod. Another was found among a pile of tools on the fantail. When questioned by Everline, neither the master nor any of the men admitted knowledge of how to operate them. Their stories were not adding up, thought Jorge. The only thing that was adding up was articulable suspicion.

Jorge eyed the instruments scattered across the deck: the rods, crowbars, hammers, screwdrivers. The sun glinted off the blade of a machete standing erect in a block of wood, its handle beckoning for a wielder. Jorge wiped sweat from his brow. Ordinary nautical tools, he told himself.

As the crew grew more agitated, the master became even more unctuous. The smile had never left his lips, though his eyes, like Silvio's, had gone nervous, nearly lunatic. "You boys almost done? Caray, aren't you hot?"

Just then, Harmon appeared, walking through the small crowd toward Everline and the master. Jorge joined them.

Everline nodded at Harmon. "What's up?"

Harmon glanced at the master, then at Steve. "Nothing. I could go for a cup of coffee though," he said. He turned to Jorge. "You know?"

"Café in this heat?" the master laughed. As if he were a member of the team, he turned to Everline. "Don't you boys want sodas instead?"

Everline smiled sweetly. "Will you excuse us please, sir?"

"Okay."

When the master returned to his crew, Everline asked, "You got coffee, for real?" Harmon nodded.

As soon as Harmon finished his story, Jorge returned his full concentration to the knot of men. A very dark crewmember wearing blue jeans and a matching denim work shirt had left the group and approached Silvio. The ensign could not ascertain their conversation, but he could make out the dark man's accent. It sounded French—Creole. Haitian. He appeared to be questioning Silvio. The man's hands were at his sides, but the muscles in his arms were tensed, and Silvio leaned back slightly, fearful.

Away from Harmon and Everline, Jorge waved the master over. The fat man hurried over. "*Sí, mi amigo?*"

Lifting his chin in the direction of the two men, he said, "What's that all about?"

"That? Oh, roommates. Young Silvio's a slob. He and Henri always fight."

"Lover's spat, huh?"

The man exploded into laughter. "*Sí, sí!* Lover's spat. Very good."

Jorge looked over the fat man's shoulder, heard a sibilant curse as Silvio's roommate turned his back to the young man. Henri's eyes were wide with anger. Harmon, across the fantail on the port side, watched the rest of the grumbling shipmates, unaware of the quarrel on Jorge's side.

Perspiration collected in the armpits of Jorge's coveralls. He had a sickening notion that the situation was deteriorating. Losing the bubble, that was the phrase for it in ship-driving jargon. Too many things occurring to safely keep track of, the big picture forfeit. A chain of events sliding toward disaster. Losing the bubble. He probed his pants pocket, his thumbnail ticking along the worn ridges of the familiar shell for comfort. He rubbed it for luck.

A few feet away, he watched Everline turn his back to the crew and pull the radio from his belt. "*Sentinel,* Bravo."

Chapter 15

"We sure could use some coffee over here!"

The excitement of his bridge team spiked as the keyword crackled over the radio. Aregood fought to appear measured as the pilothouse erupted in cheers. "All right, all right. Settle down, everyone. It's not in the bag yet, let's do it by the numbers." Yet, in the back of his mind, Aregood was excited. Ecstatic. A cocaine bust? Nothing beat a bust, nothing. First Evelyn, now this. King Neptune was smiling upon him indeed.

Still, true to his word, he realized that nothing was certain; simply having heard the keyword meant that neither contraband nor the crew had been seized yet. Aregood had been involved in busts before, on other cutters. Now was the dicey time. A seizure necessitated precision and the utmost in professionalism from every member of the boarding team and *Sentinel*'s crew, particularly from him. He banished all thoughts of promotion from his head. His crew was on *Doña Maria*, and a bust was worthless if they didn't all come back in one piece.

Aregood stepped out to the starboard bridgewing. *Sentinel* was six hundred yards off *Doña Maria*'s port quarter now. Peering through his binoculars, he could see the members of his boarding team spaced along the freighter's fantail: Harmon on the port side, Everline in the center, Vargas starboard. They formed a crescent, roughly flanking a handful of men.

The captain lowered his binoculars. Beside him stood his officer of the deck. "Mr. Dane, bump up your speed a bit. Nothing to alarm them, but close them to 300 yards. I'm going to have OPS relieve you of the deck so you can concentrate on driving."

"Aye, captain."

As his proxy gave the commands, the captain turned back to the pilothouse, where Lieutenant Griffin had stationed himself by the radio. Through the open window, Aregood said, "OPS, prepare to put SENT-1 in the water. I want Alpha suited up, briefed, and ready to go. First though, roger up to Everline." Aregood allowed himself a half-smile. "Tell him we're brewing."

Griffin grinned. "Aye aye, sir."

The enthusiasm was infectious. It had already saturated the bridge, and was spreading. Once the second boarding team was piped the entire ship would know; two teams were not needed for uneventful boardings. Like a stone thrown into a pond, that one simple word was causing ripples to radiate outward, even beyond the skin of *Sentinel*. In the Combat Information Center behind the bridge, Aregood knew Chief Radarman Collins would be preparing a SITREP about Team Bravo's discovery. The Joint Interagency Task Force watch center, headquartered in Key West, would soon be humming as well. The buzz was in the air. Only one person seemed oblivious to the buzz. "What's the matter, Irving?"

Irving shook his head. "All this excitement over a cup of coffee?"

Aregood laughed. "It's a boarding team thing. Coffee's just a keyword for contraband, more specifically cocaine. Think you might be interested in qualifying for a boarding team now, son?"

"Why all the cloak and dagger, using keywords and stuff? Why not just draw down on them?"

"It's not as simple as that. Just pulling out your gun and slapping the cuffs on before you do a full threat assessment can be dangerous. It may escalate the situation unnecessarily. There are still crewmembers throughout that freighter, on the bridge, and maybe the engine room. Our team needs maximum coordination to round them all up safely. You see, one must plan for every contingency." Irving's eyes were beginning to glaze over. Aregood continued, "Because if one of those dirtbags panics, some serious shit could blow up in everyone's faces."

"Makes sense." He glanced over the steering console, but snapped his head back at his captain. "Sir, if some shit does go down, are you sure I should be the one—."

Aregood placed his hand on the seaman's shoulder. The seaman, startled, withdrew slightly, but the captain held him fast. He lowered his voice. "Relax."

"But captain, I—."

Aregood had no time for doubt. Or whining. He tightened his grip, pressing his thumb into the soft area just beneath the collarbone until he saw one of the seaman's eyes twitch. He brought his face closer to Irving's so no one else would hear. "Why do you think I chose you as master helmsman? Because you're the best. And do you know why you're the best?"

The seaman shook his head.

"Because I said so." Aregood released him and backed away. He spoke up, friendly again. Breezy. "Don't worry, if anything happens, we're all right here. I'm not going to hang you out to dry. Now, look at that" he said, gesturing toward the front windows, and the bow beyond. From their position behind the helm, they could see the barrel of *Sentinel*'s huge, domed 76-millimeter gun, which could fire 80 shells as big as a man's leg in a minute.

"Now look at that." Aregood then pointed over the starboard bow, at the rusted freighter. "If you were them, would you want to fuck with us?"

Chapter 16

As Henri crossed the fantail, he pretended to stumble within a few feet of Everline. At the same moment, the master, with his uneasy smile, tried to get Jorge's attention. "Wait, *amigo*, wait!" Jorge ignored his distraction and yelled "Steve!" but the boarding officer had been intent on his radio. He never knew what hit him.

Wheeling to correct his feigned imbalance, Henri dropped his shoulder. Hunched over, his step quickened from a flailing shuffle to rapid, piston-like strides. At the last second, he slammed into Everline, exploding upward into the young lieutenant's kidneys. Jorge marveled as he lunged for his teammate. It was a perfect football hit. Everline toppled over the rail.

Jorge had anticipated some illicit action from the man in denim. As such, the ensign had already been elbowing past the master, lining Henri up just in case, before the Haitian had even begun his bogus stagger.

Jorge watched Everline grab for the rail as he fell. The lieutenant caught it, breaking the momentum of his fall for a second. As he swung around, however, and his legs slammed into the transom, he lost his grip. This time, Jorge was there. He grabbed for Everline's wrist, under his silver watch, just as the boarding officer's hand slipped from the rail.

Suddenly, two hundred and fifty pounds of weight slammed Jorge into the rail. The weight threatened to jolt Jorge's arm out of its socket. Over two hundred pounds of writhing, panic-stricken Everline himself, a pair of steel-toed boots, a bulletproof vest, and a belt loaded with heavy weapons dangled over the prop wash. Everline scraped the stern with his boots, but found no purchase in the hull, slick with green algae and seaweed. All he succeeded in doing was thudding into the stern again and again, twisting and turning Jorge's sore arm, yanking the ensign downward. "Steve, stop! Stop!"

Everline obeyed, and the two hundred and fifty pounds went limp in his hand. Behind him, Jorge heard mayhem. The screeching of frenzied footsteps on the deck. Frantic curses, shrieked commands. He prayed the crew wasn't going for Harmon. With his free hand, he groped to protect his holster, but as soon as he let go of the rail, his feet began to rise off the deck. He had no choice. He clutched the rail to his chest again for leverage. He wrenched his neck and screamed. "Sean, keep them off me!"

Knowing he had no hope of pulling his boarding officer back aboard, Jorge bellowed for the small boat. It was too far away to hear, but he saw an orange shape speeding toward them nonetheless. Jorge looked down again. His shipmate was staring up at him when the radio slid from his belt. It made no sound as it disappeared in the wake. Jorge imagined the propeller, submerged in the roaring waters just five feet below Everline's boots, claiming it.

Everline moaned. "Oh, God!"

Chapter 17

"Man overboard!"

Aregood spun and raised his binoculars. Through the big eyes, he could see chaos on the deck of *Doña Maria*, Harmon shouting with his hands in front of him, the crew swirling before him, moving helter-skelter like sharks before a feeding frenzy, crowding and bumping him. He saw the quartermaster reach for his holster.

Suddenly, *Sentinel* lurched, causing both Aregood and LTJG Dane to stumble. The cutter began a sharp turn to starboard. "As you were!" Dane yelled to the helmsman.

Whenever "man overboard" was shouted during drills, it was standard operating procedure for all helmsmen to turn the cutter to side the man went over, thereby kicking the stern and the screws away from him. Irving must have put the rudder over hard to starboard. Aregood was livid. "Not on here, on the goddamn freighter!"

"Wait," Dane shouted, "Vargas has him, captain!"

Aregood trained the big eyes on the freighter once more. Sure enough, Everline was suspended above the water by the ensign. The lieutenant's feet fluttered against the stern. The big officer then reached up with his free hand and grasped the wrist that held him. Even through the binoculars, Aregood could make out the strain on Vargas' face.

Aregood screamed into the bridge. "I want that small boat over there now! I don't know what's going on over there, but I want to be up that freighter's ass yesterday! Dane, full bell!"

"Aye aye. Helmsman, all ahead ten!"

"All ahead ten, aye!" replied Irving.

The cutter rumbled and shook. From the bowels of *Sentinel*, the engines worked to triple her speed immediately. Still, it would take time to close the distance, critical seconds the boarding team did not have. He scanned the fantail once more. Harmon had drawn his nine-millimeter, the crew now giving him ample room at least. Everline hung like a sack of meat.

Enraged, Aregood stormed back inside the bridge. He grabbed the microphone and keyed the ship's intercom. "All gunners mates, energize the 76-millimeter and man the starboard fifty caliber."

Griffin beheld his captain over the rims of his glasses. "Captain, the 76? Our people are on that boat!"

"Repeat, all gunners mates, energize the 76-millimeter and man the starboard fifty caliber." He slammed the microphone back into its housing and tramped over to his operations officer. "I didn't order the fucking gun fired, just manned. It's a deterrent. I want them to see it pointing down their throats when we ride up on them. Acquire the target if you don't mind while I continue to run my ship."

"Aye, sir." Griffin reached for the mounted telephone.

The captain looked over his shoulder. He caught a sheepish Irving watching and listening. "You see, son?" said Aregood. "The chain!"

Chapter 18

They hadn't lost the bubble, Jorge realized, it had popped. Fucking exploded and it had all happened in a flash. Everline, oblivious, had turned his back to the crew. No, Jorge corrected himself, the arrogant bastard had actually flared it, like the hood of a cobra. He gave them a target for Christ's sake. And with Everline's center of gravity so high, he had gone right over. It was a better hit than even Henri could have hoped for.

Now every muscle in Jorge's body was rigid, and gravity was merciless. Everline's full weight hung on his arm, which jerked his shoulder downward. His shoulder strained the muscles in his neck, his neck his jaw, and the side of his face stretched in his mouth into a rictus. Spittle flowed down his cheek. A searing pain ran the entire length of his fingertips to his temple. His head throbbed. He felt pearls of sweat bead from every pore, and salty rivulets flow into his eyes. He squeezed them shut only to see sickly orange spots flower on the backs of his lids. He was going to throw up.

It was not just physical sickness, it was terror. He could only hold on for another moment or two. Jorge clutched the gunwale to his chest as an anchor, fully realizing that his belt was exposed—

the handle of his firearm jutting into the air, asking to be grasped by anyone. Still, he dared not let go of the rail to protect his belt or he'd follow Everline right over the side. In this position, he could do nothing but imagine a phantom tug on his holster, cold steel against the back of his head. Either way, he was helpless. He began to get angry, furious at his predicament and the orange spots melted in a red cloud. Rebellion shot through his heart and gave his muscles a brief renewal. But the humidity, the sweat...he was losing his grip for good. Everline's second hand slipped off, and he twisted above the water. "Jorge, please!"

"Shut up."

Suddenly, his feet began to lift off the deck once more. He hooked a boot under a lower rung, and kicked his other leg back for balance, but he felt the suction created from the curve of his armpit give. He was going over. Just then, he heard shouting below, to his left. He shook his head, cleared his vision. It was Hosea, a few feet off the quarter, just beyond the churning waters of the propeller, the boat unable to maneuver any closer. Jorge felt buoyed. Tensing the leg that held the rung and planting his other foot on the deck, he arched his back with a final burst of strength, causing the rail to bite into his underarm even more. He wrenched his shoulder to the side, at the same time beginning to run to his left. The sweat from his underarm allowed him to slide along the rail, toward the small boat. He squeezed Everline's wrist as savagely as he could, and hurled him to the side and the waiting boat below at the same instant the lieutenant slipped away. Jorge heard a tiny, metallic pop and Everline scream. All at once, he saw a flash of brilliant silver, his own arm against the blue sky, and felt his burden, two hundred and fifty pounds, gone.

His good shoulder slammed into the deck as he ricocheted back onto the fantail. His legs flipped over his head. He rolled to a stop a few feet away against a block of wood. Pain flared up his numb right arm, past his underarm and aching shoulder, and squeezed his skull as if his head was clamped in a vice. A bitter, yellow taste burned his cheeks. He took a few steps, but his legs gave way and he fell against the gunwale. With both arms thrown over the rail, he could see SENT-2 speeding to a safe distance with Everline in the bow, grimacing and clutching his wrist, otherwise dry.

Hosea had managed to gun the boat into position without a second to spare. As the boat resumed station, Jorge watched Hosea raise his hand in a thumbs-up. That kid, thought Jorge, is going to get one hell of an evaluation. He tried to raise his own thumb in return, but noticed he was clutching Everline's silver watch. Its metal band was shredded and there was blood and hair in it. A weak laugh buckled from his chest. Suddenly, Jorge remembered the crew and spun around. He drew his pistol. Exhausted, he could not hold it up without the support of his left hand. He was flirting with unconsciousness when a great whiteness eclipsed his vision; *Sentinel* had cruised alongside the freighter. Jorge felt a sensation of *déjà vu*.

The men were docile once again. Harmon had corralled them to the center of the fantail and Locklair rounded the corner of the superstructure with his own gun raised, all under the bore of the enormous domed gun on *Sentinel*'s bow. Jorge collapsed to a sitting position, his back against the gunwale. Locklair called over to him. "Sir, you all right?"

"I'm...fine."

"Well, you look like a bag of smashed assholes."

Jorge laughed. No sound came out.

"Where's the lieutenant?"

"Hanging out." Exhausted, Jorge held out his left arm and Locklair yanked him to his feet. The sudden movement made his head swim, and he grabbed the rail again to steady himself. He took several deep breaths and shook his head. "Where's Kelly?"

"I heard all the hollering from the bridge. He wasn't up there with me."

"He's in one of the staterooms, belowdecks," Harmon called over his shoulder, the crew still in the sights of his gun. "I left him with the coffee."

Jorge nodded. He wanted to tell him that the need for codewords stopped as soon as the guns cleared their holsters, but something was wrong. He scanned the bodies of the crew. No denim. His eyes searched the rest of the fantail. Henri was nowhere to be found. Off to the side, he spotted the block of wood he had rolled into. Something about it harried his thoughts.

"Fuck!" yelled Jorge. He started for the superstructure.

The master moved to cut him off, his hands up in a conciliatory gesture. He cried, "No, *amigo*, wait. You no understand!" but Jorge, looking past him toward the superstructure, lashed out with his good arm in an upward arc, his backhand catching the fat man on the jaw. The master crashed into a pile of tools on deck. The fat man flailed and swiveled on his back like a ladybug rolling on its carapace. Jorge kept moving.

"Stay here," he instructed, already running.

Chapter 19

An uproar. Kelly crouched and spun, faced the door. Even through the bulkheads, it sounded like pandemonium topside. He fought a sudden urge to replace the decking and roll back the carpet, concealing the contraband once more, as if he was the guilty party. Being alone in the cramped stateroom, crouching beside the cocaine seemed very foolish suddenly, even dangerous. He was penned in. Trapped. He needed to get topside, to his shipmates. He sprang to the door and tried to open it. It wouldn't budge. He rattled the knob, but remembered he locked it after Harmon had left. He blew out a breath.

"Easy, Sensor, easy," he said.

He reached for his holster, the nine-millimeter. He didn't want to pull his gun unless he knew it was absolutely necessary, but he had no idea what was happening. All the more reason to have it out, his brain screamed. He drew it. He unlocked the door, flung it open, and thrust the pistol before him with both hands. He peered outside. All clear.

He started up the passageway to the ladder. In the distance, rubber soles screeched. Someone shouting. Was it Harmon? He had run as far as the intersection of the corridors when he heard pounding footsteps, someone bolting for the ladder from above. He ducked down the side corridor. He hoped it was a Coastie, but then thought a Coastie charging down the passageway was not very encouraging either. He squatted and peered down the main passageway, just enough to glimpse a man scurry down the stairs. From his vantage, he saw feet flash on the top step. No boots, Kelly thought. Crew. Then pant-legs. Jeans, not uniform. The man was three steps down when he lost his balance and bumbled the rest of the way. Something clattered against the handrail as the man negotiated the ladder, but Kelly had already pulled his head back.

Terror seized him. Everything was happening too fast. He glanced at his gun. The serrated grip felt good, too good, and suddenly that scared him more than the stranger hurrying toward him. Bits and pieces of his boarding team member training flashed through his mind. The use of force continuum: officer presence, verbal commands, intermediary weapons, deadly force. Intermediate weapons! Kelly remembered he had a belt full of non-lethal options at his disposal and relief flooded his mind for a moment. He holstered his gun and prayed this was not a deadly force scenario. He slipped his baton from its slot. He squeezed the foam grip until his fingers burned.

Down the passageway, Kelly heard the man charge, huffing a curse with every step. "*Merde! Merde! Merde!*" He sounded French. Kelly guessed he was going for the stateroom, the cocaine. He would pass by in another second. Kelly held his breath. He dropped his shoulder and placed one leg behind him, like a runner awaiting a pistol's crack. He would have to time it just right. When the man was almost upon him, he gritted his teeth and tensed every muscle. As soon as he saw a flicker of movement, he threw himself into the passageway, chin tucked, shoulder down.

He collided with the man's ribcage, slamming him into the far corner of the intersection. It felt like he had run into a tree. Kelly heard the crack of cheap plaster covering the bulkhead, air escaping from the man with a loud, almost comical "oof!" Both men fell to the floor in a heap. A machete rattled against the deck and skittered away like an angry crustacean.

"Oh fuck," said Kelly.

He scrambled to his feet.

Dazed, the crewmember groaned and rose to one knee. As he straightened, Kelly saw the man was short but compact. His denim shirt stretched tight around the chest and biceps, and his jeans around his quadriceps. In a fair fight, Kelly knew the squat man would tear him to pieces.

Kelly sidestepped between the man and his weapon. He kicked the machete behind him, further down the corridor. He flicked his wrist. The baton expanded to its full length with a shing, its weight reassuring.

"Stay down, sir."

"*Fu toi*," the man spat, and lunged for the ensign.

Kelly dodged to the side, and smashed the baton into the man's forearm. Even through the foam handle, Kelly felt the jarring vibration of the impact, the sharp crack of steel besting bone over the man's yelp. The man pitched forward, clutching his arm. Kelly swooped the baton low, then looped it over his head. Standing on the balls of his feet and stretched to his full height, he screamed. He summoned all the frustration from his months aboard *Sentinel*, the helplessness of his grandfather's phone call, his humiliation in a Key West bar, and with all the fear and fury in his heart, he brought it down squarely across the man's back. The man's air was driven out in a hot rush. The blow flattened him to the deck. Kelly backed away, baton raised, poised for another strike. The man did not move.

Suddenly, another set of pounding footsteps. This time, he did not hesitate. He reached for his gun, but forgot about the baton in his drawing hand. As he fumbled, he heard his own name being yelled. Jorge was running at him, gun aimed for the central mass of his body. Kelly ducked, threw up the baton. "Whoa!" he yelled. "It's me!"

Jorge stopped his full sprint a few feet from Kelly. He remained in a ready stance, but lowered his gun with both hands. Kelly's first thought was that someone had piped swim call; his friend was soaked through with perspiration. He watched Jorge survey the scene: the French-sounding man unconscious and sprawled on deck, a machete down the hall, and Kelly, his baton extended. Both ensigns blinked at each other. Both chests heaved.

Jorge holstered his gun. "You okay?"

"I'm okay."

"Where's your gun? Are you fucking nuts?"

"Who's he?"

"Kelly, Henri. Henri, Kelly."

"Damn, Jorge. You look like shit."

Jorge nodded. "Uh huh," he said, then fell to his knees and vomited on Henri.

Chapter 20

It had been a swift affair. He had ordered the ship to a full bell, then cut the engines immediately. The burst of speed was enough to catch the freighter, but not enough to overtake it. The captain almost wished he could have seen it from that derelict crew's point of view, or even better yet, through his boarding team's eyes: *Sentinel*, like a galleon of yore, presenting its broadside. All roughhousing ceased instantly. Order had been restored.

With his ship at a safe distance, Aregood leaned against a post on the bridgewing's platform, watching his boarding team go about their business across the water. Once the situation had stabilized, the full story made it over to *Sentinel*. Everline, the buffoon, was shaken but back aboard *Doña Maria*, relaying information from her bridge: the crew had been smuggling a large shipment of cocaine from Barranquilla to Port au Prince, then most likely to Miami. A young member of the crew had made suspicious comments to the assistant boarding officer, who in turn informed the boarding officer. Apparently, the young crewmember shared a stateroom with another man, the assailant, who had pilfered some contraband for himself. The assailant must have sensed something had gone wrong, and either out of concern for the shipment in general or his own personal stash, had bolted for the evidence, assaulting two Coasties in the process.

Perhaps if Everline and the rest of Bravo had kept the bubble, the boarding would not have gone so haywire in the first place. There will need to be extensive re-training, Aregood thought, but overall he was pleased. They had been lucky. None of his boys had been seriously hurt, and they had scored a major bust. In fact, in order to gauge the full extent of drugs onboard, a full dockside boarding would be required. Most of the freighter's crew still feigned ignorance of any contraband, so *Sentinel* would need to escort *Doña Maria* to a port where they had the capability to access any hidden compartments. In other words, tear the ship apart.

As soon as he had received Everline's first radio report that the crew had been secured, he began writing the press release and the bullets for his brag sheet in his mind. It did not matter that he himself had not set foot on the freighter; he was ultimately responsible for the actions of every Coastie under his command, be it a successful bust or collision, good or bad. That's how the chain worked. Even when it was bad, sometimes all it took was a little polishing to bring out the shine. He would gloss over Everline's bungle and instead use as his centerpiece the Cuban.

Reports also came from *Doña Maria* intimating that Sensor had played a large role, but there was no juice in that angle. No, he thought, it was the Cuban: Jorge Vargas, assistant boarding officer, the young refugee who had been plucked from the ocean, now an officer in the very service that had saved his life, had just saved his first life. The life of a fellow Coastie.

"Captain?"

Aregood turned his gaze from the freighter to his operations officer. "Yes, OPS?"

"Sir, I recommend we begin swapping out the team. They're bound to be exhausted."

"Have Alpha start relieving them. And have some food sent over." Griffin turned for the inside of the bridge, but Aregood called for him. "Got pretty hairy there for a minute, eh?"

"Yes, sir. It sure did."

"The blood gets flowing like that, tempers flare. I just want you to know I'm not angry."

"For what, sir?"

"For questioning my judgment in front of the others."

Griffin opened his mouth to reply when the executive officer stepped onto the bridgewing. "Captain, you wanted to know about options for the dockside boarding?"

"What have you got?"

"If you'll both follow me to the chart table."

Aregood and Griffin followed Tyndale to the quartermaster's station. A large chart of the South Caribbean had been laid out, detailing the surrounding islands. "We have a few choices, sir." Tyndale ran his finger across the nautical map, indicating possible ports. "But as far as time and distance go, not to mention jurisdiction and the resources for an extensive search, there's really only one logical spot." He tapped a slender brown mass due north of their current position.

Aregood smiled. It really was too good to be true.

Chapter 21

Jorge winced as he rubbed his ribs, working the immense bruise he could already feel blooming on his right flank. The heat was bearable now and a small breeze had even kicked up. It stirred his short hair as Kelly approached, beaming. Kelly placed his hands on the rail where hours before Jorge had held Everline for all he was worth. They looked at the men in custody.

None of the crewmembers had been bound except Henri, who sat handcuffed, his legs sprawled in front of him. His head lolled. Every so often, another crewmember would spit or curse at the Haitian. Jorge overheard them chastising in Spanish and Creole. Silvio looked sick, on the verge of tears. Locklair stood watch over all of them, enjoying the spectacle. He leaned against the bulkhead, his hand on his holster, emitting a low, steady giggle.

Kelly walked over. "How are you feeling?"

Jorge nodded at the Haitian. "Better than that guy."

"He had it coming."

"He's lucky. And so are you, you jackass. Next time, pull your gun."

"I know, I know. I just…" He paused, squinting into the sun. "You do a hundred boardings, but you never really expect anything like this to happen, you know? I could've shot a guy today. I could have killed him."

"Hey, fuck him. Normal people do not run around with machetes."

"You should embroider that on a pillow."

"I'm serious. He almost turned Steve into chum." He touched his side, winced. "I'd have shot him on general principle."

"I didn't know about Steve." Both men looked out over the expanse of ocean. The sun cut a brilliant swath on the water's surface straight to the freighter. Kelly shivered like it was not blazing. Neither spoke. Jorge listened to the water lap against the hull. Suddenly, Kelly pitched forward, began to wheeze.

"What's wrong?"

"You puked…all over him!" He choked out his sentence in a fit of laughter.

Jorge joined in. He saw the dazed, handcuffed man and pointed at him. "It's in his hair!"

Henri stirred. Both men howled.

Everline approached. He rubbed his wrist until they settled down. "Harmon's on the bridge with the master. *Sentinel*'s trying to figure out our next move. The small boat's on the way over to swap us out."

"You look like you need to take a shit," Jorge said.

"Jorge, man," said the lieutenant, "I just wanted to say—."

"Forget it. Just pronounce my name right from now on and we'll call it even."

Everline nodded. He cleared his throat and turned to Kelly. "Nice catch, Sensor." Everline offered a hand and Kelly shook it warily. Then Everline burst into laughter. "Nice catch to both of you!" he said, thrusting his hand to Jorge. Jorge bore down on it and gave it several mighty shakes.

"Motherfuck, Jorge! You already broke the damn wrist."

"Sorry...chum."

"You boots really are a couple of assholes."

Jorge laughed.

"Look," Steve continued, clutching his wrist, "my hand is shot. I've got to go. But this ship has to stay manned, and after all the excitement, preferably with fresh bodies. I'm giving you two the option before the captain changes his mind."

"I'm getting off of this piece of shit as fast as I can," said Jorge.

"I'll wait. I'm in no rush. Besides," continued Kelly, jerking a thumb at the huddled crew, "I think they like me over here."

"Fine by me," Everline said. "All right, the boat's here. Let's go."

Jorge walked to *Doña Maria*'s port side where the rope ladder thudded against the hull. As they donned their life vests again, new men from *Sentinel* came over the side. As soon as the last man from Team Alpha came aboard, Everline straddled the gunwale. He moved slowly, using only one hand to grab the ladder. Jorge hooked his hand under the collar of Everline's vest. "I'm not catching your ass twice."

"This is my last patrol. I could've been fish food on my last patrol if you hadn't—."

"Just fucking go already!"

Moments later, Jorge had climbed down the ladder himself and jumped into the ready boat. Hosea congratulated him. "Nice hands, Jorge."

He slapped the seaman's back. "Nice driving, Bob. Now get us the hell out of here."

"Hold tight."

The engines roared and the boat surged forward. Jorge held onto one of the ratlines attached to the pontoon. His arm was still sore, but the pain receded as the boat planed along, inches from the crystal waters. The heat was replaced by a fine mist blowing into his face. He felt it against his eyelids.

When he opened them again, *Sentinel* loomed in front of him. Hosea nosed his small boat up against the white hull, and the deckies on *Sentinel* and the crew in the boat exchanged lines. The ladder was thrown down and Jorge was the first to climb it. As he pulled himself up, blood felt like it was pooling in his head. He was drowsy.

He drew his nine-millimeter and ejected the cartridge. As he peered into the guts of the gun to ensure a bullet was not left in the chamber, Chief Norris approached him. "You're wanted on the bridge, Mr. Vargas."

Jorge avoided taking the main passageway. He knew if the air conditioning cooled him for even a minute, he might not find the strength to move beyond it. He took the outside route, shedding his life jacket along the way. It made a shucking sound as it peeled away from his clammy coveralls. The bulletproof vest underneath stuck to him, the undershirt beneath that was sopping. His body felt very heavy, like just another piece of gear to haul.

When he arrived, the captain clapped. One by one, everyone added to the applause. A corner of his mouth rose involuntarily. He had never seen the captain or the bridge team in such good spirits. He felt relieved; he had half-expected an ass-chewing. The captain put his hand on the ensign's shoulder. "Guess all that time pumping iron in the helo hangar paid off!"

"For Steve anyway."

"Ha! For Steve. Outstanding."

"Sir?"

"I just wanted to keep you and the rest of the team informed of what we need to do next. For now, we're going to keep some of you on as prize crew until we can open her up dockside. As quartermaster, Harmon will stay for navigation purposes." Then, sounding like it were an afterthought, "We'll need some officer presence as well. Sensor's not qualified yet, so he stays…"

If Aregood had wanted a reaction, Jorge was too drained to give one. He had hit the wall.

"All right, son, you look exhausted. Go get some sleep. I'll want a full briefing when you get up."

"Aye, sir. Thanks." Jorge raised his hand in salute and his shoulder burned. "Permission to go below?"

Aregood returned the salute. "By the way, you'll have the conn tomorrow."

"The conn?" Jorge blinked, felt drunk in the sun. "Where did you say we were going again?" he heard himself ask.

"I didn't. We're going to Guantanamo," said the captain. The word sliced through Jorge's torpor. "Cuba."

Chapter 22

Except for the port and starboard running lights, a red sphere on the left side of *Sentinel*'s bow, green on the right, the cutter ran dark and silent in the distance like a ghost ship out of nautical lore. Kelly looked at the tiny ruby and emerald on his class ring that now flanked the hollow where his goodie once resided, then back to the pale silhouette of the ship that trailed him at a few thousand yards. He had scoured the stateroom to no avail. The price to pay for the seizure, he thought. And resurrecting my career. There was no mistaking who found the cocaine and who subdued the Haitian. His grandfather would understand. Hell, he'll be thrilled.

Harmon approached from the inside of the ship. It struck Kelly as odd how little time it took them all to grow accustomed to the freighter, walking around like they owned it. Which, he supposed, they did.

"See the comet?" asked Harmon.

"Where?"

Kelly followed Harmon's finger to a blurred area overhead, as if someone had tried to rub it out of the sky. "Beautiful," said the ensign.

"You know, the tail isn't actually following the comet. It's leading it. Has something to do with gravity. Ever seen a green flash?"

"Green flash?"

"If the conditions are just right at sunset, clear day, perfect horizon, then just as the top of the sun dips out of sight, boom, green flash.

"The coolest thing I've ever seen is a moonbow, white rainbow at night. Have you seen that?"

"I was on watch with you when you saw it."

"All this celestial talk reminds me I owe you some money."

"Don't worry about it. We'll take it out of the budget."

"Oh no. If His Majesty found out, you'd end up on his shitlist too. Trust me, it's not a fun place to be."

"What were you just looking at?"

"My ring." Kelly held up his hand. "I lost the stone when I found the stuff."

"You've got some shitty luck, sir."

"Come on, we're not even on *Sentinel*. It's Kelly."

"You've got some shitty luck, Kelly."

"That's all changing, starting now. With this. If anything will get the crew to realize I'm not a leper, a bust ought to do the trick." He looked at Harmon. The quartermaster looked uneasy. "What? Spit it out."

"I don't know. Maybe you could just lighten up some? I think people get the perception that you're a little...stiff."

"Bullshit!"

"You're always going on and on about tradition." He pointed toward *Sentinel*. "The guys over there don't care about that shit. They just want to do their jobs and get home. It's not like we're singing sea-shanties all day. We're not on a square rigger. It's not a crusade twenty-four hours a day."

"Maybe you have a point."

"Look, you want me to talk to the guys or something?"

"No, I don't need the quartermaster fighting my battles for me."

"See, right there. That's condescending! You may be an officer, but you're no older than I am."

Kelly held up his hands in capitulation. "Not how I meant it."

"And that ring. Who actually wears their Academy ring to sea anyway? On a working ship?"

Kelly smiled. "Feel better?"

Harmon ran his fingers through his hair. He started laughing. "Yeah."

Both men looked up at the stars and the blurred area of the sky. "You ever have the urge to fall off the radar? Just sort of get lost?"

"I'm a quartermaster." He cracked a smile. "My whole job is keeping us on track, boot."

"Yeah, where's your track taking you?"

"After this tour, my enlistment's done. Done. Don't get me wrong, the Guard's cool and all. I've seen comets and green flashes and moonbows, I've gotten drunk in more Caribbean bars than American bars, and today, I almost shot someone today. I got my money's worth and I won't feel bad at all shaking hands with Uncle Sam and moving on. I'm heading back to Maryland to my family and my girlfriend. I'm going back to school. You?"

"Well, I've got to admit I've had some interesting offers, and today was pretty hairy for a while, but for once this, sailing right here, this is how I pictured it."

Chapter 23

At the conn, amid a packed bridge team, Jorge felt a prickly heat on the back of his neck. He scratched it with his sore arm, then became conscious of that, heavy and swollen, curling away like a Fiddler crab's claw. He glanced at Aregood. The captain, watching him, only nodded.

Jorge stepped out to the bridgewing and found a spot on the promenade in front of the bridge. He had waited the entire transit for a stray remark, something. Will this be your first time in Cuba? None came. He turned his attention to the bay *Sentinel* now approached. A tugboat was steaming out to assist *Doña Maria* to a berth. *Sentinel* trailed the freighter. As the tug chugged alongside the freighter, he permitted himself a view of the landscape. Small, tree-topped mountains flanked either side of the harbor's mouth. To the right, an observatory was perched at the highest visible point, as if standing guard. He wondered if the trees on those mountains were hanging heavy with the fruits of his youth: overripe spotted bananas, crisp green mangoes, papayas, guavas. Don't delude yourself, he thought. Beyond those trees, over armed sentries and barbed wire fences, was another Cuba altogether.

"What's the score, Mr. Vargas?" the lookout, an eighteen year old seaman named Gray asked.

"Huh?"

"Pocketball, sir."

Jorge looked down. He realized his hand was deep in his pocket, rubbing his shell. He sprang to within two inches of the seaman's face. "What the fuck are you looking at me for? You're the lookout. So look out!"

The seaman had not had the time to retract his smile. It hung, sick and frozen, as Jorge breathed on him. Trembling, Gray leaned back and brought his binoculars to his chest, adding a few more inches distance. "Go away, Gray," said Jorge.

The lookout darted back to the bridgewing.

Jorge heard the starboard bearing taker begin his countdown. Once he heard the proper bearing, Jorge sounded off. "Helmsman, right fifteen degrees rudder!"

After the ship was moored and liberty had been piped, Jorge changed into shorts and sandals and walked down to the wardroom when he was certain it would be deserted. He was mistaken. When he entered, Kelly looked up from the message board. He wore a fresh sunburn and was in need of a shower. Grease from the freighter smeared his face and coveralls. Without a greeting, Kelly asked, "Did you see this?"

"See what?"

"The SITREP on the bust. Some names are omitted." He dropped the metal clipboard on the table as if it were contagious. Above the clatter: "Guess who's?"

Jorge picked it up and scanned the attached document. It was a copy; it had already been transmitted to shore. "There's mine..."

"Yeah, there's yours. But you're not the one whose career's in the fucking toilet."

Jorge bristled. "I shouldn't be in it?"

"All I'm saying is that I found the shit."

"By accident."

"What the hell's the matter with you? I still found it. I think I deserve a modicum of credit."

"You saying I don't?"

"This could have helped me make rank!" he said, pointing at clipboard, "You don't need the help with your career. This was my last chance!"

"It must suck, not being the golden boy for once."

"And you are?"

"The CO's pretty happy with me for once."

Kelly spread his hands. "Of course he is!"

Jorge raised his chin. "What's that supposed to mean?"

"Look around, man. Where are we? He doesn't respect you. You're just a tool to him. A narrative."

Jorge's balled his fists. "Maybe so, but for someone who hates the man, you sure think the same." Jorge pushed open the wardroom door and did not stop moving until he was outside, bounding down the gangway and into the shaded cabin of a liberty van on the pier. He slammed the door behind him. He looked at the driver. Gray's face drained of color.

"Gray, just get me to a bar within two minutes and we'll call it even."

Gray hit the gas.

An hour later, Jorge sat in a corner of the Guantanamo Bay Officer's Club. There were military reminders everywhere, banners, pictures of aircraft, command insignia, but the club was air-conditioned, deserted on a Tuesday afternoon. He preferred it that way. In the middle of his second beer, Aregood entered the club. Jorge stared at the man as he stopped at a bank of phones, hunched over a receiver and speaking softly, too softly for Jorge to hear. Jorge thought of calling Nancy, but thought better of it. After some time, Aregood hung up and strolled over.

"Seat taken?"

Jorge shook his head.

The waitress came over and Aregood ordered two more beers.

"The wife?" Jorge asked.

"Sure."

"Why is my name the only one mentioned on the SITREP?"

The waitress returned with their beers and Aregood flashed her a bright smile. He turned to Jorge and hoisted his mug. "To a safe, successful seizure."

Jorge raised his and they drank. "But why me? Why only me."

Aregood's smile faded. "Let's be frank here. I couldn't very well mention Everline, could I? As I'm sure you recall, he wasn't even on board for the heavy lifting."

Jorge smiled, despite himself. "But what about Sensor. He found the stuff."

Aregood leaned back and smiled. "You're a good friend. That's a very admirable quality, but whether you accept it or not, your friend has an attitude problem. And believe it or not, I'm trying to help him. The same way I'm not humiliating Steve in a report the entire fleet will read. I take care of things my way, in-house. But that's neither here nor there. The bottom line, Jorge, is with Steve out of the picture that left you, as the assistant boarding officer, the next highest-ranking officer on that freighter. So you get the credit. Believe me, if something had gone wrong, you'd get the fid. That's how it works."

"I guess, sir."

"No guessing involved, son. It's Chain of Command 101. Been that way at sea for thousands of years and it's not changing anytime soon, so get used to it. You're a natural born ship driver and you're tough as nails, but when you accept that simple truth, I'll see command afloat in your future."

Jorge gave him a pinched stare over the top of his mug.

"Don't look so suspicious," Aregood said, "you made *Sentinel* look damn good out there. You just made your career. And I won't lie to you, you helped mine as well." Aregood raised his beer. "I take care of my own."

The captain took a long pull from his bottle and the ensign followed. Jorge decided to push his luck. "And Kelly?"

"Don't worry, Sensor will get his day in court. Now, get out of here. It's a beautiful day. The crew is having a pier party, go celebrate. This is on me."

"No, sir."

"That's an order."

Jorge exited the bar feeling much lighter than when he entered. With the sky sharp and blue enough to make his eyes water, he decided to walk back to the ship rather than wait for the van. He passed the Bachelor Officer's Quarters, then the Exchange, until he reached a part of the road lined with dense stalks topped by palm fronds. When he was sure no military vehicles were coming, he closed his eyes and let the orange light play on the backs of his eyelids. He heard the hutías, the cane rats hidden in the trees, chitter at him from above. He could almost smell the empanadas, the neighborhood fritangera folding over dough filled with egg and cheese, crimping the sides and frying them creations in a vat of oil. It smelled so salty and rich. Not every memory that jumped from behind the trees was horrible.

Despite the beauty of the day, when he emerged from the forested area by the buildings near the docks, he felt a measure of relief. The industrial sector, filled with warehouses and workshops, offered no hints of the Cuba of his youth. In the Eighties, during the height of the Cold War, Guantanamo Bay was crowded, lively. But this was the mid-Nineties and the dockside section resembled a ghost town. Far down the beach, a rusted jeep sat abandoned in the low tide, its wheels long ago flattened from a joyride gone awry by an army of crab pincers. In one of the slips, Jorge could hear the shrill sound of metal grinding from the bowels of *Doña Maria*; the engineers were belowdecks prying her open for her secrets. Jorge kept walking.

At the foot of the pier, the sound of reggae wafted toward him. The pier party was in full swing, such as it was. Everyone was more subdued than when they had descended upon Key West. Pier parties were a common practice among cutters when they pulled into a dull port. Cases and cases of beer were bought from the nearest store, while the in port officer of the deck unlocked the liquor locker and let the crew retrieve their bottles of duty-free alcohol purchased at their more exotic destinations. It was cheap and the scenery tropical, and after the last few days with *Doña Maria*, the crew was tired. Sagging in lawn chairs in the shadow of *Sentinel* was as crazy as they could manage.

As soon as Jorge set foot on the long, concrete pier, they began whooping and beckoning for the ensign to join them. Locklair pitched him a can.

"We got started without you."

"It don't GITMO better than this," said Jorge, and tipped his beer.

Jorge sank into a lawn chair, sipped his beer, and stared out toward the harbor's mouth and the sparkling ocean beyond. He turned over every word Aregood had said, looking for hidden clues or intent. Suddenly, it grew quiet around him. He turned from the water.

Dressed in navy blue shorts, docksiders and a white cotton shirt, Kelly approached the fringe of revelers. No one offered him a beer. Bob Marley asked, "Could You Be Loved?" Other than that, the only other sounds were a few, isolated snickers.

Jorge followed Kelly's gaze as he surveyed the crowd. Irving smirked. Harmon stared at his own feet. Before Jorge could speak up, Kelly spun on one heel and strode toward the liberty van. "Gray, let's go," he said in a loud, clear voice, oddly devoid of embarrassment. The seaman, who had been talking to a cluster of deckies, rushed after the ensign. In seconds, they were gone. The party's din resumed.

When Jorge saw Seaman Irving break from a group of deckies to grab a beer, he slid from his chair. As Irving reached inside a cooler, Jorge sidled up unnoticed and closed the lid with his foot, just hard enough to snag the seaman's arm. Irving looked up. "Hey, Mr. Vargas."

"Hey, Irving." He watched the lanky seaman squirm.

"What's up?" His left eye twitched as he chuckled.

"Just having some fun, man. You?"

"Just trying to get a beer."

"Oh." Jorge took a deep breath, looked out over the harbor.

After a few moments, Irving offered a nervous laugh. "Sir?"

"Oh, I'm sorry." Jorge stared down at him then, leaning forward, shifting his weight to the cooler's lid until Irving winced.

"Ow! Give!"

"You been talking, Irving?"

"I don't know what you're talking ab-ow!" Jorge twisted his torso and drove his leg down. The music was loud and the crowd raucous enough that no one heard the seaman yelp, or cared if they did. Jorge didn't care which.

"Irving, I want you to listen to me. You listening?" Irving bit his lip and nodded. The seaman's arm was caught in the soft just above the elbow. "Good," Jorge continued. "If I hear that you've said another word about any of my friends again or God help you, me, I will rip your arms off and hand them to you. Understand?"

"Yes!"

"Excuse me?"

"Yessir."

"That's better." Jorge let up. Irving jerked away from the cooler. He rubbed his elbow, his face red with strain. He began to turn away, but Jorge stopped him. "Hey."

The ensign signaled for the beer. The helmsman frowned and tossed it over.

Within half an hour, the van returned. Behind the wheel, Gray was laughing. Kelly stepped out, carrying a long, flat box in front of him. Without a word, he marched to the perimeter of the large circle of lawn chairs, then through it. The crew grew silent once again. Someone shut off the portable stereo.

Kelly looked from face to face, then hoisted the box over his head. He looked last at Jorge, then dropped the box. It hit the concrete with a gravelly smack and its sides ruptured, spilling forth magazine after magazine of naked women. Pornography spread out like falling dominoes on the deck.

Harmon looked at the pile, then back at the ensign. "Holy shit."

Suddenly, the crew broke form their lawn chairs and charged forward, scooping up the magazines at the ensign's feet. Locklair picked up a magazine by his foot and bellowed, "Get this man a fucking beer already!"

Reggae once again flooded the pier. Tears streamed down Jorge's face, he laughed so hard.

Two hours later, the sun set the bay ablaze. The men were all drunk, and lolling in a ring of low lawn chairs like covered wagons around the ocean's fire. Jorge watched Kelly from afar as his friend engaged in drunken conversations about women, the service, life at sea. Drowsy, with his legs sprawled in front of him and a cold bottle on his thigh, Jorge realized he had had plenty of those conversations with the crew, but his friend had not.

"Officers and enlisted, man," Locklair said. "You guys did it for the money, we did it for the freedom."

"But on *Sentinel*," said Harmon, "we all get screwed."

"I didn't do it for the money." said Kelly and the crew howled.

Jorge grinned. The sun was down now, and he felt only the heavy, heady need to doze. He would catch up to his friend later, but for now, he gave him some space. He let Kelly have Cuba, the closest he could come to an apology.

Chapter 24

Sentinel set out to sea when *Doña Maria*'s affairs were in order. With Cuba a day behind them, Aregood sat in his cabin and mulled over the fate of the freighter. *Sentinel*'s engineers had offloaded all of the cargo, accessed every hold and every space, and pumped all of the tanks. Their efforts revealed over four thousand pounds of cocaine in triple-wrapped bags. *Doña Maria* had been riddled with it as if it were a cancer: in the spaces below the main engines, in tanks within the fuel tanks, even drilled into the mast.

The cocaine would be sent to U.S. Customs in Miami, first for evidence, then for destruction. A case was also being prepared against the master and some members of the crew. If that Haitian had kept his cool, Aregood guessed, the crew probably could have returned to their homeport, wherever that actually was, with *Doña Maria*. Most masters and crew feigned ignorance of the contraband in their midst, and usually got away with it. This time, the master and the Haitian were in custody and the rest of the crew detained, most likely awaiting repatriation to their respective countries. And for now, *Doña Maria* belonged to the United States government.

Whether or not she was returned, resold, or scrapped into a million razor blades made no difference to Aregood; she had already given it all up.

That left one thing: capturing the information in his brag sheet. It was late, quiet. He sat in front of the computer, poised to write, but twirled the point of his marlinspike in his palm. It was strange. There were no more obstacles to attaining captain; a four thousand pound coke bust clinched it. All he had to do was write it up, but all he could think about was her.

Talking to Evelyn in Guantanamo had only made matters worse. He could barely concentrate. Her crooked grin, nearly a smirk. Her round bottom. Desire rushed below. Whenever it did, thoughts of his family involuntary rushed in after and desire was replaced by the heavy ache of guilt, like his chest had been poured with cement. No, not guilt, he thought. Claustrophobia. He wanted to return to Key West, but within two weeks, *Sentinel* would return to homeport in Portsmouth, Virginia, and even he, as the cutter's captain, could do nothing about it. For the present, he thanked Neptune he was at sea.

He wished he had asked Evelyn for a picture. He was not sure whether it would have helped; there was already too much emotion running rampant inside him. Only writing her letters seemed to calm him. It was one-sided and not at all immediate, but it was still communication. It would have to do. For the first time since assuming command of *Sentinel*, he postponed making an entry in his brag sheet for the night. He turned off his computer and removed a sheet of paper from his desk. Evelyn, he began when there was a knock on his door. Aregood draped his arm over the salutation. Tyndale entered.

"Evening, Rich."

"Evening, sir. This just came into Radio. I figured you might want to see it first." He handed the captain a blue folder. Aregood opened it and read the contents.

"Where is he now?" asked the captain.

"On the bridge. Watch."

Aregood placed his marlinspike on the desk. He spun it like a bottle. "Well, it's a message. Put it on the message board with all the rest and route it to the bridge."

"Captain, shouldn't we—."

"Route it."

Chapter 25

It was near midnight, and Kelly leaned against the post of the port bridgewing. He stood on the small platform twenty-five feet above the water, listening to the flat sea hiss underneath. The comet was still overhead. Despite the omission of his name on the SITREP and his conversation with Jorge in the wardroom, the last few days had been his best since first setting foot aboard *Sentinel*.

Though no official credit was bound to come his way for the bust, after over eight months of ostracizing him, the crew had finally come around. Even Everline gave him plenty of space by relegating himself to the opposite bridgewing, leaving Kelly to run the bridge as he saw fit.

And in two weeks, Kelly would be home.

Sentinel seemed to slice off slivers of salt air as she peeled through the night water, and the ensign breathed deeply.

"Sir?"

Harmon's form could be seen in the doorway, silhouetted in the glow of the countless tiny lights from the pilothouse. The massive form of Everline stood behind him.

Something in the quartermaster's tone gave Kelly pause, but the ensign laughed. "How have I sinned against the crown now?"

Harmon stood speechless.

"Sean?"

"Kelly," Everline said, "this was on the message board."

Kelly.

Harmon held out the metal clipboard. Kelly jerked his penlight from his belt.

"What is it?"

The red glow of the penlight darted across the page. Standard Coast Guard message format, like the SITREP. From Integrated Support Command Portsmouth, Virginia. Ombudsman. "Regret to inform" in even, impersonal type. The ensign's heart knocked in his chest. His concentration shattered, he scanned the rest, catching only flashes of the text. His own name, then "Jack Sensor..."

The metal clipboard clanged against the deck. Kelly dropped next. He heard keening, realized it was coming from him. He looked up and saw the comet still trailing them, a blur in the sky. He saw the dark faces of the two men, blurry now too. Tears streamed down his face now, and caught in the glow of the port running light, each one looked for a moment like a ruby before the wind bore them aft and away.

Chapter 26

Jorge stood on the forecastle of *Sentinel*, surrounded by the members of Deck Department, who stood ready to drop anchor into Virginia's Elizabeth River. It was a precaution; the water was calm and the weather warm for an April day. So his mind wandered to his fiancée, who stood somewhere on the pier ahead of him. He hoped.

Coming home was like the crew's very own holiday. Spotting their loved ones' faces on the pier was the Fourth of July, their first kiss New Year's Eve. On the forecastle, the mood was buoyant. Laughter was raucous and sudden. The deckies traded jabs. This particular Special Sea Detail, from the buoy at the mouth of the Chesapeake Bay, over the southern tunnel of the Chesapeake Bay Bridge-Tunnel's twenty-mile span, and through the ship channel to the Portsmouth Coast Guard base seemed to be the slowest two hours of Jorge's life.

He turned from the pier and looked up at the promenade in front of the bridge. He saw Everline, at the end of his final patrol, bringing the cutter in for its homecoming. His hands were splayed on the rail in front of him like a conquering hero, and although the sleeve of his blue windbreaker concealed it, Jorge knew covered his wrist. Everline tipped his cover to Jorge, and the ensign nodded back. Flanking the big officer were XO and OPS, ready to offer advice if Everline found himself in a nautical tight spot.

Somewhere beyond Jorge's view, roaming the bridge, was the captain.

The ensign walked to the starboard side of the forecastle and gazed up. He could see the bridgewing clearly, where Harmon shot bearings to the landmarks. Beside him stood Kelly. He stared forward as if in a trance. Harmon called out his bearings, and the ensign logged them, nothing more.

The night Kelly had been informed of his grandfather's death, a phone call rousted Jorge from a deep sleep. It was Harmon on the bridge. "Get up here now. It's Kelly," the quartermaster had said, but the tone in his voice jarred him; he dashed to the bridge in his boxer shorts and a tee shirt. When he reached the top of the steps, he realized that he had not had time to acquire his night vision. Hairline fissures of light escaped from the consoles, and in their aggregate glow, he could just make out that the pilothouse was deserted with the exception of a lone figure, the helmsman. "Out there," the silhouette said. It sounded like Hosea.

Jorge fumbled to the door leading to the port bridgewing. The moon, the stars, and the comet high overhead provided a few more lumens of low, dusky light. Jorge made out the backs of a few more silhouettes, all congregated on the bridgewing. One massive, Everline. Another smaller one, Harmon. Another lookout Jorge couldn't identify.

"What's going on?"

The group of figures parted, and Jorge saw a heap on the platform. For a second, the object looked so lifeless, he thought it was Oscar, the life-sized mannequin the shipdrivers used for the man overboard drills. With alarm, he realized the heap was alive when it lurched, and Jorge heard the showery sound of vomit spilling. The seas were like glass. Something was very wrong. He crouched next to Kelly. He put his hand on his friend's heaving shoulder.

"Come on, man, this is ridiculous even for you."

In a low whisper, one of the silhouettes said, "His grandfather."

"No," said Jorge. He looked up into group as if he could discern their features.

Another figure: "He hasn't said a word."

Jorge crept closer to the outline of Kelly. He whispered to his friend. "Hey buddy…"

No answer.

"Steve?"

"Right here, Jorge."

"You took back the deck and conn?"

"Yeah, I got it."

"All right, I'm taking him below," he said, straining to see more faceless figures now.

"Back to your stations everybody," snapped Everline. "Give them some fucking room!"

"Hey," Jorge said, "can you hear me? We're going to get you out of here, then we'll get you off this boat. All right?"

"Jorge." The voice was thick but calm and just loud enough for the two of them. "I don't think I can walk."

"That's all right." Jorge, still closer to blindness than sight, slipped his arm under Kelly's shoulder and pulled Kelly's arm around his neck to hoist the heap of his friend to his feet. "Can you see?" he asked.

"Yeah, I can see."

"Then we'll make it."

It was in that fashion, guiding one another, the ensigns returned to their stateroom. Jorge put Kelly in the bottom rack and called Griffin. Though this was a personnel matter falling under the domain of Tyndale as executive officer, Jorge felt it prudent to first inform OPS. It was past midnight, but the lieutenant agreed to fill out a memorandum immediately, requesting leave for the ensign, and a helicopter pick-up from Guantanamo. Outside of their stateroom, Griffin explained to Jorge since they were just a day out of Cuba, with flight operations scheduled for the morning anyway, there should be no problems; Kelly would likely be back in the States within thirty-six hours. These types of cases were fairly routine for Guantanamo; the base officials would know how to handle everything.

"Was telling him on watch routine, too?" Jorge asked.

Griffin looked down and adjusted is glasses. "I can assure you," he responded, "I never saw that message."

He began to say more, struggled with it briefly, then turned quickly and strode down the passageway back to his own stateroom.

Jorge's eyes swept the pier for Nancy's sandy blonde hair. He passed each eager face, once, twice, his heart sinking lower each time, but to no avail. She was not among the crowd. Perhaps she was unable get the day off from work, he hoped. Right, he thought.

Soon, the lines went over, and the ship's whistle sounded. After two months of sunrises at sea, hundreds of arduous evolutions, storms and squalls, blood, sweat, tears, and vomit, and the addition of a snowflake sticker on the side of the bridge signifying their latest seizure, *Sentinel* was moored. Home. Within seconds of the granting of liberty, the crew flowed down the brow in a human stream that emptied into the arms of its loved ones. Jorge went to the flight deck, and from his vantage there watched the mass of people from both sides clog the gangway, friends and family rushing up to the crew hustling down to meet them. There were congregations on the pier, the fantail, the brow itself. Bear hugs and sloppy kisses abounded, "public displays of affection" be damned. Despite himself, the scene made him smile.

He was lost in the crowd's reveling below when he felt a presence at the railing beside him. It was the captain. Jorge's hackles rose at the sight of him.

"Jorge." The captain nodded.

Jorge looked away.

The captain ignored him. Instead, he raised his arms and called for everyone's attention below. The two hundred and fifty crew and civilians gathered on the stern and pier fell silent. Aregood's voice boomed. "Excuse me, everyone, excuse me! For those of you who don't know me, my name is Commander Kevin Aregood, captain of *Sentinel*. I don't normally do this, but I just wanted to take a moment of your time to address how much I appreciate you being here today. It's very important to me that I thank you for welcoming this diligent crew back from another rigorous patrol. Believe me, I know how difficult it is to be separated from your loved ones, but sometimes it is necessary in order for this crew to accomplish all of the amazing things it does every patrol."

Suddenly, Aregood flung his arm around Jorge. Jorge tried to shrink back, but found that his captain held him fast around the neck. "Thanks to your loved ones, and especially this guy here, Ensign Jorge Vargas," the captain ruffled the ensign's cap with his free hand for emphasis. "*Sentinel* seized over four thousand pounds, two tons, of cocaine headed for our shores, our streets, and our children!"

Applause broke out from the families below. Jorge saw flashes from cameras below, some from families, some professional.

"You should all be very proud of this crew. I know I am, that's why I'm granting them a full week of stand-down!"

This time the cheers erupted from the crew.

"And ladies, these guys have been working very hard over the last two months." The captain looked to his left and right, then brought the back of his hand to his mouth in a confidential gesture. "Go easy on them."

The crowd broke into rowdy laughter, followed by even more shouts and applause from the women. Without a word, Aregood released Jorge and started down the steps, his hands raised as the families cheered his descent. Jorge felt sick, dirty.

"Kevin!"

Jorge watched Aregood set foot on the fantail where a husky woman nearly bowled him over. When he caught his balance, the captain's arms seemed to float in the air above the woman for a moment before settling in an embrace. A few feet next to the woman stood a skinny, sullen boy. When the woman released him, Aregood walked over and thrust his hand out to the boy.

Aregood corralled the two up the ladder to the flight deck, back toward Jorge. The steps were narrow and the captain followed behind his wife with his hand on the small of her back. Jorge had never seen the man this anxious. A smile curled on his lips. He saluted

"Captain," he said.

The captain ignored him.

A half-hour later, only a smattering of people remained on the pier. Jorge had changed into civilian clothes and was walking down the brow when a voice at the quarterdeck shack caught him short.

"Apologize."

Jorge turned around. There she was, leaning against the watch shack, arms folded, sandy blonde hair swaying in the breeze off the water.

"I don't need an explanation and I don't want any backtalk," Nancy continued. "Just. Apologize." He dropped his seabag and began inching toward her, returning her smirk.

Nancy did not budge from her spot against the shack. "I'm serious."

Jorge nodded gravely.

"I'm serious, Jorge."

He pounced. Before she could move, his arms were around her in a tight embrace. "Get off of me!" she laughed, and blows rained on Jorge's back. After a good showing, she returned his embrace.

"You are such a colossal asshole, Vargas. Epic."

"I know." She smelled like lilacs.

"I am sorry."

"I know."

"No," he said, pulling back. "I am. And I'll do it."

"What do you mean?"

"Key West. I'm in."

"You mean it?"

"Anything you want. Where were you anyway?"

"Hiding in the car. Teaching you a lesson."

"That's fucked up."

They drove down the lane leading off base. Bradford pear trees lined both sides, their tiny petals blew off in the breeze and swirled around the car like confetti. Once off base, Jorge filled her in on the patrol since Key West: the bust, Cuba, and Kelly's grandfather. How Aregood denied the leave request. XO delivering the news, Kelly going for him, and he and OPS restraining him. Doc sedating him. The delirious moaning all night long.

Jorge shuddered.

"The funeral?"

Jorge shook his head.

Nancy brought both hands to her mouth. "Jorge we've got to go back and get him. I'll cook him a meal, something."

"He's gone. I missed him. He slipped away as soon as the lines went over. I imagine he's heading to Ocean City."

In their Virginia Beach apartment, Jorge thought about calling Newark, but after two months at sea, he was alone, finally, with his fiancée. He dropped his bags and pulled her close.

"For the record," she said, "you're still an asshole."

She unfastened her belt and slid her jeans over her smooth thighs. The whisper of it made the hairs on Jorge's neck stand on end. She fidgeted with her toes in her pantlegs for a moment, then stepped out of her jeans.

Jorge smirked. "What was all that talk about a meal?"

"Jorge," she said, unhooking her bra, "you know I can't cook."

Chapter 27

Kelly had the car windows down, as he always did during the approach. A few miles out, he could detect the thick, bittersweet smell of the swath of the marshes that rimmed the mainland and preceded the island. To Kelly, that rich smell of the wetlands of creatures in their tidal pools, was home. As he approached Great Egg Harbor Bay, between Ocean City and the mainland, he glanced at the side of the road. Tall stalks of the reed grass mingled with the mud and brackish waters, their feathery heads nodding him in. He remembered crabbing here as a boy with his grandfather. He could still picture snails fastened to the reeds just above the black mud, Fiddler crabs scavenging in the high grasses. Fish teemed, bluefish, striped bass, fluke, and flounder. Gulls, terns, egrets, and ospreys, pulling them from the brine and dropping shellfish onto the rocks to get at their meat. It was his grandfather who revealed all of this to him. The food chain. The real chain of command. Kelly stepped on the gas.

When he reached the apex of the bridge that connected the mainland to the island, Ocean City suddenly lay out before him. Beyond it, the Atlantic. To his left, electric light illuminated the northern end of the island; even in April, the glow of the boardwalk, and Atlantic City beyond, was visible. The southern end, the quiet end, was where they lived, but at the foot of the bridge he turned toward the boardwalk and the lights.

Bud had agreed to meet Kelly for dinner at Bob's Grill, a boardwalk eatery with a clear view of the beach. Kelly parked and scaled the ramp to the boardwalk. When he reached the top, the entire length of the boardwalk was in view, curling to the right along the natural contour of the island. The fine ocean spray veiled the sharper edges, and most of the shops were empty and dark. A few mainstays remained open and provided enough of a glow for Kelly to make out some landmarks: the Music Pier Convention Hall, the Ferris wheel, the waterslides farther down.

The tables in Bob's Grill were new, with gray counters and mauve booths, but everything felt old. Black and white photographs of the Ocean City Beach Patrol in their swimsuits, from every year since the turn of the century, lined the walls. Tonight, the place was empty except for a few elderly patrons. Kelly could hear the quiet clinks of their coffee cups on the saucers over the surf outside.

In a booth close to the windows sat a man with a ring of white hair around the bottom of a bald pate. When Kelly entered, the man stood and brought three fingers of his meaty hand up to his eyebrow.

"'Anchors Aweigh!'" he said.

Kelly tried a smile and returned the salute. "'Anchors Aweigh' is the navy."

Thick in the arms and chest and with his perpetual tan, Bud Docimo looked less like a lawyer than a trawler captain. Yet when Kelly's parents were killed in a car accident on the Garden State Parkway, it was Bud who helped Jack adopt him. Since then, he had been a friend. I need all I can get right now, thought Kelly. He extended his hand and Bud took it, pulling him off balance and into a tight hug.

"I'm sorry, boy."

"I know. It's good to see you, Bud."

"Have a seat. Eat yet?"

"I'm not hungry."

"Bull. You've lost too much weight."

Bud signaled for the waitress. Kelly looked at his watch and scratched his chin. Aside from not eating, he had not been sleeping much either. Dreams had made it difficult. A bony teenage waitress waited at the end of their table.

"Eggs?" he asked. It was hard to focus.

"Breakfast is only served—." Bud cleared his throat, loudly. Her pointy shoulders flinched and she left quickly, without another word. Kelly thought that Bud would have made a fine captain indeed.

"I'm sorry I made you meet me out here. The last time I was in your office was my parents…"

"Say no more. Formality's the last thing you and I need to worry about." He slid a long, business envelope across the table. The envelope was so white it hurt his eyes. He flipped it over. A signet with the New Jersey state emblem in relief sealed the flap, across which read, "John W. Sensor: Last Will and Testament, Living Will and Durable Power of Attorney." Bud drank his coffee in silence as Kelly broke the seal and read the contents.

Kelly's food came and he put the documents off to the side. The scrambled eggs looked Day-Glo in the fluorescent light, and the rich smell that wafted off of them had a hint of the marshes. It turned his stomach. He finished his coffee, and that cleared his head enough to admit he did not understand what he had just been reading.

"That's what I'm here for," Bud said. "I'm your ambassador to the mind-numbing argot of legalese. Jack and I had spoken about this before, and though you are the executor of the will he charged me with ensuring that the process was as easy on you as possible, if anything should happen. For starters, you are Jack's only living relative, so not only are you the executor, you're the sole heir of his estate. I'll go into the legal ins and outs with you later, after you get some rest, but bottom line: your grandfather invested wisely. His pensions from the bread company, the settlement from your parents, free college thanks to the Academy…"

"Free. A quarter-million dollars worth of education and training shoved up my ass a nickel at a time."

Bud smiled. "Even so, Jack had a handsome sum of money with no appreciable debt. Even with the burial costs—."

"How was the funeral?" It was painful to hear Bud in lawyer mode again after fifteen years.

"It was nice, Kelly, really nice. That neighbor lady of yours, Ms. Thompson, she took care of a lot of the details. Jack had a lot of friends. He was a real charmer, your grandfather. If I ever said half the stuff he got away with, the women would knock me ass over tincups. He would've made a great lawyer. Now," Bud replaced his fisherman's smile with his lawyer's expression. "Again, bottom line, you've got quite a nice nest egg. On top of the investments, there's your home, bought and paid for."

"Put it on the market."

"Excuse me?"

"The man was my home."

It was ten o'clock. Kelly had elected to take care of as much of the paperwork as possible at Bob's. His plan was to so exhaust himself with legal minutiae that entering the empty house for the first time would not be so much a hurdle as a necessity. So far, it seemed to be working. Kelly drove south along West Avenue with his eyelids at half-mast. A few blocks before his street, he crossed over to Central, closer to the ocean. It was deserted now as Kelly coasted to a stop in front of the house. The wind off the beach had picked up, but Kelly barely registered the balls of foam rolling across the road. He fit his key into the lock and stepped inside. The smell hit him at once, old cigar smoke mixed with the salt air, but it was too much to think of now. Kelly wasted no time with the lights. The only necessity now was sleep. He climbed the stairs in the dark, dropped his bags on the deck, then fell into the rack. No, he thought, not deck, not rack. Floor, bed were his last thoughts before being sucked into the black undertow.

In the morning, Kelly showered and went straight to the grave. It was over the bridge, back across the marshes, in the neighboring town of Marmora. He did not expect to be happy about the any of it, but nothing was right. The plot was still fresh, covered with earth barely two weeks old. There was no headstone yet, only a plastic marker bearing Jack's full name. Next to the plot was the grave of his grandmother, gone since Kelly was a baby. With its even ground and weathered headstone, it was an institution by comparison. Kelly looked at the baby grass that poked sporadically through the fresh earth covering his grandfather. It looked anemic. Malnourished. Kelly balled his fists.

He drove back to Ocean City and the funeral home. He selected a headstone and made the remaining arrangements, but there were not many. Everything was over. Kelly spent the rest of the day wandering the town, avoiding the house.

After dark, Kelly returned to the house. He lingered outside for a while, sitting on the front deck. Out of habit, he lit a candle to keep the mosquitoes away, but it was only April. He was alone. Finally, he went inside. Again, he did not bother with the lights. He stumbled through the living room, past the mantle and the framed shellback certificate above it, and up the stairs. He paused outside Jack's room, then went in.

The first thing that hit him was the hint of Old Spice. Then objects began to take shape in the dark. There was the bed, made. Rolaids and loose change in a small dish on the dresser. The clutter on his nightstand organized, all at ninety-degree angles. There was another deck off the bedroom and he rolled back the sliding glass door. Across the street, he could see the ocean, calmer tonight, with the moon barely above it, cutting a swath right toward him. As a teenager, that same swath sometimes drew him to the beach, as if the moon had cleared a path just for him, and before he knew it, he would be standing in waist deep water, staring at the moon.

That same beach was where Mrs. Thompson found him. She had brought him a cup of coffee, Bud told him, as she did every morning Jack fished the beach. Only this time, he was down in the wet sand, his pole beside him, the waves lapping at his ankles. Kelly thought it over. His grandfather had lost his wife to cancer, then his daughter and son-in-law, then inherited a boy at sixty. Raised him alone, thank you very much. Nothing would stop him from getting back out there.

"Damn it, Pop."

As he stepped back inside the bedroom, the moonlight over his shoulder caught something white on the nightstand.

He turned on the bedside lamp. It was an envelope not yet sealed. He sat on the bed and looked at the front, but it was blank. He unfolded the pages inside and his heart slammed in his chest.

Hey there Charlie Brown,

I figured I'd write you an old-fashioned letter. I know how much it means to get letters underway, even if it's from your grandpop and not some fraulein. A letter's a letter. And you didn't sound too happy when I spoke with you from Key West. Did you know I was in Key West before? I was there for three months for sonar school. I left there as a third class, and boy was I ever glad to leave. The heat was unbearable and there was nothing down there to keep your mind off of it! There was one bar, a plank across two barrels with a guy selling nickel beers. I hear it's a lot of fun now. We'll compare notes when you get home.

The real reason I'm writing is I wanted to tell you again about Donnell. I know I've told you before but it bears repeating.

It was the morning of May 3, 1944, and I'd just gotten off my sonar watch. On a destroyer escort like Donnell, they have some bunks on the messdeck, and that's where mine was. I was tired, but there was no way I was going to get any sleep there during breakfast, so I hot-racked. A buddy of mine was eating so I used his bunk. This bunk was amidships, and the messdeck was in the tail end of the ship.

I'd been asleep for about ten minutes when the torpedo hit. One second, I'm in the rack, the next, on the deck with my shoes blown clean off my feet! I didn't know what the hell was going on, but I knew something was wrong. I saw sunlight. It was a hole and I climbed like the devil. Simple as that.

Sixty-nine feet of Donnell's stern was blown off, messdeck and all. Everyone in there had either been blown to bits or washed out to sea. One guy was blown clear over the mast, still on his mattress. He broke his back when he hit the water in front of the ship. A lifeboat got to him and he lived, but he was never the same upstairs.

Anyway, the ship stayed afloat, and she was towed by a destroyer to France, where her generators lit the city of Cherbourg until the end of the war. Altogether, twenty-nine men died, twenty-five were badly wounded. After that, we spent a couple of months in a rest camp in Ireland. I was eighteen.

It was just chance, pure dumb luck that I had made it. For every city lit by a generator, a ship somewhere had gone down, and for every boy like me there was a boy who chose a meal instead of a nap. Life at sea has its ups and downs and God forgive me, when you asked me for sea stories, I'm afraid I only gave you the ups. And the next thing I know you're all grown up and out to sea yourself, sounding blue. Go easy on yourself, Charlie Brown. You don't have anything to prove to anyone, least of all me.

That's enough blabbing from the old man. We'll talk when you get back. I've got to run, fish to kiss and ladies to catch, you know.

Love,
Pop

Kelly read the letter two more times then shut the light. He had known about *Donnell*, but had he remembered the details? Had he ignored them? Probably, he thought. He fell back on his grandfather's bed and stared at the stars through the skylight. A salty breeze blew into the room. Kelly considered his options.

After an hour, he went downstairs and out the back door, to the utility closet where the fishing poles were kept. He grabbed one of the ocean rods.

On the beach, the sand was cool. He got halfway to the water and realized the letter was still in his hand. He tucked it into his pocket and followed the swath to the water's edge. Kelly pulled the hollow ring from his finger and knelt over the pole in the damp sand. The fishing line ended with a lead sinker, but a smaller line branched off the main line and ended with an orange floater. Kelly removed the floater and replaced it with his ring. He tied several, sturdy knots in the transparent wire around the ring. The line was heavy with two sinkers now. Kelly smiled a bit. How many of his grandfather's rigs had he snapped as a little boy that first summer, before he got the hang of casting? Kelly smiled a bit. Enough to exasperate the old man, though Jack had always tried not to show it. He flipped the reel's guard over and pinched the line. He paused for a moment, then reared back with his arms and torso, and after the tip of the pole whipped a tiny circle in the air, he exploded forward.

Kelly numbered a good cast as one of the most satisfying sensations he had ever experienced. The sinker and the hollow ring soared toward the dark horizon. When the tackle reached its zenith, Kelly clamped his hand over the running line and jerked the rod back. There was a moment of resistance, then a plink somewhere along the line, and the tip of the pole swung free, weightless. The line recoiled, curling invisible loops in the wind. In seconds, the empty line was reeled in and Kelly was halfway up the beach, running the back of his hand under his nose and imagining another empty shell resting on the bottom.

At sunrise, he was on the bridge, the car packed with only those mementos he deemed essential: letters, photographs, the shellback certificate laid carefully on the backseat, his seabag crammed in the trunk. Bud had agreed to arrange for movers in the coming weeks and anything else that needed doing. They would coordinate any unfinished business by telephone.

He drove through the marshes again, passing the cattails and spartina and bayberry, scaring up the laughing gulls along the causeway that picked at the crushed turtle carcasses. It was chilly. He took one last breath of marsh air and rolled the window up. The only unfinished business that concerned him now was aboard *Sentinel*.

Chapter 28

Off the coast of South Carolina, Tropical Storm Bertha had churned herself into a hurricane and was heading toward the Hampton Roads region. Dane had called to alert Jorge that *Sentinel* had upgraded its readiness status. They would evade it at sea. The ship would need to be ready to get underway in six hours, so the crew would need to be assembled onboard within three. Jorge looked at his watch. Noon. He would be underway again by six p.m. By nightfall, they would be leaving Chesapeake Bay.

Jorge understood the logic of this as a sailor, but it did not mean he liked it.

"Wait," said Nancy, "explain this to me again." She sat on their bed as he packed. "Why are you going out again when a hurricane is coming?"

"Because," he said, flinging a pair of boxer shorts into his academy-issue duffel bag, "if the ship is moored and the hurricane actually hits here, it could destroy the *Sentinel*. Ships best evade hurricanes at sea."

"But you just came home."

"I know."

She was right. And Jorge needed a break. This past patrol had been, in some respects, worse than the one before. Leading up to the patrol, Jorge had spent little time with Kelly. When his friend was at work, he was circumspect, and left as soon as liberty was piped. When they finally put out to sea, he barely spoke, barely ate. Then the promotion lists came over the message traffic. Jorge had been selected for lieutenant junior grade, Kelly had not. As a final insult, Aregood had made captain. What alarmed Jorge was that Kelly no longer seemed to care.

Jorge tried to engage him, but it was like he was a different person. Other than standing his break-in watches or working out, Kelly stayed in the stateroom.

"Promise me the next billet will be on land."

"I'll only be gone a couple of days."

"I don't like this. It makes me nervous."

"You'll be fine. Just keep the TV on. If the storm gets too close, go to my parents' house."

"I'm not worried about me."

Jorge sat on the bed next to his fiancée and slipped his arm around her waist. "Babe, it's called storm evasion. Besides, she'll turn. They all do."

She wiped her eyes. "I don't know what's wrong with me."

"I can try to take your mind off it. We still have a few hours…."

Instead of making love, Nancy curled up against him, resting her head on his chest. He tried to maneuver for a kiss, but she wouldn't budge. When he realized she was asleep, he reached to switch off the bedside lamp but thought better of letting in the outside gloom.

At three, Jorge got the final call, kissed his groggy fiancée, grabbed his bag, and was out the door in ten minutes. He had plenty of time to get to the ship, but he hated to rush, and the longer he waited, the more hectic he knew it was going to be onboard. As the gate guard waved him onto the base, it felt more like October than July. The sky was gray, too dark for an afternoon, like the day after Daylight Savings Time. Despite the wind and the drizzle, the weather was warm and muggy, disorienting Jorge further, sending an electric tingle up his spine. He scratched his neck. Bertha was already throwing enfilades of storm clouds as far north as Virginia, despite its slow transit up the coast. The hurricane warning flags, two red ensigns with black centers, snapped atop the base flagpole.

He parked his car in a spot two spaces away from Kelly's Honda and made his way to the pier. In the distance, black smoke rose from *Sentinel*'s stacks. They've lit off the mains already, Jorge thought, it's official. As he approached the quarterdeck, Dane stepped out of the watch shack with a clipboard, scratching off names. "Port brief in the wardroom at 1700. Underway 1730."

"Who has the conn?"

"Congratulations."

"Great."

Jorge crossed the flight deck and looked out over the basin, out toward the breakwater. He noted the flood tide then hustled inside.

The lights were on in the stateroom, but Kelly was under the covers of his top bunk. Jorge tossed his bag on his rack.

"What are you doing?"

"Fever. Captain knows."

"And he cares?"

"Since he found out about making captain, I don't think he needs to amuse himself with me anymore."

"Any idea where we're going?"

"Out to sea, I imagine. It's how we evaded all of last summer's storms."

The ensigns chatted for a while; Kelly huddled in his rack and Jorge in a chair, feet propped on his desk. Despite the fever, Kelly was in good spirits, lively even. They had spent a lot of time like this, Jorge thought, and was pleased to have things somewhat back to normal between them. At five of five, Jorge rose and stretched. When he stepped for the door, Kelly said, "Hey."

"Yeah?"

"Take care up there."

Jorge laughed. "Sure."

"I'm serious. Watch your step. How did the old sailors say it? Keep your weather-eye lifting, Jorge."

"What is it with everybody today?"

The department heads and chiefs were already gathered in the wardroom when Jorge entered. He found a seat at the long table. Aregood shot him a look and said, "Finally. Go ahead, Mark."

Dane had tacked up three charts, the first of the Elizabeth River, the second of the lower Chesapeake, and the third of the entire bay. A line representing their proposed track snaked its way throughout each chart, ending finally at an anchorage at the mouth of the Potomac River, north of the shipping lanes.

"What's this?" asked Jorge.

"Last minute change of plans," Dane said. "District has decided to send the cutters up the bay en masse instead of scattering us at sea. *Bear*, *Forward*, and *Legare* are heading out now." Then to the captain: "Mr. Vargas will have the conn on the way up, so with your permission, captain, we'll set Special Sea Detail in fifteen minutes."

"Make it so," Aregood said.

Twenty minutes later, the ship's horn sounded three short blasts as *Sentinel* backed out of her berth and swung into the Elizabeth River. Flanked by the captain and OPS on the promenade in front of the bridge, Jorge came up to twelve knots. Soon *Sentinel* cleared the piers of the Norfolk Navy Base, passed over the tunnel connecting Willoughby Spit to Hampton, and turned into the broad lower bay, toward the Chesapeake Bay Bridge-Tunnel's eighteen-mile span and the Atlantic beyond. Once safely inside the lower bay, Dane made a pipe for all non-essential personnel to lay belowdecks; the wind and chop was not yet severe, but the decks were slippery and dusk was approaching. Within two miles of the great bridge, Jorge ordered left rudder and more speed, and in seconds, Norfolk was astern of them and *Sentinel* sped due north at sixteen knots into the heart of the Chesapeake Bay, toward the Potomac.

Early darkness encroached on the bay. From his vantage, he could not see any tall man-made structures, and the few visible lights on the low bluffs along the shoreline seemed so different from the mountainous islands of the Caribbean they so often patrolled. To Jorge, it seemed like they were sailing back in time, to the colonial era Jorge had read about in maritime history class. As they approached the Potomac at ten o'clock, night visibility had lessened with the mounting rain until Jorge could see nothing of the low landscape. Soon the only visible glow was that which *Sentinel* threw off herself. The bridge energized the ship's horn to blast every minute.

As they left the shipping channel for the lee of the Potomac's northern shore, Jorge asked to be relieved. As the First Lieutenant in charge of Deck Department, he wanted to experience the sight of the anchor dropped in less than ideal conditions, and it did not get less perfect than tonight. On the forecastle, Chief Norris stood behind the hawse pipes and watched his boys, illuminated by the deck lights, make the starboard anchor ready for letting go. He offered Jorge a hardhat without looking at him, then cupped his hand over the ear of his sound powered phone and said "aye" into the mouthpiece.

"Let go!" shouted the chief.

"Let go, aye!" replied Hosea, pulling the locking pin out of the chain stopper, making way for Locklair, sledgehammer in hand, to knock the locking ring away. Both men jumped back as the thick chain, like a cobra about to strike, leaped off the deck then shot down through the hawse pipe, down to the water's edge. Jorge heard the anchor splash. He smelled the acrid tang of rust in the air as the chain roared across the deck and felt the ching-ching-ching of it vibrating through his steel-toed boots. He pulled up the collar of his slicker as the whole ship shuddered. After a moment, the speed of the chain slackened, and Norris applied the brake to keep the chain from piling up over the anchor. Soon, the ship drifted downstream then stopped altogether. The sound of the waves against the hull had replaced the rattling echo of the chain.

"Anchor's set!" yelled the chief. He turned to Jorge. "It ain't so much the anchor that keeps a ship in place," he said, "it's the weight of the chain. We'll ready the port anchor just in case."

The winds blew steadily at thirty-five knots and there was a good chop on now, but once the bridge determined that *Sentinel* was not dragging, the Anchor Detail was secured and Jorge, with no watch to stand until morning, left the forecastle. He looked at his watch: 2230. With 30 minutes the galley would be serving midrats, but he was more tired than hungry. He opted for the stateroom.

The stateroom was black. Instead of waking Kelly or switching to red, Jorge stretched out in his bottom rack. He interlaced his fingers behind his head and sighed. The weather would harry *Sentinel* all night, he figured, but for now, the waters of the bay nudged the cutter in a pleasant rhythm. He would just rest his eyes.

Chapter 29

From his cabin, Aregood read the message traffic. Previous weather bulletins had Bertha making landfall in eastern North Carolina, but the storm had turned northeastward again and was chugging up the coast, blowing sustained winds of forty to fifty knots. It had glanced Portsmouth, but it had dropped below hurricane strength, and the damage was limited to minor flooding and some downed trees and power lines. We'll be in for a snotty night, he thought, but nothing serious.

He decided to catch some rack while he could. It seemed like he had just closed his eyes when the phone rang.

"Captain, this is Dane. It's really blowing up here. Last fix shows us dragging anchor."

"What time is it?"

"0200 hours, sir. Should I set the anchor detail?"

Aregood mulled it over for a moment.

"Captain?"

"No, just get me Norris and Locklair. XO and OPS, too. And I want Irving on the helm."

"Aye, sir."

When Aregood reached the bridge, visibility was nil. He opened the door to the bridgewing, and was greeted by the howl of fifty-knot winds. Cold rain pelted his face. He pulled his ball cap down and looked up into the superstructure, but saw nothing outside the nimbus of their own anchor lights at the top of the mast. A blast from their ship's horn jangled him, but it alerted other vessels in the vicinity of their presence. Aregood grinned. A real sailor's night.

When he stepped back inside, Norris and Locklair had been rousted and were chatting with Hosea, waiting for their vision to adjust. A groggy Irving was relieving the helmsman. Aregood consulted with Dane and looked at the radar, trying to tune out the bands of rain and sea clutter, but all it showed was a great yellow blob.

"Dane, latest fix?"

"Still dragging southerly, sir," Dane reported. "No danger of shoal, but we're dragging in the direction of the channel. We're already a mile outside the drop circle."

"No sweat, my boy." Aregood could feel his blood beginning to rush. "I'll take the conn."

"Sir?"

"I just want to have a little fun. Have the plant clutch in the engines."

"Aye, sir. Winds are fifty knots, seas confused—."

"I got it, I got it," he said, waving the young lieutenant off, then shouted, "This is

the captain, I have the conn!"

The bridge team responded in unison. Aregood sent Norris, Locklair, and Hosea down to the forecastle and told them to stand by. He rolled down one of the starboard windows and the sudden wind blew the hats off everyone inside. "I'll be outside!" he yelled over the howl. To his XO and OPS Boss, he said, "Let's go, boys!"

Aregood laughed as he watched the cover fly off his executive officer's head and into the blustery night. Tyndale cursed, but the man's words were lost in the wind. He gave the executive officer a shot in the arm. "Come on, Rich, this is what it's all about!" Even the saturnine operations officer let a smile escape.

The rain stung the skin and the air was filled with foam and bellowing. A hurricane downgraded to a tropical storm in the sheltered Chesapeake Bay was no raging sea, but it was a turbulent body of water nonetheless.

He turned toward OPS. "Get me Sensor."

"I thought he was down hard, sir."

Aregood waved off the comment. "This is character building."

With both engines now online, Aregood shouted down to Norris to weigh anchor. Once the anchor was clear of the bottom, the captain planned to maneuver *Sentinel* back to the drop circle, only this time he would pay out plenty of extra chain to keep her in place.

OPS returned a moment later. "Sensor's not in his rack, sir."

"It's two-thirty in the morning."

Dane stuck his head out the window. "Captain, there's a lot of incoming merchant traffic and we're still drifting, sir."

"Don't get your panties in a bunch, Dane. We'll have the anchor clear in a minute. OPS, go check the messdeck."

"I thought we might set a full sea detail, sir?"

"I don't need all of that. We'll do this the old-fashioned way."

"Sir?"

"OPS, find Sensor. Now."

"Sir, I would like the log to reflect that I strongly recommend we set the Special Sea Detail. The Anchor Detail, as well."

"OPS, quit being such a pussy and fetch me the boy!"

"Aye aye, sir."

As he watched Griffin leave, and wondered when the officer corps had gone so utterly soft, the ship's whistle boomed again, startling his officers. He and the XO stared at one another. In the howl of the gale, it took the captain a second to realize it had not been their horn.

"Dane, get on the radio and broadcast our position. Find out exactly where that boat is. XO, tell Chief to double-time it with that anchor."

"Aye," said both men and vanished.

The order made it to the forecastle, and in response to the rapid hauling, the cutter pivoted on the anchor chain. Aregood watched from the bridgewing. As the cutter swung, he ordered speed to get north of the channel as quickly as possible.

"All ahead eight!" Aregood shouted through the window.

"Command?" Irving shouted. He cupped his ear toward the window.

"Irving, mind your fucking helm! I said all ahead eight!"

Sentinel's horn blasted at the minute interval, and as it's boom faded, he caught the tail end of the other ship's horn. The piggybacked blasts made it difficult to get a bearing on the other ship, but it sounded like it was somewhere off their starboard beam. He peered into darkness, saw nothing.

Dane ran outside with his radio report. "It's a commercial fishing vessel, sir, inbound for the Potomac."

"In the channel?"

"Coming out of the channel to the anchorages, sir. Like us."

Aregood was trying to picture it in his head, the two ships were approaching the same area from different angles, when the horns blared again, *Sentinel*'s obscuring the inbound vessel. "Turn off that fucking horn so I can hear! Dane, keep talking to them!" Aregood shouted over the wind. After another minute, the other horn boomed off the starboard bow.

"Right full rudder! All ahead full!" he shouted. He did not listen for the command repeated back, but craned his neck over *Sentinel*'s side, listening for the other ship and trying to pierce the gloom. At a thousand yards, he made out a hazy port running light, high enough off the water to indicate a large boat, its red light glaring at him through the murk like a wary eye. At right full rudder, with the quick kick of the engines he had ordered, they should pass well beneath the fishing boat, he thought. A little close, maybe five hundred yards, but not too close. Aregood ordered one short blast, signifying their intention of a right turn. In the distance, one short blast was sounded back, indicating the boat's agreement. The captain breathed easy. He would wait until the red eye passed to their left before selecting a course.

Though he could not discern his surroundings, the ship beneath his feet told him something was off. In a right turn, *Sentinel* should heel to the left as the sea met and resisted its turning face. *Sentinel* was heeling right. He looked up and peered into the downpour. The red eye remained fixed.

Aregood spun for the window.

"Irving, repeat my last command!"

"Left full rudder, all ahead full, sir!"

"My God."

Aregood scrambled and tried to mouth the right commands, but five short and deafening blasts shook him, the danger signal. To which boat it belonged the captain could no longer tell.

He heard the rush of the water and braced.

Chapter 30

He stirred a second before, sensing something was not quite right. Maybe an errant noise, but all was quiet. Perhaps something in the movement of the ship or the wave action had raised the hair on his arms.

He was flung from his rack then, striking his head on its post. He heard screaming, his world black and blaring and aslant. Objects rolled helter-skelter over him on the deck like animals scurrying across a black forest floor. He recoiled. His heart slammed in his chest, and his head ached from a fresh knot and the effort of deciphering his lunatic surroundings. His arm brushed against something cold and solid. He touched the smooth face, big and heavy. The filing cabinet. Drilled into the bulkhead. Stable.

He groped for the handle and pulled himself to his feet. Things fell into place then, the dimensions of his room, his ship, his life, just as he heard the clanging reports of the boat's sudden slide, her pots and pans and innards spilling everywhere. It felt like the tempest outside had smacked the boat with the flat of her hand, knocking *Sentinel* onto her side, dipping her low into the dark, sloshing water.

Sentinel finally righted herself with dreadful slowness. And that scream, he thought. He realized it was not from a man, but from the ship herself. The rending of metal. There was a second of calm, and then Jorge's budding senses were shattered again by the bleating of a klaxon.

Collision alarm.

Jorge was still blind, and his brain still revolted at the dark. The schooner all over again. He reached for the toggle and wrenched it back and forth. The room remained pitch black.

"Kelly!"

When he heard no answer, Jorge lunged for the racks, reaching for his friend. Jorge held onto the post with one hand and swept the upper rack with his free hand, feeling empty space where his roommate should be. He patted the mattress, then the pillow. He stood patting for several seconds, disoriented and not making the connection that his friend was not there until he heard the pounding of footsteps outside his stateroom. He cursed himself for being an idiot and reached for his belt. A second later, his penknife cut a red beam across Kelly's rack. He could still see the impression left by a body. A postcard peeked out from underneath the pillow. It took Jorge a moment to realize it was his own rack. He shook his head and shown his light at Kelly's rack: empty. He continued the sweep of his beam across the room. Trashed. Books, uniforms, and toiletries strewn across the deck. Jorge danced around the deck's flotsam toward the head and flung the door open, empty as well. He fled to the corridor.

Officers' Country was red in the glow of the battle lanterns, and men ran past him shouting that *Sentinel* had been struck. The ship's loudspeakers boomed, "Collision, starboard side. All hands man your General Quarters stations."

As he ran, it dawned on Jorge that he had not been awakened by the collision alarm, but by the collision itself. That kind of mistake could only mean bad business on the bridge, he thought.

He scrambled down the ladder to his General Quarters assignment, the damage control locker on the main deck. When his steel-toed boots hit the deck, he heard a splash and his stomach clenched. Rivulets of water trickled past his soles in the narrow passageway, running blood red in the crimson light of the battle lanterns. He ran in the direction of the flow.

A small crew of boatswain mates had gathered by the locker. Gray sat against the bulkhead, eyes wide. Jorge grabbed him by the shoulders. "What happened?"

"Your head's bleeding, sir," said Gray, blinking.

"Gray!"

The petty officer pointed to a tight ring of seamen, standing motionless, surrounding the scuttle to the lower decks, the petty officer berthing areas and the Radio Room below that. Jorge muscled his way inside them and looked down. He hoped to see a long stairway leading down to the berthing areas, then one going deeper into the bowels of the ship, but all he saw was blackness. It took him a moment to realize that it was not darkness, but the sea. Flush with the scuttle was salt water. It gurgled and spat at him.

He looked at Gray. "Was there anyone else?" he yelled.

The seaman shook his head. "Too fast," he said.

Jorge ran quick calculations. *Sentinel* already felt heavy and swollen beneath his boots. How long had it been since the screaming hull woke him? How much time had he spent in the stateroom, then how long to get down here? It seemed like full, slow minutes stretching between then and now, but in truth, he knew that it had been only seconds. A riven hull. Full racks of sleeping men blasted by founts of hurricane water. Free communication with the sea.

"Jesus. Help me shut this."

"We can't—."

"Gray, they're already gone. We have to hurry."

Chief Norris, Hosea, and a throng of engineers and boatswain's mates had arrived and surrounded Jorge now. The water spilled over the lip of the scuttle. The men piled on, and with their collective strength, the hatch slammed home. Water sprayed in protest between the scuttle's hatch and its housing until Jorge spun the wheel on top, tightening it. The water slowed to a trickle. Jorge screamed and strained the muscles of his arms and back once more and the entrance sealed with a gasp. Then quiet.

Chapter 31

The long green table, a common expression in the Coast Guard for a captain's mast or court-martial. Aregood figured he would be standing before one, facing a panel of stoic higher-ups, but when he arrived at Atlantic Area Headquarters in downtown Portsmouth, he faced one man. Admiral Roger Stokes controlled all Coast Guard operations on the East Coast sat alone behind the cherry desk of his spacious office. Over his shoulder, the Elizabeth River sparkled in the summer sunlight. Any other time, Aregood would have relished a visit with the Commander of Atlantic Area, but today, he stood at attention in the doorway, studying him.

Unaware of his visitor, the admiral was engrossed in a report. No doubt the investigation, thought Aregood. He looked as an admiral should look, Aregood thought, square-jawed, tough but manicured. With over thirty years in the Guard, the huge collection of ribbons above his left breast pocket resembled a colorful solar panel. Aregood had always held him in awe, ever since his own ensign tour on Stokes' cutter, when he thought Captain Stokes looked just as a captain should.

Aregood cleared his throat. "Admiral."

Admiral Stokes looked up. He picked up his papers and rapped them on his desk, sliding them into a manila folder. The admiral walked around to the front of his desk and leaned against it, arms folded. The admiral watched Aregood for a long time, a queer look on his face, one Aregood had never seen before. "I still picture you as an ensign, you know. Keeps me young by default, I suppose."

"Please, sir. You're hardly old."

The admiral ignored the remark. "Come in, Commander."

Commander. So that's how it would be.

Stokes beckoned Aregood to a couch in the sitting area of the office. The admiral chose a high-backed leather chair. Aregood felt adrift on the long couch.

"Sad day, Kevin."

"I know, sir. I'm sorry to put you in this situation."

"What situation is that?"

"Of having to reprimand me, sir."

The Admiral leaned back in his chair. "I think we have two different situations in mind."

"Sir?"

"I was referring to the twenty-one Coast Guardsmen who died. And the six civilians."

"Of course, sir. That's what I meant."

"Here." Stokes flung the folder onto the table. "I wanted you to have a look at it, beforehand. I had questions, between you and me."

Aregood skipped to the "Findings of Fact" section and scanned. It read pretty much as he figured it would. Low visibility. Dragging anchor. Relieving the conn without getting a full report. Failing to set a proper anchor watch or special sea detail, despite recommendations to do so by the operations officer. Mistaken helm commands. *Sentinel* making contradictory turning signals....

The bow of the 110-foot longliner *Gloria May* had pierced *Sentinel*'s hull. As fate would have it, due to the wave action, the fishing boat slid down the face of a wave, just as *Sentinel* reared up and away on the crest of another, and the cutter was struck below her waterline. After the collision, things became blurry for the captain, and the report actually helped him to piece things together. The damaged cutter remained afloat, but *Gloria May* had not fared as well. As *Sentinel* settled back into the water after the strike, she pushed the bow of *Gloria May* down into the sloshing water, cracking her open. Six dead on its way to the bottom of the bay, all hands. Fortunately for his own laid-open cutter, the other Portsmouth cutters were anchored nearby and were able to render assistance within minutes. *Sentinel* was towed to the Coast Guard Yards in Baltimore for repair, her survivors remaining onboard for the transit. Aregood reread "survivors." It stung.

"See something funny, Commander?"

"I see sixty pages, sir, but not the heart of the matter. I don't feel the hurricane's winds or——."

"Spare me. I see twenty-seven dead. And you had the conn."

Aregood stared at his shoes. They shone so clear he could see himself in them. The admiral continued.

"You severely underestimated the situation. You put a jackass on the helm. I interviewed him personally and what in God's name were you thinking? Not to mention you seemed more preoccupied with getting a single ensign on the bridge than a proper compliment of watchstanders. Why was that?"

"Ensign Sensor, sir," he said, "He's my...protégé."

"Was," said the admiral.

"Yes, sir."

"Do you have any idea how difficult you've made it for the rest of us to do our jobs now? Our resources are stretched so thin that I'm sitting on a proposal right now to cut Atlantic Area operations across the board by ten percent. Just to save money. Ten percent less patrols, because we can't afford the fuel, and now this. The worst Coast Guard tragedy since *Blackthorn*. In view of the shore for Christ's sake."

"Sir, if I may, with the proper spin, we could——."

"Spin?" Stokes slapped the leather arm of his chair. "This isn't politics, Commander! People are dead and you were at the wheel. You have no say in this!"

"What's going to happen now?"

"What would you do if you were me?" Aregood tried to form and answer, but panic cinched his throat. Stokes did not wait for a response. "The ship's logs and the testimony of the witnesses all bear out the same chain of disaster."

Witnesses, thought Aregood.

"Look. You've had a great career and you've done a lot for this service, and in my own way, I feel partially responsible. Maybe I could have trained you better, I don't know. Regardless, the court martial will occur in two days, after which, you'll be allowed to retire quietly."

"Admiral, no. Wait, please!"

"You'll have your pension and full benefits, son. It'll be just like going on leave. You just won't come back."

Aregood could not believe it. His throat turned bone dry. "*Sentinel?*"

"Until we find a permanent replacement, Lieutenant Commander Tyndale will take care of your men."

Tyndale. It all made sense now. He looked at his hands. They were trembling. He drew a deep breath in and shut his eyes. When he opened them again, he was steady. "Admiral, I'm not sure how, but it is my belief that Rich Tyndale somehow engineered this collision. He has always coveted my command."

Though he was already sitting, Stokes seemed to collapse into his chair. He blinked, his mouth agape. It took him several moments to compose a sentence, but he finally said, "You've been through an ordeal, so I'm going to ignore that remark. But it's my recommendation that you seek professional help."

"Admiral, I've been betrayed."

Stokes lunged forward and grabbed Aregood by a shoulderboard. He shook him and Aregood heard his shirt tear where it attached to the epaulet. "Men are dead." He punctuated each word with a hard shake. He shoved Aregood back into the couch. Stokes stood over him, pointing. "From your ship, under your command, with you at the conn!"

Aregood sat motionless. He stared at the file in front of him. Finally, Stokes collapsed into his own chair again.

"I called your house yesterday. I spoke with Lisa," said the admiral.

The file gave way to an orange glow. He sat motionless, feeling nothing but the pulse of his heart in a tick of his face, and the blazing of his own eyes. Stokes continued. "She says you haven't been home in days. I don't think your family problems are germane to this investigation, but go home. You need all the support you can get right now."

Aregood laughed bitterly. "Support." He looked at the ceiling to clear his clouding eyes.

Stokes pinched the bridge of his nose with his thumb and forefinger. "I was hoping to help steer you through this, but you obviously need more help than I can give you. Seek counseling. That's an order. Dismissed."

Aregood rose to attention, pinning his shoulders back like the ears of a feral dog.

"Someone is responsible, Admiral. I'll find out who and you'll see."

"Get out of my sight. After the court martial, I never want you to see you in that uniform again."

Aregood walked out the door. He passed Vargas, the next officer to be interviewed. Further down the corridor, Tyndale was bent at a water fountain and Aregood charged. The tackle felt good, and he landed several satisfying blows before he heard the shouting and felt the strong arms hauling him away.

Chapter 32

None of it seemed real yet, twenty-one friends and shipmates gone. Every day since the tragedy had been unreal as well. From the rainy morning Nancy showed up at the Baltimore Yards, out of her mind with panic and sobbing in the shadow of the torn ship, to today's trip to LANTAREA where Aregood lost it.

Still in uniform, he went straight from his interview with Admiral Stokes to downtown Norfolk. As he stood outside the eight-story red brick building on Botetourt Street, his hands were shaking. As he rode the elevator up, he rubbed the seashell in one pocket, and from the other, he pulled the bent postcard. Before he could read it again, the doors opened and there was the door to Kelly's apartment. He had just jammed the card back into his pocket when he noticed the door was ajar.

He opened the door and peaked inside. A bald and burly man stood in the center of Kelly's den, going through the drawers of his oak desk. Jorge sneaked inside, crouched as he might on a boarding. Without turning around, the man said, "Friend or foe?"

"What?"

"Simple question," he said. He turned around and offered Jorge a hearty smile. "Coastie, I presume?"

"Jorge Vargas. Who the hell are you?"

"Bud Docimo. I'm from Ocean City. The family's lawyer actually." He shook his head. "How did you know Kelly?"

Jorge was suddenly unsure how to identify himself. Classmate? Shipmate? "He's my friend."

"Me, too. I guess we're the only family left then." Bud pointed to some boxes. "So you won't mind pitching in then."

With two of them, they had the apartment cleared by dark. Bud had arranged for a truck to collect the furniture, leaving the more personal effects to the two of them. Bud pulled nautical books from the shelves while Jorge cleared a rack full of compact discs from the Beatles, the Beach Boys, Frank Sinatra. He boxed up old videotapes, Cagney and Bogart movies, and took down framed posters of vintage movies from the wall: *The Caine Mutiny*, *White Heat*, and *The Mark of Zorro*. Jorge smirked. Old man's taste, he thought.

He called Nancy and told her he would not be home for dinner. Instead, Bud followed him as he drove into Norfolk's Ghent district for steaks. In a quiet southwestern grille on Colley Avenue, the man from Ocean City offered anecdotes about a younger Kelly, and Jorge filled him in on their more colorful escapades from the Academy and *Sentinel*. Jorge took an immediate liking to the weathered, old fellow and wished they had met under sunnier circumstances.

"Bud, one thing has been bothering me. Did you pack the shellback certificate? I didn't see it."

"I don't recall. Maybe I packed it before you got there."

"There weren't as many pictures either. I remember Kelly always had a ton of pictures of his grandfather around the apartment."

Bud contemplated this as he took a healthy pull of lager. "He was pretty unhappy on that the ship, wasn't he?"

"What makes you say that?"

"Just things I picked up from Jack."

"I think he didn't want his grandfather to worry, but yeah, he was not happy."

"Why not?"

"Well, he buried his grandfather a few months ago."

"No," Bud said, "he didn't."

After a moment, Jorge nodded.

"I received a very large check in the mail just before I came down here," Bud

said, "large enough to settle his estate." He studied the beer bottle, then Jorge. "Large enough for a burial."

"What are you saying?"

"I think this collision is muddling the real issue, son."

"What issue?"

"The kid's had a tough go of it from Day One. First his parents. Then Jack. Disillusionment, depression. Doesn't take a genius."

Jorge made a sour face. "I refuse to believe that."

"You know him better than I do, but one thing's for sure, he wasn't just getting his grandfather's affairs in order, he was getting his own together as well."

"No." He rubbed his brow as if trying to process these new, troubled thoughts, but in truth, he just wanted to shield his eyes in front of this man.

"Either way, Jorge, what's say we just let him rest in peace." He held his bottle out. Jorge could not speak, so he nodded and without looking clinked it with his own. The two men ate the rest of their meals in silence until the check came and Jorge reached for it. Bud snatched it up. "Don't even think about it, kid."

Outside the steakhouse, Jorge thanked Bud for dinner.

"Anytime. And when you guys come up to Ocean City for the...well, I'll take you and your fiancée out for a nice seafood dinner if you're up for it."

"Do you have a place to stay tonight? Nancy would love to meet you."

"Oh, I appreciate it, but I do my driving at night."

They shook hands.

"You Coasties are alright." Without another word, he gave Jorge a shot in the arm and marched up Colley Avenue toward his car. Jorge waved. The man waved back as he drove past.

Alone in front of Magnolia's the wind had picked up and it was chilly on the street. He had not expected to be out this late. It suddenly occurred to Jorge that he was a few short months away from becoming a married man. It seemed too far away. Even the twenty-minute ride back to Nancy and his warm bed seemed too long from where he stood. He pulled the postcard from his pocket and stared at it under the street lamp, trying to figure it out one last time. The front, a photograph taken from the water, showed the length of a pier lined with people, all facing the same direction, staring out over the sea. Some people stood, some sat on the edge of the pier, letting their feet dangle over the water. The reddish hue and golden reflections indicated they were present in anticipation of a sunset. Cumulus clouds floated overhead and hotels loomed in the background. In the foreground, the people looked warm and cheerful. In the lower left corner, "Key West" was written in gold script.

Jorge flipped the card over. Blank. He dropped it in a trashcan and hustled up Colley Avenue.

Chapter 33

What a difference a few states make, Kelly marveled, wheeling his Sportster into the dusty parking lot of a Georgia roadside diner. Leaving rainy Virginia and North Carolina, he had gotten off to a slow start. He was still a new rider, traveling only a few hours a time, whenever the sun poked through the gloom long enough to dry out the pavement, and bunking in roadside motels the rest of the time. But now, the sky was blue and cloudless, and the Georgia heat bore down on the gravel like a weighted thing. He cut the ignition and dismounted in a haze of dry, summer dust. It was chalky and he held his breath as he tugged the straps that lashed his seabag to the back of the bike. Confident it was still secure, he strolled toward the front door, plugged two quarters into a newspaper dispenser and removed a copy, then found a window table inside to keep an eye on the motorcycle and the seabag that now contained his only remaining possessions.

Kelly was on his second cup of coffee when he read a small headline on page four. He was so shocked he knocked his cup over and spilled coffee all over the paper. "Shit," he yelled, then ran past the counter with the waitress calling after him. He fumbled two more quarters into the machine outside and yanked another copy out and opened it on the spot. The sun was so bright on the white page he had to squint to read the newsprint.

When he returned to his table, it was already clean and there was a fresh cup of coffee. He slid into the booth and spread the paper in front of him, careful not to spill, and reread the article's headline. "Search Continues for Missing in Coast Guard Collision."

Norfolk, VA

The search for the missing in the July 13 Potomac River collision between Coast Guard Cutter Sentinel *and the fishing boat* Gloria May *continued yesterday without success. Divers have been on site attempting to salvage the sunken fishing vessel, while assorted Coast Guard boats and aircraft continue the search for their missing brethren. Several bodies of Coast Guardsmen were recovered belowdecks before* Sentinel *was towed to Baltimore, MD, and the likelihood of finding survivors in the bay is grim, according to Admiral Roger Stokes, Commander of Atlantic Area Operations. "The force and placement of the collision along with the sea conditions at the time," the Admiral said, "makes hope for finding more survivors difficult at this point." The Admiral went on to state that the purpose of the search will soon shift in focus from rescue to recovery, and that the cutter's captain, CDR Kevin Aregood is under investigation.*

The collision is the worst Coast Guard tragedy since January 28, 1980, when the USCGC Blackthorn, *a 180-foot buoy tender, and 23 of its crewmembers were lost after a collision with the U.S. tankship* Capricorn *in Tampa Bay. The Chesapeake Bay itself is no stranger to Coast Guard tragedy - on October 20, 1978, the training cutter* Cayahoga *was on a weekend training cruise to Baltimore, when she was struck amidships by an Argentinean motorship, also off the mouth of the Potomac River, resulting in eleven deaths.*

USCGC Sentinel *was commissioned in 1983. Her career highlights include 14 narcotics busts, most recently a large cocaine seizure in March in the Windward Passage...*

Kelly called the waitress over and asked if she had any of yesterday's newspapers. She produced a copy from behind the counter. The articles inside had more information, including a list of the missing. Kelly searched the list for Jorge and let out a small cry of relief when he could not find the name. He wanted to call—what if Jorge had not found the postcard in the melee or did not understand it—but thought better of it.

He sank back in the booth, closed his eyes. It was all too much to take in. He brought a trembling hand to his brow and reread the names.

"Jesus Christ," he said. "Harmon."

And Gaskey. And Hosea. And Locklair....

And Sensor.

Sensor. His eyes widened and he shot upright. They were searching for him, but in the wrong place and the wrong context, and only for another few days it seemed. His case would not have to bear the result of a suicide investigation. They would assume Kelly Sensor was caught belowdecks and sucked out to sea, or above decks and washed overboard. Either way, he was presumed dead.

I'm free, he thought.

After all this time, he marveled. He had planned meticulously and trained vigorously. He was lean in body and mind, no time or movements wasted since returning from Ocean City for the last time.

Kelly could still picture his view from the fantail, looking out at the increasing chop of the Chesapeake Bay, dressed in a black wetsuit with flippers in hand, the Bay-Bridge Tunnel closing in the distance. From drills and other evasions, he knew the weather decks would be secured, so when they passed over the tunnel on their way out to sea, no one would see or stop him from leaping overboard and swimming for the rocks a half-mile away. He readied himself, and tried to savor his last two miles sailed on *Sentinel*. There had been no vomiting for months, no nightmares. The skin under his wetsuit itched and tingled. He felt wired and ready.

As he took a giant, open-mouthed breath, he heard the latch of the watertight door behind him being thrown. He dove behind SENT-2 in its cradle, breaking the skin of the wetsuit's knee and palm on the non-skid deck surface. He dropped a flipper. It bounced underneath the boat, toward the door.

Crouched, he peered from around the davits and saw Tyndale emerge. The XO surveyed the fantail. He approached SENT-2 and Kelly ducked again behind the davit. He felt the XO give a cursory tug on one of the straps that held the rigid-hull inflatable firm. Kelly clenched his fists and creased his brow, tensing into a tight ball and willing himself to blend right down into the non-skid, invisible, but after a few leaden moments he heard the XO grunt, bend over and grab the flipper, just out of Kelly's reach. The ensign held his breath.

"Fucking deckies," said the XO, then tossed the flipper over the side. Kelly uttered a silent curse as it whizzed past like a dark bird. He heard Tyndale mutter something, then after a quiet moment, open the watertight door once more. Once he heard the latch dogged from the inside and he was sure he was alone again, Kelly stood and looked at the bridge-tunnel, then at his remaining flipper.

As he did so, the bridge-tunnel started to slip away before his eyes. Beneath him, the cutter heaved, the telltale feel of its turning. The span of the bridge was sliding from the bow in front of him off to the starboard side.

"No!"

Sentinel was cutting between the buoy gates, leaving the channel on a northbound course. His mouth hung open in shock as he realized that for all of his months of planning, he was undone by a simple decision he had not anticipated: *Sentinel* was evading in the bay, not at sea. By his estimation, the bridge-tunnel was still two miles away. Kelly watched his lifeline drift out of reach and nausea flooded his stomach. His sea legs lost their memory and he grabbed for the rail.

In the part of his mind that still processed rational thought, he realized absently that every second he waited, *Sentinel* steamed even farther away from his salvation at sixteen knots, that each additional foot churned ahead was a raging mistake, and his body was burning with what he could only describe as the opposite of fever. It was not nausea. It was adrenaline. He believed that if he did not soon feel the cooling touch of the waves, he would surely combust. His vision flared red with the blood pulsing in his temples and he backed himself against the bulkhead. He sprung off of it, and charged down the deck, which seemed to narrow and telescope away from him with each pounding step like a cruel joke, which only made the deck look more like a runway, and with as much power as his body possessed, he cast himself into the sea.

Sailing over the rail like a dream, both arms locked forward clutching the single flipper like a game-winning football, his legs uncoiled and kicked out behind, his torso tensed in mid-air, holding his breath and rigging himself in to be as streamlined as possible, a black knife sailing well clear of those screws which could either suck him forever into *Sentinel*'s endless push forward or triple the distance of his jump. Sailing, sailing, until the reality of the Chesapeake rushed up to meet him like a stinging palm across his cheek to tell him there was no turning back now.

Even after Kelly hit the surface, he still felt like he was falling. In the propeller's roiling wake, there were equal amounts of air in the water and water in the air, and despite Kelly's frantic strokes, he went under. He knew this because his eyes stung and saltwater seeped into his wetsuit though the tears at his palm and knee, burning his new cuts there. Under the chaos of the wash, where the sea maintained some substance, a hard current coiled around his legs like a tentacle and jerked him down. Reeling, every direction he swam toward felt wrong, and he quickly became lost beneath the surface. His strokes became disorganized, dissolved into simple flailing. He held his only breath, and then grasped his knees, curling into a ball to wait for the wake to stop tossing him. His eardrums felt tight in his head as he spiraled down, and he realized then just how far he was from the surface. He waited for his entire life to pass before his eyes, like everyone always said it would, but only those events that led him to this predicament repeated themselves and his panic gave way to anger. How insane he was for jumping off a perfectly good boat with a hurricane on the way. At least, he thought, he was away from Aregood now, out from under him. Some great victory. Even in his last moments, he thought, all he could manage to think of was that damned man.

He closed his eyes and prayed it would not hurt.

"Why are you crying, Charlie Brown?"

Kelly opened his eyes and looked back at the strand of Ocean City. He was farther out than he'd ever been, well past the other kids. The waves broke over Pop's waist, and his grandfather was the tallest person he knew.

"It's over my head."

"Then you're only making more water for yourself by crying."

"Stop laughing, I'm going to drown."

"Come on, you're on my shoulders."

"Then what if you drown?"

"When I was your age, I'd already swallowed a gallon of saltwater. It's good for you. Boy, I can't believe your parents never taught you how to swim."

"What if I go under?"

"You know how to kick, right? Doggie-paddle?"

"Yeah."

"Well, if you go under, just open your eyes."

"That stings." He heard the faint tinkling of the bell on the street vendor's cart and squirmed again on his grandfather's broad shoulders, nearly toppling them both. Other kids were in full sprint across the hot sand in pursuit of bomb pops, Italian water ice, and frozen candy bars.

"I want a water ice."

"Are you listening to me, pal?"

"Sorry."

"Open your eyes and blow some bubbles. Just follow the bubbles and kick your way to the surface. That's swimming."

"That's all?"

"You'd be surprised, Charlie Brown."

Kelly opened his eyes. He felt the grip of the wake subside and his body stopped tumbling. The water still heaved him about, but it was no longer an aerated churn, but a deep, even teal, so when he blew out a tiny breath, he saw nothing in the murk. Kelly expelled all of the air in his lungs and saw a thin, white trail arc away from his face. He kicked and pulled, frantic behind the bubbles, his throat and chest empty and ready to rupture, and when his head broke the surface, a streak of foam blowing off a wave top stung his face and filled his gasping mouth with bitter seawater. He coughed and gagged and went under again, but there had been a blessed moment of air, and it was enough to fight back to the surface. He found his equilibrium and treaded water. On the crest of a wave, Kelly saw *Sentinel*'s mast light in the distance, shrinking as it continued north. He waited for the next crest and swung his head to the east and through sheets of hissing spray was the Chesapeake Bay Bridge-Tunnel, its yellow street lamps at their even intervals lit up like the most beautiful string of Christmas lights he had ever seen. After a few awkward tries and some more saltwater in his lungs, he rolled onto his back and fit his right foot into the flipper and started a steady crawl toward the break in the lights—the southern tunnel. Without the height of eye afforded by the ship, the distance seemed insurmountable, the bridge itself looked like a child's toy, but he continued anyway. The current seemed to be with him.

Kelly jockeyed for position by swimming as hard as he could in one direction, with the currents shunting him in another. If he drifted too far north, he'd be swept over the tunnel and out to sea. Too far south and he'd pass under the bridge, between the pilings and then out to sea. He was closer to the bridge-tunnel than the shore, so land was not an option. Even so, it was not a straight shot to the bridge-tunnel. He plowed forward, peeked out of a crest like a sea turtle, adjusted his course, and plowed on, encouraging himself by talking to his grandfather, sometimes his parents. He tried not to think of it as a two-mile swim with a hurricane bearing down on him, but the home stretch of a marathon.

Soon, the fishing pier jutted out from the first of the bridge-tunnel's four man-made islands. Then the pier was over his head, shielding him from the rain. Then, at eleven-thirty, five hours after jumping, he felt the rocks. Spent, he hauled his body onto the jagged boulders and collapsed, the waves still lapping at his flippered foot. He found a nook in the rocks, and too exhausted to remove his flipper, passed out in the darkness under the pier.

He awoke when the water level had risen and his body was half-submerged again. He checked his watch: 12:40 am. The wind blew a deep tone through the concrete pilings of the pier. He scrambled up the rock pile and searched for his stash.

He had driven out to the Sea Gull Pier Restaurant late the night before with everything he would need in the trunk, wrapped in a tarp. It irked him that he had to pay ten dollars just to get onto the bridge, not even to cross it, then laughed a moment later when he remembered everything he was preparing to do. He unloaded his equipment, and hid the bundle under the pier. No one saw him come or go, and to be sure, he entered the restaurant and ordered a cup of coffee. He watched the spot on the quay above his stash, then followed the long finger of the pier pointing into the bay, toward the lighted buoy gates that marked the channel.

Now, under the pier with the wind howling, that moment seemed like a month ago.

Where the pier met the rocks of the island, nestled out of sight of the fishermen and tourists, Kelly retrieved the mountain-bike he had bought as a graduation gift for himself and never once used after reporting to *Sentinel*. Tied to its handlebar was his blue Academy backpack, filled with sneakers, a towel and dry clothes, bottled water, two ham and cheese sandwiches, a chocolate bar, and one hundred dollars in cash. He tried to untie the sack but his hands shook with cold. He stuck them between his thighs for warmth and got the backpack loose a minute later, upending the water bottle and gulping it until he gasped, then moving on to one of the sandwiches, then the candy bar, devouring everything in his black wetsuit at one in the morning in the middle of a hurricane beneath the Chesapeake Bay Bridge-Tunnel's Sea Gull Fishing Pier.

"What I did for my summer vacation," he said. "By Kelly Sensor."

He tossed his flipper into the bay in favor of his sneakers and emerged from beneath the pier with his mountain bike. At that hour and in that weather, the pier was deserted and as Kelly flung the backpack over one shoulder and mounted the bike, it seemed to him that it was more like a triathlon, and the finish line was his apartment in the Ghent section of Norfolk. He pedaled into the wind, crouching over the handlebars, three-and-a-half miles from the island where he made landfall. The gale shunted the bike occasionally, and he fell twice. Now and then, headlights would blind him or a car would whoosh from behind. A few honked. Three-and-a-half miles later, the bridge-tunnel was behind him.

At the foot of the bridge, among the trees, the wind died down and his land speed increased. He pedaled until he reached the first bar, a strip joint called The Flight Deck. He grunted at the irony, and coasted the bike to the side of the building. Behind a dumpster, he removed his sneakers and unzipped the black wetsuit. It clung to him like a man-sized leech, and he cursed and wrestled with it in the rain. The howling of the wind sounded like the sky itself was trying to catch its breath and suddenly Kelly thought of *Sentinel* out there, men looking for him. He toweled off then and pulled on a pair of jeans and a sweatshirt, stuffed the hundred dollars into his pocket with quaking hands, and donned his sneakers again. He tossed the towel and backpack into a dumpster then kissed the torn, bloodied wetsuit in his hands. Behind him the bay hissed.

"Been fun," he said, then flung the wetsuit into the dumpster too.

By the time he reached the front door, his new clothes were soaked through. But the bar was so warm that drowsiness was immediate. The place was filled with young, enlisted men, Navy and Marines. With his short hair and jeans, he looked like any one of them, so no one paid him any mind as he walked to the bar. Two girls in thongs and pasties danced on a nearby stage, coaxing the sailors out of their money and looking bored while doing so.

A young bartender approached. He looked like most of the customers, buzzcut and moustache, most likely a sailor trying to earn a little part-time cash.

"Your lips are blue," the bartender said.

"Dark and Stormy," Kelly said.

"No shit, it's a hurricane. You're shivering."

"No, the drink."

"The what?"

"Just bring me a beer. And a coffee. Both. And a taxi."

"One beer, one coffee, one cab, aye."

A half-hour later, the walk from the door of the bar to the door of the taxi felt like the longest ten feet of his life, the final leg of his brutal race. After a dreamy twenty-minute ride, he fished the key out of his jeans pocket and let himself into his building. He had to pack, to get on the road and out of Norfolk before anyone realized he was gone, but he could barely stand. He shed his damp clothes, and now nine hours AWOL, fell into bed and the deepest, blackest sleep he could remember.

At seven, his alarm sounded. Panicked, he realized the night before had not been a strange dream and leapt out of bed, expecting military police to break down his door at any moment. After a few moments, he calmed down. He sat on the bed and thought it through. The worst case scenario would be if someone saw him go over the side, but the boat never turned around. No one had come looking in the bay while he was still out there. He shivered at the thought of *Sentinel* circling back and illuminating the waters with its mighty beam, hunting him in his black wetsuit. His first watch would not be until eight that morning, so it was conceivable that no one even knew he was gone yet. Possible, but not probable, and when he did come up missing, *Sentinel* would double back on their trackline and begin the search. It was likely that he was discovered missing sometime the night before and the ship was already looking for him, that Headquarters was being notified, and all nearby units were being scrambled, but no one would have any reason to go to his apartment yet. He lived alone and had no next of kin—but the thought of being under such scrutiny filled him with the desire to keep moving. He showered, ate another sandwich, and canvassed his apartment for signs that he had spent the night there. Satisfied, he sat on the couch and looked at the seabag at his feet. Yesterday afternoon, while his shipmates had packed for a day or two at sea, Kelly was gathering the supplies and heirlooms that would make the cut in his new life: as many pictures and photo albums of his family as he could carry, his grandfather's shellback certificate, toiletries, a dog-eared copy of *The Count of Monte Christo*. He grabbed the seabag and was out the door by eight a.m.

Kelly did not relish riding in the rain, but when he emerged on the street, he was pleased to see that it was only drizzling. In the parking lot on the side of the building, an old motorcycle awaited its rider, a 1971 Harley-Davidson Sportster. He had spotted the bike in the classifieds a couple of weeks after returning from Ocean City. It was a lucky find. The machine was in good condition with a 900 cubic centimeter engine and a convenient push button starter instead of the kick-start. It was listed for an even five thousand dollars, but he talked to the owner down to forty-five hundred in cash, and for another fifty, he had taken a safety course to obtain a license. No one knew he owned it, and with only a month's worth of practice, he felt by no means like the bike's master, but he felt comfortable enough to get where he needed to be.

Kelly lashed the seabag to the rise in the seat above the rear tire and swung a leg over, then leaned back against it. The items inside shifted to contour his torso. He started the ignition and the bike roared a growl that felt good in his gut and he rolled into traffic with caution. It was Saturday morning.

Kelly pulled out of the diner and onto the empty country road. He had sworn he would not do this, that he would remain cautious during the transit if not for safety's sake than at least for avoiding notice, but it seemed somehow an appropriate salute to his lost shipmates. Just this once, he thought. He revved the engine to 5000 rpm before shifting into second gear with his left foot. He stood on the pegs and leaned forward to keep the front of the Sportster from standing up and rolling onto its back. As it was, the wheel came two feet off the ground, and when it landed again, they were off like a bullet, bike and rider screaming toward Florida.

The next night, Kelly pulled off at a stucco motel in Miami and the exertions of the past few days caught up with in him. In the morning, he awoke with a light fever, so when the Cuban cleaning lady came in to make up his room, he offered her twenty dollars to bring him some food. That afternoon, with the shades drawn, lying in his fever-soaked bed in the dark, he tossed and turned, so close to his destination and desperate to stay on the move, but too weak to do so. Finally, late that night, the fever broke. At first light, shaky but bursting with new energy, he paid up and began the final leg of the trip, Route 1 through the Keys.

On the way south, it was pure summer again. There was no trace of the gray of the storm; everything was primary and vibrant. Baby blue sky, verdant palm fronds, even the double yellow line flared off the blacktop. The single southbound lane of Route 1 had enough traffic that Kelly was forced to take the Sportster slowly and taste the quality of the new air around him. Despite the fumes of the road, he gulped it like a tropical cocktail, salt-rimmed and tinged with lime. Atop the bike, the wind ruffled his shirt and the waters of the Atlantic to his left and the Gulf of Mexico to his right seemed as pale and blue and endless as anything he had ever seen. It quenched him. He had nowhere to be.

At noon, Kelly rolled into Key West. He followed Route 1 to the right, along the island's perimeter, and was greeted by the sharp smell of salt air, sea creatures, and the red and black mangroves at low tide, not unlike his beloved marshes. Along the water, the wind buffeted him once again, tugging at the buttons of his shirt as if trying to whisk it from his back. He circled the island a few times, gazing out over the shallows and getting accustomed to his new surroundings. Near the Naval Air Station, he was overtaken by a fleet of scooters and mopeds and other motorcycles, and he allowed himself to be swept up in the buzzing company of them, turning inland in the general direction of Duval and continuing down the longest street in the world.

Chapter 34

Kelly winced as he strode through the lattice entryway of The Wayfarer and saw couples lunching at the familiar iron tables. He continued toward the front door. The door chimes sounded like ice when he stepped inside, and the darkness of the bar at noon surprised him. It took a moment for his vision to adjust, and when it did he noticed the bald man grinning at him from behind the bar.

"Shit," Kelly muttered. Sober, he realized just how big Fritz was. He suddenly wished he had stopped somewhere for a drink first. A lot of drinks.

"Oh, this is too rich," Fritz said. He threw down a wet rag and flipped the heavy wooden hatch of the bar with a flick of a wrist. He sidestepped to navigate his bulk through the opening.

"Wait," said Kelly, his hands in front of him. "Hold on."

As Fritz approached, Kelly shrank and brought his right forearm up in a gesture of contrition and to shield his face from another pummeling. He twisted his upper body away.

"Please. Don't."

The bartender smiled and kept coming. "You must be a glutton for—."

When Fritz reached for him, Kelly uncoiled, driving his right fist into Fritz's groin with enough power to feel the oblique muscles of his own stomach wrench and pull. The bald man seemed to expel every molecule of oxygen in his body and doubled over. As Fritz bent down, Kelly came up, springing off the floor with his hands clasped together in one giant fist. He caught the bartender on the cheekbone. Kelly continued to drive upward so hard the cords in his back and neck lit up with pain, and the bigger man arched back and fell into the bar. His bald head nailed the brass foot railing, knocking him cold. The low hum of it vibrated along the length of the bar.

Kelly straightened and massaged his sore neck with one hand. With the other, he fished into his pocket and pulled out the teal business card. He dropped it over the man and it fluttered to the man's broad chest.

"'Anchor's Aweigh.'"

The two blows had winded him and his mouth was dry and clammy. Trying to catch his breath, he turned around, noticing for the first time the other patrons. A few men stared at him from the cherry wood booths.

"Pleased with yourself, Mr. Sensor?"

Kelly turned to see a white-haired man standing in the darkened hallway opposite the front door. He was dressed similar to their previous encounter, wearing crisp khakis and a pressed white Polo this time, something one could see in any print ad for men of any age and not likely to turn heads, and it dawned on Kelly that that was likely the point.

"Now we're square."

The Chaplain gave a wan smile. "We'll see."

Another man, lanky, with a prominent Adam's Apple peaking from his collar, emerged from the darkened corridor behind him. Kelly recognized him from the blue car from his first encounter with the Chaplain. He was taller and older than the Chaplain, raw-boned but strong-looking. The older man crouched in front of the fallen bartender and patted him on the cheek. When this did not work, he grabbed the drink nozzle from behind the bar and sprayed club soda in his face. Fritz stirred.

"He's fine. Go on."

"Thanks, Tim. Mind the bar?"

"Sure thing."

"Rule number one, Mr. Sensor," the Chaplain said, leveling ice blue eyes at Kelly, "no scenes."

"I apologize."

"Very well. Follow me."

The Chaplain led Kelly down the darkened hallway, past the kitchen and a stairway on the left, payphones and restrooms on the right, and just short of a back door that led to the alley behind the bar, the old man turned left into a small office. He sat down behind his desk while Kelly looked around the office. The furnishings were much like the rest of the bar, dark wood, seafaring lore, aerial photographs of Key West before its development. When Kelly looked at his host, he found the man staring at him again. The blue eyes unnerved him.

"What?"

"Have you held up your end of the bargain, Mr. Sensor?"

"Pardon?"

"Does anyone know you're here?"

Kelly fished into his pocket and pulled out the clipping of the article with the list of names. He pushed it across the desktop. "They think I'm dead."

The old man pulled a pair of reading glasses out of his breast pocket, and with a final cautious glance toward the younger man, read the article.

"My."

"I had nothing to do with it."

The old man relaxed at that and passed the article back. He allowed himself a smile. "Then I believe that's the strangest bit of luck I've ever seen."

"I wouldn't call it luck, sir."

"No. I suppose not."

"Can we talk fee now?"

The old man burst into laughter. "For what? You're down here free and clear under your own steam. There's no fee."

"How do you live then?"

"I don't make my money at this, Kelly. I own The Wayfarer and a couple of shops along Duval. A gallery. Beach art for the tourists, that type of thing. All very legitimate."

"I don't get it."

"Kelly, it's not like I smuggle boatloads of refugees into the country. I just lend a hand to the occasional serviceman or citizen who wants to move on. You could say I'm a part-time recruiter for the Conch Republic. Call it a hobby."

Other than escaping the ship and making his way to Key West, Kelly had not really thought beyond the immediate future. Now that it was upon him, he was impatient to know how he would live. He wanted details. The Chaplain looked at Kelly's expression and began answering questions before they were asked.

"There's a room above the kitchen. It's sparse, but it'll work for the night. Be downstairs at seven a.m."

"What then?"

"We're taking a trip."

Chapter 35

"You see, the plan from the very beginning was to kill myself."

Kelly flinched in the driver's seat of the turquoise compact. The ocean breeze was coming across the narrow Keys and through the open windows, but Kelly was still sweating. He was back on Route 1, and heading north. His obliques burned; he had pulled something yesterday. Kelly stared at the railroad tracks half-buried in the sand, running parallel to the road. He had not noticed them on the way down.

"Relax, Kelly. You're a dead man. Try to enjoy it."

Kelly squeezed the steering wheel until his palms stuck to the rubber grip. He felt a tickle of perspiration roll from his underarm. "Excuse me if I'm not as nonchalant about this as you are. I just wasn't…"

"Prepared for the mainland? Don't worry, it's a common response."

"I feel so much better, thanks."

"The sooner you get back on the horse, so to speak. Helps one adjust. Besides, we're only going to the Everglades and that's a country unto itself."

An abrupt laugh shook Kelly. "This is ridiculous. 'The Chaplain.' I don't even know your real name."

"Will it brighten your day?"

"Maybe."

"William."

"Thank you, William."

"Be as sarcastic as you like, young man, but remember, you came to me."

"I don't recall asking you to have Fritz kick my ass in your bar. You followed me."

"True. But I'm not the one who jumped off a perfectly good boat in the middle of a hurricane. Pretty drastic. I'm not the architect of your problems. I didn't bring you to Key West. I'm just the person who's helping you."

"Well, it might help if I knew why."

"Like I was saying, the original plan was to kill myself."

"I didn't think you were serious."

"Don't tell me the thought had never crossed your mind either."

Kelly tried to answer, but hesitated. The Chaplain continued.

"I enlisted in the Army in 1950, and I went in much like I imagine you did, full of vim and vigor." William cleared his throat. "Korea never really received the press of the wars preceding or following it, but I can assure you, it was a war nonetheless. In the spring of '53, half of my unit pulled a month's leave. I just never went back."

"Just like that?"

"Just like that."

"Come on. What set you off?"

The Chaplain inspected a cuticle and said, "I saw a friend of mine slicing ears off some Chinese Communists for a necklace once. Tony Carango from New York. Didn't even faze me. The next morning, Tony and I were standing next to each other at Personnel Inspection. The lieutenant said his creases were sharp. I got gigged for my shoes." When he finished with the cuticle, William picked a piece of lint from his khakis. "Made me furious, nearly out of my mind with it. It wasn't even that he took the ears. And then it hit me."

"What?"

"I was bothered that nothing bothered me anymore. Never mind the ears, but those shoes..." The Chaplain forced a laugh, but it died quickly. "Well, I wasn't very impressed with myself after that."

"So Key West then."

"All I wanted to do was go home to Pennsylvania, but when I finally got there, I was restless, anxious. Utterly lost without my comrades. Pathetic, really. I drank like Prohibition was coming back.

"One night, I was in some dive, and sitting at the end of the bar were a couple of WWII vets chatting with the bartender, and one of them was telling stories of Florida. I leaned over in my chair and listened how this guy had been stationed there for his sonar training. To my drunk ears, just the word itself, Florida, sounded like a song. You'd think I'd never heard of it before, but there it was, blooming right in front of me: white sand, endless water, locals keeping to themselves, working hard by day, and crazed with the moon and liquor by night. Finally, I asked where exactly in Florida this place was. The vet made a face. 'Key West. Place is goddamn hot and uncivilized,' were his exact words, I remember. 'Uncivilized' clinched it for me."

Kelly drove into Islamorada, and the Chaplain grew quiet again, as if the denizens might overhear his story. Ten minutes later, the collection of shops and beach resorts tapered off and the Chaplain continued.

"This soldier wasn't going to cash out without a party. Some of my pals had been discharged already, wounded or otherwise, and others were on leave like me, so I decided to round up as many of them as I could to bring with me to the end of the road. One friend of mine had just gotten married. When I showed up on his doorstep and asked him to come, he looked at me in the eye and sensed right away something was up, so he took a pass and told me to be careful. He knew. Looking back, it's hard to believe how many of them just up and came with me, but it was a different time.

"So I continued the Pied Piper routine and the caravan just got bigger and bigger on its way down. Finally, we arrived. Picture the Wild West set in paradise and that was Key West in the early Fifties. Inordinate amounts of booze, women, and fights. To us, it was Heaven and I scarcely remember any of it. Other than Korea, it was the first time some of these boys had ever been out of their home states. Someone hooted that I had done a far better job leading them on the path to glory than our unit chaplain ever had, and with alcohol being such a powerful adhesive, the nickname stuck.

"Pretty soon though, it was time to saddle up and head north again; North and South Korea were in negotiations and the war was all but finished, but we were still due back. Before we were to leave, I gathered everyone on the southernmost point, where that buoy sits today, and announced that it was nice knowing them, but I wasn't going anywhere. It was the end of the line. We had all said it, of course, at one time or another, either here in the States or over in the jungle, but this time, the fellas knew I wasn't budging. I figured I'd wish them well, wave them off, and that night, I would take a walk on the beach and put a bullet in my head.

"Just then, Tim Newman steps forward. 'I'll stick around,' he said. Now, Tim had to be the tallest, lankiest kid ever to step out of Tennessee, and to look at him, you wondered how he never got picked off, but he was a natural outdoorsman. Fishing, hunting, trapping, you name it, a real can-do sort of fellow. His enlistment was already up and he was a bona fide civilian when we all left Korea, free and clear.

"I pulled him aside, more begging him than trying to explain. 'You don't understand, I'm not going back. Ever.' But he did understand. He read me just fine. All he said was, 'Fishing's too good to leave.' and that was that. All of a sudden I realized I didn't have to go back to Korea nor did I have to die; I could have a future right here. I was so overwhelmed with hope and gratitude for this third option that I swore to the fellas that I would always be there for them. Not just in the figurative sense, but the literal. I would be a lighthouse keeper. I'd help their kids, their grandkids…I was feeling pretty magnanimous at the time," the Chaplain laughed. "And believe me, they held me to it."

"So they left and you stayed?"

"Ever since."

"I appreciate you telling me."

"What about you?"

"I'm ashamed to admit it's nothing like that. Not even close."

"How's that?"

Kelly surprised himself by telling the Chaplain everything. He began with his parents, led him through the halcyon days with his grandfather, his time at the Academy and his friendship with Jorge, onto *Sentinel* and the shellback incident and the feud it had spurred with his captain. The news of his grandfather, the funeral missed. By the time he finished, they were nearly through the Keys.

"I feel like a fool. I don't hate the military. It just…wasn't what I thought it would be."

"You wanted glory."

Kelly winced.

"There's nothing wrong with it, son. So did I." The Chaplain leaned forward in his seat, waving his hands about the car, gesturing to the seas. "I wanted the honor of the battlefield; you wanted the romance of the high seas! We wanted a crusade."

Kelly laughed. "I feel so ridiculous."

"In the end, neither of us felt much like heroes."

"My troubles sound pretty trivial compared to Korea."

"There are no trivial reasons for wanting to make your life better. I was tired of war. You were tired of being a cedarbird."

"Cedarbird?"

"Old Key West term. Someone who blindly follows orders, who allows themselves to be taken advantage of," he explained. "You and I may be a lot of things, but one thing we have in common is that we both decided to call our own shots. We're nobody's cedarbirds."

"Don't you worry about getting caught?"

The Chaplain pursed his lips and remained silent for a moment. "In the islands, there are men who make their living taking tourists out to swim with sharks. Day in and day out, they swim in shark-infested waters. They even feed them. At first, I imagine it's terrifying, but you can't be terrified every day of your life. You get used to it or you can't do your job. After a while even the sharks think of you as scenery."

"That doesn't sound very comforting, William."

William laughed. "You have the occasional dream about getting bit. A small price to pay, considering."

"Considering?"

"We're free to crusade."

"So there's no guilt about deserting?"

He tugged the brim of his hat to shade his eyes and reclined his seat. "You've heard of a captain's practice of a letting his crew go early on a particularly beautiful day?"

"You never met my captain."

"From now on, don't think of it as deserting. Just think of it as sunshine liberty."

They reached the mainland by noon and continued through Miami, finally turning due west on I-75 and leaving the skyscrapers of Fort Lauderdale for the primeval landscape of the Everglades. An hour into the territory, after passing countless diners and airboat rental shops, the Chaplain told Kelly to pull a gravel lot.

The Lazy Gator was a general store that sat on a high shell mound that sloped immediately behind the wooden structure down to boat docks and the glades beyond. To look at, the tall grasses and curling waterways were reminiscent of Kelly's New Jersey marshlands, but the texture and scents were different. There was no breeze to knock down the shell dust or stymie the heat as Kelly and the Chaplain approached the store.

A young man sat at a picnic table in the shade of a slash pine on the edge of The Lazy Gator's clearing. Halfway up the trunks of the trees clung bright clusters of stiff-leafed wild pines. They looked like red porcupines and Kelly watched them with suspicion for movement against the sharp sky. The Chaplain embraced the man.

"Herbert, how have you been?"

"Good, sir." Herbert's head was shaved, and he seemed even more uncomfortable than Kelly, which put Kelly at ease. Herbert looked a few years Kelly's senior, but he was afraid the man might skitter up a pine at any second like some speckled tree lizard.

The Chaplain turned to Kelly. "I'd like you to meet Herbert. He's what you might call an alumnus. Class of the Gulf War." Herbert cast Kelly a sideways glance, and gave Kelly a quick handshake.

"Pleased to meet you," said Kelly.

Herbert said nothing, made a jerky waving motion.

The Chaplain took over. "Well, Herbert, why don't you tell us who you've just met."

Now with something to do, Herbert came alive. He fished into a backpack and produced a manila folder. "Jonathan Richardson."

The Chaplain turned to Kelly wearing a satisfied grin and thrust his hand forward.

"Who's that?" said Kelly.

"That's you," said the Chaplain. "Jonathan."

Herbert handed the folder over to the Chaplain. "Same drill. Both certificates."

Kelly was stunned. When he was aboard *Sentinel*, he focused on escape, and when he had escaped, he focused on arriving in Key West. Throughout, he had vaguely supposed he would no longer be able to identify himself as Kelly Sensor, but until now, had never contemplated the mechanics of it. The new name tasted bitter on his tongue. He felt a tremendous sadness and desire to apologize to his grandfather.

The Chaplain grasped both of Herbert's shoulders.

"When are you going to take a vacation and come on down to see us again?"

"I been pretty busy, sir."

"Nonsense. You know where we are and you're always welcome. You and young Jonathan here should paint the town."

"I'll see what I can do."

"And I'll see what I can do on my end. Maybe introduce you to some more nice girls at the Upstairz Lounge."

Herbert blushed. "There ain't any nice girls at the Upstairz Lounge, Chaplain."

"Depends on your definition of nice, Herbert."

This elicited a laugh from the anxious man and he loosened up enough to give both men a real handshake before returning to his car. Kelly and the Chaplain stayed for a lunch of gator tail and sandwiches and the old man let Kelly eat in quiet. As they headed east back through the Glades, the Chaplain explained Herbert. "Corpsman in the Gulf War. Got tired of seeing all of his friends get diseases he couldn't identify. Shame, really. He's a nice boy, but he had a hard time adjusting to it."

Kelly did not feel like talking but answered by reflex. "Like what?"

"Absolute freedom. Having no obligations is wonderful, for a while. But any military man, even those few who choose our path need some semblance of structure, a schedule, an outlet, something, anything to occupy his time and give it meaning, or he'll lose his marbles. Trust me, I speak from experience. Herbert was on that track, but with his medical background, I helped place him with a small hospital on the Gulf Coast. He doesn't much look like it, but he's happier now. He feels useful." The Chaplain opened the manila folder. "And he's certainly useful to us."

As Kelly drove, the Chaplain held up two documents: a birth certificate for Jonathan Richardson, born September 21, 1973 and a death certificate, August 16, 1977. "Keep the birth certificate, destroy the death certificate, and voilà, you can apply for your new social security number, driver's license, the works."

"That's it?"

"Simple as 1-2-3. The people of Key West mind their own business, and certainly don't give a damn about yours. And so Jonathan Richardson walks the earth once more."

"I feel like a ghost."

"Don't get superstitious on me, son. You're hardly the first person to come to Key West to drop out."

When they returned to Route 1 and flashes of the glittering blue waters could be seen beyond the tangle of trees on the roadside, Kelly felt at ease for the first time since the morning. The sadness remained, but the anxiety of the morning evaporated the farther south he drove and was replaced instead by a calm curiosity.

"Wait, you said before that you spoke from experience. Who lost it?"

"I've seen vets, men as young as you, not survive their first year. Mostly Vietnam vets, but still."

"Jesus."

Before Kelly could ask if he felt responsible, William spoke up. "All I can offer is a second chance. Even with a head start, some people just can't outrun themselves."

Kelly nodded.

"I haven't moved tons of people, Kelly. It began with some of my friends from Korea, their sons from Vietnam, and so forth. A few fellows in the right time and place, such as yourself. Just a

217

little word of mouth operation, but I've moved enough people that I've learned a few lessons. That's why I'm giving you a deadline."

"For what?"

"For your plan to stay out of trouble. Learned through trial and error. You're less likely to falter if you have a plan. Stay here, move on. Find work, be a bum. I don't care. But in a week's time, I want your plan. You can stay above the bar in the meantime."

"Did you have a plan? Other than kill yourself?"

William laughed and said, "We were lucky. I ventured into business and this operation, and both have made me very happy. Tim helped with it too in the beginning, but he preferred fishing. Between the two of us, we were able to get him into the shrimping business. He owns *Lady Joanna*."

Ahead of them, Kelly could see dozens of Winnebagos and trailers lining both sides of the road on the next key, and several old-timers fishing in the shallows behind the trees or playing cards or just sitting on the side of the road in folding chairs watching the sun dance on the wavelets of the Gulf and ocean. He had not noticed them on the transit north.

"What's that all about?" Kelly asked.

"Snowbirds."

He had never heard the term before. The scores of elderly, sun-browned and serene, soothed him as he passed. He imagined a phalanx of their silver-chrome trailers bearing him like Neptune past Key West, past Cuba even, across the main, as far south as he had ever been. For the first time all day, he felt the promise of his new circumstance, and for the rest of his drive, he turned the word over and over on his tongue.

Still, eight hours in the car under a beating sun had left Kelly drained, and when he and the Chaplain returned to The Wayfarer, he wanted nothing more than to get to his room above the bar and lay down in the cool, quiet darkness. He needed time to sort out the events of the day, to get to know Jonathan Richardson. He slumped on a barstool first. A drink might help, he thought.

"Punk," said Fritz.

"Ma'am," said Kelly.

"Look," the Chaplain said, easing onto a stool, "It's done, Fritz. He's in the fold. And Kelly, I told you to leave everything behind. That includes prejudices, too. Part of the deal."

Kelly looked at Fritz, the size of him and the expression on his face, and realized he would never catch him by surprise again, so it seemed wise to make amends. "I'm fine with that."

"Fritz?" asked William.

The bartender folded his arms. After a moment, he looked off to the side. "Whatever."

"Wonderful. Shake."

"William, come on." protested Fritz. The Chaplain subdued him with a steely glance, and the bartender relented and extended a meaty hand. The Chaplain turned his attention to Kelly.

"This is going to hurt, isn't it?" asked Kelly. He offered his hand, but the wind chimes tinkled instead as the front door opened. Fritz's eyebrows arched and his expression brightened.

Relieved, Kelly let go of his breath and searched for the cause of Fritz's sudden mood swing in the mirror behind the bar. A slim young woman in an oil-smudged tank top approached. Her top offered Kelly a healthy glimpse of her skin, and as she strolled closer to the bar he found himself admiring her tone. Honey, Kelly thought, then corrected himself. Caramel. When she removed her ball cap and tousled her curly coal bob, his chest burned as if he was in the bay once more, breaking the surface after skipping too many breaths.

"Sugarcane!" yelled Fritz.

She smiled as she lifted the hatch to get behind the bar. She stretched up to the bartender and wrapped her arms around his neck, and he straightened, lifting her off the floor. She laughed as he swung her around, exposing a small dolphin tattoo, blue and shiny, as if it had leapt straight from his grandfather's shellback certificate onto the small of her back. She planted a kiss on his bald pate with her full lips, punctuating it with a loud smacking noise. Kelly noticed her exposed midriff, the long muscles of her stomach, and her firm breasts pressed against the bartender's swollen bicep. He looked away and shifted in his seat.

As she fixed herself a drink, she noticed the blue bruise on the back of Fritz's head.

"Ouch, honey."

"It's nothing." He glared at Kelly. "Nothing at all."

"Penelope, we have a guest," the Chaplain said. With her arm still slung around Fritz, she turned her head to Kelly, noticing him for the first time. He offered his brightest smile.

"Another stray," she said.

Fritz stifled a laugh and the Chaplain shouted "Penelope!" in dismay, but she continued to look straight into his face with such disinterest that for a moment he thought she was looking past him, straight through him, searching for something better. His cheeks burned.

"Relax." She offered Kelly a cocky grin. "Just having a little fun."

Her smirk was sharp and taunting. A smile, Kelly thought, that Jorge might smile. He reconfigured his expression to give her the least satisfaction. He stared her down until her smile lost its luster.

"I'm Piper," she said finally.

"Penelope is *Lady Joanna*'s first mate. And when she's not being so rude, she's also my daughter."

"Don't talk about me like I'm not here, Pop," she said, looking away from Kelly's gaze finally. Kelly looked away then too.

"Penelope, this is a friend of mine. Behave yourself."

"Well, does he have a name?"

"Of course," said the Chaplain. "This is Jonathan—."

"Jack," said Kelly. He cleared his throat. "Call me Jack."

Chapter 36

She infuriated him, but one look at Piper had reminded him of just how long it had been since he had thought about women, about anything other than his career or revenge or escape. Now it was all he thought about. Maybe it was getting off the ship finally, maybe it was the island itself, with its new sights and scents, reminding him he was alive. Drunk as he was, and climbing the wooden planks toward the Upstairz Lounge, Kelly decided he no longer cared why.

He paid the cover and settled into a seat in front of the stage. A booming AC/DC song shook the walls and the overhead was filled with a layer of smoke. He looked around at the rest of the clientele, lone middle-aged men and small groups of rowdy college students, all armed with dollar bills folded like tents in front of them. Kelly ordered another Dark and Stormy as a curvy blonde, writhing onstage, slithered over to him on her stomach.

"Hi, sugar."

"Hello."

"I'm Starr." As she drew closer, she arched her back and tossed her hair. She raised her upper body off of the stage, as a Cobra might its hood, giving Kelly a full view of her breasts, too firm and round to be natural, but compelling nonetheless. As she loomed over him, a rosy nipple passed an inch from his eye, close enough to feel her warmth. This close, her tan looked even deeper, and her white teeth and painted fingernails gleamed under the black lights. "With two R's," she said.

"Of course," said Kelly.

"What's your name?"

"It's Jack."

"You don't sound too sure, Jack."

"No, it's Jack."

"You look too serious, Jack."

"I'm sorry. I'm drunk."

"Don't worry, Jack," she pouted. She rolled onto her back and kicked her legs straight up in the air in one fluid motion, putting a wall of flesh between their faces. She ran her glowing fingernails up the backs of her legs. They left fading white trails on her skin, and he followed their trajectory north, up toward her hard calves, all the way up to the dagger points of her stiletto heels. She bent one knee at a time, dropping each leg, and Kelly followed each heel as it traced tiny spirals into the air. His head felt like it was filled with cotton candy. Suddenly, she opened her legs in a giant smile, revealing her face once more. "Be happy!"

Kelly laughed, but stopped when he noticed the next round of dancers taking the stage. One wore a pastiche of a military uniform, complete with an officer's cap and golden epaulets. By the end of the next song, it would be discarded.

"Jack?"

"I'm sorry. Some other time." He dropped a handful of bills on the bar and left the way he had come, out the front door and down the steps onto Duval. The wind cooled his brow, but everywhere on the street were women, luscious and half-clad. Instead, he opted for his room above The Wayfarer. It was dark and lonely there, but safe. People streamed past him on the sidewalk, and he was set to join them southward when he heard something that incensed him.

"Hey there, stray?"

He turned around and tried to focus. People were passing in and out of his vision, jostling him as they passed, but one striking figure remained still, hands on her hips. She wore a short sundress, and her full lips were painted. His vision snapped into place when she smiled that cocky smile. He rushed at her. He grabbed her by both arms and screamed into that maddening face.

"Don't call me that!"

As soon as he realized he was touching her, the street stopped spinning. His arms fell to his sides. Her startled expression burned off the remaining vapors in his head.

"Fuck," he said. "I'm sorry."

Piper opened her mouth to speak, but Kelly looked toward two men approaching him. They had not even reached him yet but were already shouting. Not big enough to be bouncers, Kelly thought, just a couple of fraternity boys on summer break. Good Samaritans, or more likely, two guys looking to score points. In their khaki shorts and polo shirts, they looked identical to Kelly and he thought he might be seeing double, except one wore a red University of Georgia ball cap and the other an orange University of Tennessee visor.

"Hey, you! Tough guy!" one of them yelled.

"Look, fellas," Kelly said. "We don't want any trouble."

The Georgia ball cap shoved him. Over his shoulder, an orange University of Tennessee visor sidled up to Piper and put his arm around her.

"We're fine," she said. "You can go."

"Are you sure?"

Piper erupted into the Tennessee visor's face. "Do I have a sign on me that says 'Touch Me'? Go the fuck away!"

"Fine. Cunt."

Piper brought her knee to the man's groin. Kelly barely registered the motion. The man went down. As he yelled, Kelly seized Georgia ball cap and jerked down hard, throwing the man off balance. As he stumbled toward him, Kelly drove his knee into the kid's thigh, where his boarding team training had taught him a large nerve ran. Sure enough, Georgia's leg buckled, and using the forward momentum, Kelly pivoted and flung him at his friend, who was getting back on his feet.

Piper grabbed Kelly by the wrist and yanked him away, running north. As they dashed up Duval, Kelly could hear the rising commotion behind him, and ahead of him, the last thing he expected to hear, laughter. She led him to the entrance of Rick's and when the bouncer saw her coming, he cleared the way. She darted past him.

"Hi, James!"

He nodded. "Lady Piper."

Without breaking stride, she slipped past him like quicksilver and bounded up the steps, into the safety of the club's second level. Kelly stopped at the base of the stairs and turned around. The college boys were giving chase, Tennessee ahead, Georgia limping behind. They were shouting. He turned toward the bouncer, a huge black man nearly the size of Fritz.

"How much to keep them out?"

"You're with Piper. Don't worry about it."

Kelly slapped twenty dollars into his palm. "Thanks just the same."

"Cheers," said James.

At the top of the stairs, Kelly adjusted to the darkness and scanned for Piper. She appeared beside him with two shots. She looked delighted. "Tequila," she yelled over the music. He looked at her sideways, but accepted the shot.

"Probably the last thing I need tonight."

"You're more fun this way," She raised her glass. "Welcome to Key West."

Kelly touched her glass and downed his shot. He stifled a grimace. Piper brought the back of her hand to her mouth for a moment, and Kelly noticed her conceal a grimace of her own.

"Another shot?" he asked.

"After you," she said.

After a second round, they found an open spot at the bar. "So how do you know my father?" she asked.

"Friend." Kelly took a sip of his drink. "Of my family."

"How come I've never heard of you then?"

"Does your father know everything about you?"

"Are you a wanted man?"

"You tell me."

Piper burst into laughter. "Do they make women with brains where you're from?"

Kelly laughed too. It felt good. When their giggling tapered off, he said, "You're father is just…providing a little guidance." Kelly hailed the bartender. "Two more," he said.

"No," Piper said, and yanked him toward the dance floor.

Kelly stood his ground, tugging her back. "Oh, no. I haven't danced in way too long."

"Since when?" she asked. It was more of a dare than a question.

Since I was in dress whites, he thought, a pretty redhead on my arm, the heft of the new ring on my finger. "A long time ago."

"Not afraid, are you?"

Kelly hesitated long enough for her to seize his hand again. Before he knew it, he was keeping time with her on the dance floor.

He had forgotten how good it felt to dance, how freeing it was. After a while, he stopped caring how he looked and lost himself in the music. Finally, "Dancing Queen" blared from the speakers, and drunk men grabbed their girlfriends and spun and flung them across the floor. Piper started back for the bar, but Kelly wrapped one arm around her waist and clasped her hand. She seemed startled for a moment, but Kelly nodded and smiled. "Like this," he said, taking command.

From the Academy ballroom lessons, and tips from his grandfather, Kelly knew that the key to swing was not in the twirls, but in the footwork. There was much grace and joy to be found in just the simple synchronicity of that footwork, of two people settling into one rhythm, and by the second verse, Kelly believed that Piper had discovered them as well. By the second chorus, the footwork was second nature enough that he ventured some turns. He spun her out and pulled her back in, and they fell right back into step. Her laughter trilled in his ear. People made room for them.

As the song subsided for something slower, her eyes looked as if someone had turned on a light inside of her head. When he found her lips, they were flavored with rum. She responded with a boozy kiss, arms flung around his neck, and his heart fluttered like a steel drum, the last thing he remembered before waking up with her in his room above The Wayfarer.

Kelly's head felt like a coconut fit to burst. He wasn't sure which would cause the rupture first, the dawn light beaming through the window where his guest had just flown up the blinds with a vicious tug, or the racketing sound of it. Her fervor to get dressed and to make as much noise as possible in the doing could not be good, he thought.

"Where are you going?" he asked.

"That would fall under the category of none of your business."

Apparently, this was serious. As she held her tangled sundress over her head, Kelly stared at her behind, and just above it, in the small of her back, the tattoo of the tiny, blue dolphin. As soon as he sat up and reached for it, the sundress fell like a curtain down her back and it was gone. "Did we…?"

"Yeah." She would not look at him.

"Well, was it fun?" he tried to joke to brighten her mood. It sounded lame and he knew it.

"Doubtful," she said. She spun on her heel toward the door and over her shoulder said, "It won't happen again."

He was about to ask what he had done wrong but she was moving too quickly. He sprung out of bed and blocked her path to the door, touching her arm, lightly. He remembered how fast she was with a knee. She pulled her arm back as if burned. Kelly offered his palms. She turned her head away from him.

"What is it?" he yelled.

"You're naked!"

To appease her he moved back toward the bed, ripped off the sheet and wrapped it around his waist. As he did so, she grabbed the doorknob. He lunged toward the door again.

"Could you wait for just one second? Please?"

"I just want to get out of here before the bar opens."

Kelly looked at his watch. "It's zero six, I mean, it's only six A.M."

She folded her arms and waited for him to move.

"Fine," he said. "Can we meet later then?"

"This was a mistake."

"Why?"

"I don't even know you."

Her eyes were shiny and Kelly wanted nothing more than to keep her from crying. He reached out to her again. She stepped back.

"Then get to know me."

"I don't want to know you, Jack. You're a stray."

Kelly fought the urge to throttle her. He stepped aside. "Fine then. Get out, you spoiled brat."

"Brat?"

"We're done." This time he reached for the door. "Out."

She planted her feet. Kelly could tell she was ready for another round.

"Before I throw you out," he added.

She strolled through the door and he slammed it after her, then immediately closed the blinds. He crawled back into bed, but he could not sleep for his headache and his anger. He decided on a shower, but the spray from the nozzle pounded on his skull until he sank into the tub and let the faucet run instead.

He couldn't remember the last time he had taken a bath. The last five years of his life had been bay showers at the Academy, and on the cutter, sea showers. Sitting in the hot water, the muscles in his neck and back relaxed, and both the ache in his head and his anger seemed to drain from his extremities. He tried to remember his night with Piper.

It would probably take more than a box of dirty magazines to win her over, he thought.

At noon, Kelly shuffled down to the bar. Searching for the most shade, he sat in the corner booth farthest from the door and windows and ordered a Cuban press. He heard wind chimes and when he looked up, the Chaplain was strolling towards him. Kelly held his head in his hands and wondered if William already knew.

"Morning! Have you given any thought to our previous discussion?" asked the Chaplain.

"Has it been a week yet?" Kelly grumbled.

"No, but you're smarter than that."

"I was thinking I might stick around, for a little while, at least."

"Not to turn into some libertine, I hope."

Kelly winced. "No, I think I've gotten that out of my system in a single night." The food came and he muttered, "Oh, thank God."

"You'll need a job."

"I have money."

"You'll need a job anyway."

"What about here?"

"That could work, I suppose. If you play nice behind the bar with Fritz."

"I was thinking more along the lines of investing."

"Were you now?"

Kelly looked at his plate. "It was an idea."

"I'd still want you behind the bar for a while to learn the ropes and such."

Kelly thought about it and nodded. "That's not a problem."

The Chaplain broke into a winsome smile, as if he had planned it this way since their first meeting under the banyan tree.

"Your daughter's a real charmer," he said, tearing a hunk of the Cuban.

"I'm afraid that without her mother around, no one really taught her the finer points of femininity. Don't take it personally."

"Where's her mother?"

"I have no idea."

"Sorry. None of my business."

"We're a little late for pretense now, Jack. Let's just say her mother, quite a bit younger than me when we first met, was not the maternal type. She left when Penelope was four." The Chaplain walked to the bar and returned with an iced tea. "She seemed quite curious about you though."

Kelly shrugged, pretending not to care. "Yeah?"

"I just thought I'd let you know."

Kelly blushed. "Anyway, I was saying I might like to invest." He looked at the ledger that the Chaplain carried with him. "In everything."

The Chaplain raised an eyebrow. He slid the ledger across the table and said, "Commit this to memory." He then raised his iced tea. "To sunshine liberty."

Silent, Tim steered *Lady Joanna* down the main ship channel, while William studied the shore from the pilothouse. The Chaplain had asked his old friend to give their new charge a tour of the island from the water. "Rule Number One," said William, "always have a plan. Always. And have contingencies for your plans. Have backups for your contingencies, and when all else fails, have a trapdoor. An escape just in case."

"You make it sound like the Army is going to bust through your door any minute," said Kelly.

The water sparkled and gulls cried over the chugging shrimper, but Kelly was seated, engrossed in the ledger. There were names and entries dating back to the mid-1950's. Every person, military or otherwise, the Chaplain had ever placed was listed, along with every contact made, every person who offered aid or shelter along the way, and how to reach them all. Just as William had described on the drive to the Everglades, the entries were bunched together during dates concurrent with wars, thinning out in times of peace, especially within the last few years. Toward the end of the book, dated March of this year, he found his own name, Kelly Sensor, an account of his first visit to The Wayfarer and their meeting the next day. 'Forecast: Probable,' it read. It detailed his latest arrival in Key West, and the last entry was yesterday, with his new name, and though he had never noticed The Chaplain write in it today, the word 'apprentice.' Kelly smirked. Clever devil, he thought. Suddenly, he looked up. "Wait a minute, that couldn't happen, could it? Them finding you?"

The Chaplain did not turn around. "Unlikely, but anything is possible. You have to be ready."

He closed the ledger and joined the Chaplain at the window. The shade of *Lady Joanna*'s pilothouse gave them a reprieve from blunt summer heat, and the wind wafting in through the window mingled salt, diesel fumes, and the ever-present smell of shrimp ingrained in the deck below. Off their beam was Mallory Square. This afternoon, there were no cruise ships moored to block their view. A few tourists lunched on the docks and sun-browned crews polished the fiberglass hulls of white catamarans and fishing boats for charter. Kelly offered the ledger. "Pretty sizable network you've established. Very impressive."

"That's your copy."

Kelly laughed. "Don't miss a beat, do you?"

"*Semper Paratus.*"

Kelly smiled. Both men watched a sailboat slip its berth and pass abeam, heading north. Once in the channel and astern of *Lady Joanna*, the sailboat let fly its spinnaker. Across the water, Kelly could hear the faint pop as the canvas was puffed full and taut like a balloon. "Why me though?"

"Seriously?"

"Of course."

"You seemed right for the job."

"Come on."

"I'm not a young man anymore, Kelly. I want more time with my daughter," he said, and gesturing to the island, "and my friends. But just because I can't do it forever doesn't mean there shouldn't be a lighthouse keeper. And then you barrel into my bar, drunk and heartbroken. It was like looking in a very old mirror." Still looking at his island, William said, "It was a sign."

"I don't know about signs."

"Oh, make no mistake. We're all connected." Kelly made a face, and when William saw his expression, he laughed. "You don't believe me?"

"Nope."

"You will. Regardless, the job is yours if you want it."

"I don't know if this will create problems, sir." He took a deep breath. "I think I'm interested in your daughter."

The Chaplain burst into laughter. "Are you trying to prove my point?"

Kelly's cruise on *Lady Joanna* reminded him of the promise he had made to himself during his very first visit to Key West, to witness the sunset celebration at Mallory Square. That night, he walked north along Duval toward the cruise ship berths. The street performers carried out their stunts and jokes and magic, until it was time for the assembled to raise their cups to the setting sun. They erupted finally into cheers when the red rim of the sun disappeared below the waters of the Gulf of Mexico.

Staring at the sun so long left spots on Kelly's eyes and played tricks on his vision. Dotted by orange-red balls of light, an image of Piper appeared, from the first time he met her: bent ball cap, tank top, smooth arms. He blinked a few times, and the balls disappeared, but Piper did not. He stifled a smile, huffed instead. "What are you doing here?" he asked.

"Best place to catch the sunset, despite all you conch wannabes." When Kelly ignored her barb, she said, "It's close to *Joanna*."

Kelly nodded.

"Do I look like a spoiled brat to you?"

Kelly looked away.

"Look at me. I get my hands dirty. I work for everything I've ever earned. I wanted to join the Navy, but my father went ballistic."

Imagine that, he thought.

"Why are you smiling?" she asked, annoyed.

"You're just like a fucking squall. Smooth sailing one minute and then out of blue, pow! Do you realize the only time you're even civil to me is when I'm mean to you? Or when you're drunk? You're unfathomable!"

"Unfathomable? Are you for real?"

"Unfathomable."

"Who are you exactly?"

"Just some stray."

She laughed despite herself.

"One chance," he said. "A proper date."

"I'll think about it."

"And tonight doesn't count."

They promenaded down Mallory Square. The sun was long gone now, and one by one, the lights of the surrounding boats and hotels were coming on. Piper told him about her wild youth in Key West. He imagined she had given her father quite a bit of grief. He could not stop stealing glances at her. When they reached the end of the esplanade, the lights over her shoulder took on a distinct pattern. He pulled back.

"What's wrong?" she asked.

Twenty yards across the water, the bow of *Sentinel* loomed at him. Kelly stumbled backward as if the ship were about to impact the esplanade. The hard landing on the concrete jangled his senses. He saw the ship was moored.

Piper crouched beside him. "Jack?"

He stared at the cutter.

"What's going on?" she asked.

"Clumsy. Let's head back," he said.

"You're lucky this wasn't the date, you spaz."

She hauled him to his feet and they headed back the way they had come. He had forgotten *Mohawk* and *Thetis*, two of *Sentinel*'s 270-foot sister ships, were stationed in Key West. He glanced over his shoulder toward the receding cutter. Every day, others like it came and went, carrying Coast Guardsmen who might recognize him. He would have to be more vigilant. *Semper Paratus*, he thought.

Chapter 37

Piper chose the particulars of their first date. She insisted, and Kelly obliged without argument, until she turned her car back onto Route 1, heading north into the Keys.

"What's wrong with you?" asked Piper.

"For conchs, your family doesn't like to stay on the island very much."

"Do you want this to be our first date or our only date?"

"Where are we going?"

"Surprise."

Kelly shook his head.

After two hours, Piper turned off into a small community of rental cottages in Islamorada. She drove through the maze of units and palm trees until the Gulf was in view. A weathered dock extended to a small, thatched gazebo. On the left side of the dock, two small skiffs rocked in the slight breeze, and on the right, a pond enclosed by a rock seawall. Piper stepped onto the dock and pointed toward the pond.

"We're going swimming?"

"Not us. Look."

Kelly walked onto the dock and looked at the water. At first, he did not realize what he was seeing when a yellowtail as big as his leg cruised past. Then more shapes glided in and out of view: tarpon, grouper, bonefish, dolphin. All silently jockeying into position in front of him, then sliding away. Kelly crouched down, amazed. It would take him a lifetime to catch as many fish this size from his beach in Ocean City. That thought brought a sudden tinge of sadness, but there were too many fish to marvel at.

"They're beautiful."

"Dad mentioned you liked to fish."

Kelly watched a snook brush a drum. "I feel like I'm eight years old."

"That's how I feel every time we haul back the nets."

The sun was going down on the Gulf side behind her. She wore a short, orange sundress with tiny flowers on it. A small sweater hugged her chest. Her hair was down and curled and fluttered in the breeze, and she wore the barest of make-up and an awkward sweetness.

"Thank you for this. Really."

She turned and walked back down the pier. "We have reservations."

"See you later, guys," he said, then jogged after her.

The Green Turtle Inn was a cozy restaurant on the Atlantic side of US-1. An aroma of fried fish mingled with pasta greeted him at the door. A bar ran the length of the small front room which was populated by half a dozen tables and a piano. An old lady sat at the piano and played "Yellow Bird." When she finished, she raised a scrunched hand toward Piper and bobbed it. Kelly watched Piper mimic the lady's twisted hand and waved it back at her. The lady smiled like a loon.

Piper nudged Kelly. "It's the turtle wave," she said.

"Huh?"

"Just do it."

Kelly scrunched his hand into what he thought a turtle's head looked like and bandied it for the lady. He felt like an idiot, but the lady's smile doubled and she broke into "The Girl From Ipanema." Kelly scanned the walls of the restaurant. They were covered with hundreds of photographs of patrons throughout the years, and common to nearly every picture was an elderly gentleman with piercing black eyes. When Kelly's gaze returned to Piper, he noticed the same old man hugging her.

"Piper, dear!"

"How's tricks, Henry?"

"Tricks," he tittered. "You're devilish."

When Kelly approached, Henry glared at him and the man's smile vanished. His eyes grew so intense Kelly thought he had offended him in some way. Suddenly, Henry turned back to Piper and his face lit up again. "Let me escort you to your table, dear." He led Piper across the room and she gave Kelly a smile over her shoulder.

Once seated, a waitress came over with two gin and tonics. "This is on Henry," she said. "He'll be over in a bit to explain."

When the waitress left them, Kelly asked, "What's with the codger?"

"He's a mentalist."

"What's a mentalist?"

"He can do tricks with his mind."

"Right." But the notion of a mind reader made Kelly anxious. He remembered the man's unnerving stare. "What kind of tricks?"

"Guess what's in your pockets, that sort of thing. This is his place. You can come in here once and not come back again for five years and he'll remember your name. He's a bit of a local celebrity. Cruise ships sometimes bring him to sea for their guests."

"So," Kelly said, "go fish."

"Go fish," Piper smiled.

"What made you decide to be a shrimper?"

"Don't you mean why would a girl want to be a shrimper?"

"No, why would this girl want to be a shrimper."

"I love the water."

"Lots of girls love the water. Most don't sling fish."

"Fair enough. When I was little, I loved watching the fishing boats return with their catches. I always got a thrill out of watching the fisherman haul fish twice my size onto the docks for everyone to see, but I wanted to be out there, where the action was. I begged Uncle Tim to take me with him on *Joanna*. After a year, when they realized I hadn't outgrown it, they finally relented. I had to stay in the pilothouse the whole time with Pop, of course, but it was the most exciting thing I had ever seen, the anticipation of those nets being hauled back and wondering what kinds of animals were in them. Then suddenly, it looked like the whole sea floor spilled out onto that deck. Creatures skittered everywhere, pink and white and blue, clicking like crazy in the sun. I don't know," she sipped her drink, "when that net unfurled, it was like...I don't know...."

"Sunken treasure," said Kelly.

"Sunken treasure," she said. She brushed a dark lock from her eyes and stared

into her drink. He noticed she was blushing. "So," she recovered, "what's your dream?"

"Mine?"

"Sure."

"I don't know anymore...."

The question stumped him. For the last year, he had had only plans, not dreams. "I always wanted to be the captain of my own boat."

"Like in the Navy?"

Kelly laughed. "Something like that."

"You don't have to be in the Navy to have your own boat, you know."

Kelly was about to ask Where the hell were you six years ago? when he felt a presence over him. He opened his eyes to see Henry looking down on him with a grave expression.

"Please accept my apologies, sir." Henry turned toward Kelly with a grave expression. "I pride myself as being the premier mentalist of the Florida Keys."

"I don't follow...."

"I'm terribly embarrassed, sir. I can't remember your name."

After dinner, Kelly and Piper stopped at the rooftop bar of Papa Joe's for a drink before making the long drive south. They ordered Coronas and walked down to the boat docks to watch a cabin cruiser chug into a berth. Kelly stared out at the Gulf, but the darkness beyond the lanterns of the dock was absolute. He looked behind them, into the black wall of the tree line at the shore. "What's that squawking?"

"Cormorants nest in those trees. In the daytime, you can see the branches stained white with their shit."

"Romantic."

Piper laughed. "Poor Henry. You really stumped him. It was kind of sad when you told him your name was Jack and he asked, 'Really?' For a moment, I thought he might cry."

"Poor Henry," Kelly said.

Piper dropped her chin and looked up at him. "Your name is Jack, isn't it?"

"You're the one who pals around with mentalists," he said. "You tell me."

She furrowed her brow and stared at him. "Oh, believe me. I can read your mind."

"Try me."

"You want to spend the night with me."

"Again."

She walked toward him, and before he knew it, she was in his space, right in front of him, filling his vision with her face. He could smell her hair, apples and tea. She leaned forward and kissed him so lightly that once it was over, he doubted it had even happened.

"I'm a mentalist," she said, "not a genie." She raised her chin and just as quickly, spun on one heel and walked back toward the Gulf.

Kelly followed her down to the docks.

"Look," she said. The man from the cabin cruiser had lit a cigarette as he tossed some offal into the water. Kelly noticed his catch, two bonefish and a massive grouper, hanging on a gibbet rising from the dock. With the breeze dead, the air was heavy with the smell of them and the offal and the still water around them.

"Nice fish," said Kelly.

"Thanks." He scratched the scalp under his ball cap, then donned a pair of work gloves. He reached into the bucket beside him, then held his cupped hands over the water. The offal made a raining sound as it hit the shallow water at the neck of the dock. The man dipped his hands into the bucket again, then dropped his bundle a few feet away. Kelly watched the care with which the man went about his tasks, and raised an eyebrow at the bucket.

"Skins," said the man.

He pointed at the water. A minute later, two black shapes cruised into the small nimbus of light from the overhead lanterns. They nosed up to the skins on the bottom, dorsal fins breaking the dark green surface for a silvery instant, then slipped back under as they curled back and forth. The shark pups were only two-foot long, but Kelly identified tiny remoras already attached. He focused on a scrap on the bottom. A pup glided over it, and without slowing or giving the tiniest shake of its smooth head, the scrap was gone when the shark had passed. Kelly watched this over and over until it lulled him into a kind of trance. The sharks curled back and forth for a time until the floor was picked clean, then melted back into the darkness at the edge of the lantern's shine as quietly as they had come.

The man gathered his gear and touched the bill of his ball cap in farewell. Piper waved and Kelly nodded, but neither said a word. On the way back to the car, Kelly reached for Piper's hand, listening to the shells of the parking lot crunch under their feet.

Chapter 38

Key West was not where he wanted to be, or anywhere on land for that matter, but it was his destination regardless. To Aregood, the clouds over Route 1 looked like hostile countries on a foreign chart. He took several deep breaths, but tethered to land, the clean ocean smells he had loved breathing so much were now laden with the rot of vegetation. Pools of stagnant water alongside the road. Still, Key West had Evelyn, and a fresh start maybe, and that was more than he could say for anywhere else.

The divorce had been quick. Lisa got the house, and half of the retirement he was forced to take after the competency hearings. Still, he didn't care. He was free of her. What stung was the end of his career, the indignity of going from captain to civilian in an instant. That they wouldn't listen to reason. He had given the Coast Guard twenty years, and they had beached him without a second thought.

When he arrived at her condo on Petronia Street, the early September heat draped itself over him like a damp quilt and the walk from the gate to her front door was uncomfortable. He was not sure at that moment what he wanted more, her or a shower.

Halfway to the door, he saw the note. Dropping his seabag, he stared at it, dumbfounded, as if it was written in another language.

Sloppy Joe's on Duval.
On foot. No car!
Trust me,
E

"Are you fucking kidding me?" he mumbled.

He threw his seabag onto the front seat of his car and stormed westward. He remembered the way from their very first encounter at Hog's Breath Saloon and from years' worth of port calls to the tiny island, and the walk was well over a mile. On a normal day, this would not have been a problem, but the blue jeans he wore clung to his legs in the humid afternoon. Pointy palm leaves tickled his collar as he passed down Petronia. He scratched his neck red.

At the end of the avenue, he encountered the Key West Cemetery. Petronia resumed on the other side of the burial ground, and as the sky threatened rain, Aregood cut through. Once inside though, he paused to behold a monument to the battleship USS Maine. Perched high atop a stone column, a century old sailor stood at attention, an oar at his side, his hand frozen in salute. It struck Aregood as poignant how the sailor, despite such tragedy, remained at attention, focused for eternity on his duty. Then he noticed the sailor was saluting with his left hand, not the customary right, and the hand itself was more cupped than rigid.

Aregood stepped forward for a closer look. He shielded his eyes with his hand, peering up into the sailor's face, and he realized then that the Maine sailor was doing just the same, scanning the horizon. It dawned on him that this sailor was searching for his lost shipmates. Aregood stepped back. He looked around. In every direction, headstones and obelisks pointed heavenward. The memorial of José Marti stared back at him, in sympathy or reproach, Aregood could not tell. He drew himself as erect as the sailor in front of him.

"It wasn't my fault," he said.

The wind had picked up. Aregood hurried along.

With the cemetery behind him, he tried to think about Evelyn again. It occurred to him that he had not in fact driven. He had grumbled about it surely, perspiration had soaked his shirt, and it looked as if any second that the clouds would open up on him, but he had walked. Once he had read her note, it had never occurred to him not to. Taking orders, he thought. He allowed himself a small smile.

Thunder rumbled as Petronia intersected Duval and the air, heavy with mist, weighed all of the smells down. By now, his damp clothes chafed along his body as he strode past St. Paul's Episcopal Church, past one bar after another. Finally, with Sloppy Joe's in view, the skies cracked and dumped sheets of cool rain on him. The rain fell straight down, chasing the locals back to their cars and homes, the tourists into the bars and shops. Aregood marched north unfazed; the water running down his collar washed away the clamminess and soothed his raw neck. At Sloppy Joe's, the crowd rimming the open-air entrance made way for him.

He surveyed the bar. The rain outside made the huge room dim, but the atmosphere was festive. Flags of every nation hung from the ceiling and two huge billfish decorated the walls. Cruise ship tourists wearing Hawaiian shirts populated nearly every table and they were entertained by a boogie-woogie man banging out bayou songs on a piano with his foot.

Aregood strode over to the bar across the room and ordered a rum and Coke and some paper towels. Patting his neck, he glanced sideways and saw her sitting alone in the middle of the room. He was pleased to see she was growing out her hair. He took his drinks to the table. He face brightened but she did not get up.

"You're all wet," she said.

"All washed up, one might say." He did not return her smile, but took a seat across the table. "What was the point of my little constitutional?"

"I wanted you to sweat."

"I was hoping we might do that together."

"To purge, I mean."

"Fine then. Why here?"

"Total immersion. Best way to learn a new language."

"And what language would that be?"

"Conch, darling," she said, beaming.

"How about a kiss," he said, reaching for her hand, "and we'll call it even."

Just then, the piano man, a Hemingway look-a-like with white hair and a wild beard began a bluesy version of "Blueberry Hill."

"One more thing," she said.

"I've come a long way, Evelyn."

She grabbed his arm. "Dance with me."

He looked around him. "It's lunchtime." he said. It was the only valid reason he could offer.

"The sun's over the yardarm somewhere," she said. "Come on. Dance with me."

She took his hand. When he realized she would pull him from the seat if necessary, causing an even greater scene, he stood. Aregood focused on a giant cow dolphin over the bar. He stared at its bulbous forehead in the grainy afternoon light, the gold on its belly, the blue on its back, and the tips of its outstretched fins. It was the one object in the bar he empathized with. A fish out of the water and nailed to the wall. He felt as if the entire bar were staring at the two of them, and when he ventured a look, he discovered that he was correct.

But everyone was smiling. Some even looked envious. Then all he was aware of was her arms around his neck, her hips swaying against his. He smelled lilacs on her neck. His shoulders relaxed.

She granted him a long, lurid kiss and he no longer cared about the other patrons.

They spent the day drinking. By dusk, the whole bar was overflowing, so they stumbled outside. Aregood headed south. Evelyn tugged him north.

"Come on," she said, "to the sunset."

By now, the weather had cleared and they arrived at Mallory Square just in time to hear the crowd hush and watch the glaring sun hover over the waves. As Aregood watched it touch the horizon, he imagined he could hear it hissing, being extinguished.

"Evelyn," he said. She had her arms around his waist and her head on his chest. "Thank you for letting me stay with you while I get back on my feet. It won't take long, I assure you."

"I was hoping it might be a while."

He smiled and kissed her. "And thank you for today."

"You deserved a carefree day."

"Carefree." Suddenly, Aregood turned sour. "It's funny. The nautical term for what has been done to me is that I've been relieved of command. 'Relieved.' Isn't that ironic?"

Evelyn said nothing, but squeezed his hand.

"All I ever wanted was to be a good officer. And everything just…spun out of control."

"But it wasn't your fault, right?"

He had explained to Evelyn what had happened to *Sentinel*, but he had not gone into the full chain of events on the bridge that night; it would only confuse her. He still did not understand them completely himself. Of that alone, he conceded, perhaps he was culpable. "If I'm guilty of anything," he said, "it's that I tended to believe in the best of my shipmates. And good sailors died because of my trust."

"You were let down. It happens to good people."

"I guess you're right." Aregood hugged her. "I'm relieved with you, Evelyn."

While no one was looking, Evelyn cupped his groin and whispered in his ear. "I've put you through enough for one night. Ready to go home?"

"Oh yes," he laughed.

On Petronia, they made love until they were hungry, then wandered into the kitchen at midnight. Still slick with sweat, Evelyn's body was tanned and firm, and in the glow of the refrigerator's light the kitchen looked strange and new. He felt younger, alive.

They made love again and drifted off to sleep. At dawn, Aregood awoke and pulled back the covers, hoping not to disturb Evelyn. He stood and stretched, and the cool air pumped by the air conditioner raised goose flesh on his naked skin. He tiptoed to the bathroom. A few rays of light shone through the closed blinds, and hooking his finger between them, he was greeted with a sanguine dawn. He craned his neck and peered out the window and over the tree line. The sky was a brilliant rose, but the old mariner's rhyme about storms floated up from the sailor's part of Aregood's brain.

Red sky at night, sailors delight. Red sky at morning, sailors take warning.

He shivered again. It was an old mariner's superstition and the worst had already happened. He shuffled back to bed and the comfort of Evelyn's warm body.

Chapter 39

Kelly preferred structure, thrived on it, so on a busy night, the pace staggered him. It was September and in two months of tending bar at The Wayfarer, the only thing he could compare it to was the bridge in the middle of General Quarters, and watching Fritz navigate with such precision gave him an appreciation for the man's composure, even if it aggravated him.

"Fuck!" Kelly said, fumbling with a bottle. A crowd was forming behind him, and the murmurs he heard were less than supportive.

At the other end of the bar Fritz was ringing up an order and pouring two drinks at once. "What?" he asked.

"Manhattan!" Kelly yelled. "Whiskey, vermouth…"

"Bitters."

"Right." Kelly stepped back from the bar and scanned the shelves.

"Any day, dear," a customer said.

Kelly waved his hand without turning around. "Doing my best here, sir."

Fritz strolled up with a bottle and brushed Kelly aside. "Watch." He added a dash of bitters and commandeered Kelly's drink, dumping it into a shaker and rattling off the steps as if he were reading them. "Combine everything into a shaker with ice, stir, strain into a chilled cocktail glass, chilled, then add a cherry." He held his creation up to the light. "Voilà."

Kelly nodded his assent. He was impressed that a man who could tear a phone book in half could specialize in such delicate work.

"Then serve," Fritz added, presenting the drink to the peeved customer with a slight bow.

The man with the Manhattan smiled at Fritz, then, looking at Kelly asked, "Amateur night?" Fritz laughed and the customer threaded his way back through the crowd.

"Thanks."

"Anytime, boy scout."

Together, Kelly and Fritz worked through the backlog until a steady rhythm was in place. Finally, the crowd thinned enough for Kelly to take a break.

"All these mixed drinks," he said. "Doesn't anybody ever want a beer?"

"This is a nice establishment with a predominantly gay clientele, Jack. The keg stands and date rapes are up the street."

They heard the wind chimes at the door and both turned to watch Piper enter the bar. During the day, Kelly slept and studied the ledger, or spent time with William learning the operation. At night, he tended bar. Any time off belonged to her. Her hair was pulled back and her sable clothes stretched taut across her firm stomach and chest. She looked lithe and sleek and severe. She leaned across the bar and pecked Fritz on the cheek.

"Jack ready?" she asked.

"He's about as useful as breasts on a nun anyway, sugarcane. Just give us another minute, okay?"

"Play nice boys," she said, and walked outside.

Kelly turned to Fritz. "What's wrong?"

"To be honest…nothing. Yet."

"Yet?"

"Look, Jack, you get a fresh start, same as everyone else. That's the deal everyone gets. And I have to give you credit. You've come a long way. William believes in you and she looks happier than I've seen her in a long time, so I'm giving you the benefit of the doubt. They're family to me. If you hurt them, I hurt you. No posturing or beating my chest. I'll just hurt you, Jack."

Fritz smiled, but it was cold and comforted Kelly not at all. He added, "You got the drop on me last time. We both know you'll never be that lucky again."

"I'll make you a deal, Fritz," Kelly said. "If I hurt her then you have my permission, no, my blessing to kill me." He extended his hand.

The bartender grinned and took it. "Deal."

Kelly flipped the bar back and made his way to the door. Standing on the spot where Fritz picked him off the floor months before, Kelly turned around.

"Why didn't I see you in the ledger then?"

Fritz's back straightened and his chin lifted. "I came here after I was drummed out. I'm not hiding anything from anyone."

Moments later, Piper and Kelly sat in the backseat of a cab heading toward the northern end of Duval. It was a typical summer night in the Keys, rich with humidity, and the traffic was too slow and the relative breeze too leaden to provide relief. Still, Piper nuzzled up to Kelly. They stopped the cab at Rick's and when James saw them coming he rubbed his hands together. "Lady Piper," he said, "you are dressed to kill."

"I'm dressed for action. Jack promised to take me dancing until dawn."

"You know the cover."

She kissed the bouncer on the cheek. He let her pass.

"You're easy, James," said Kelly.

"And you'll never make it to dawn."

Kelly was about to agree, but the screeching of car brakes cut him short, followed by the blaring of several car horns.

"The idiots are out en force tonight," James said, craning his neck. "Better catch up to your queen. She looks like she means business."

"What about my cover?" Kelly shut his eyes and puckered his lips.

James jerked his thumb toward the stairs. "Consider it waived."

Kelly reached the top of the stairs when he heard a disturbance below. He started to make his way back down the stairs to see if there was a scuffle, but Piper hooked his arm. "Let's go!"

The crowd was heavy and the music raucous. After a few songs, Kelly was drenched with perspiration. He looked at Piper. A few locks of hair came loose and shaded her eyes as she danced, and her smile smoldered beneath them and the pulsing of the pink lights. He reached out for her but she shimmied away.

"Come on," she said.

In an instant, she was off the dance floor and darting past the bar. Confused, Kelly started after her, fighting to keep up. As he wove through the crowd, bumping men and women as he hurried along, he could see her over heads and shoulders, turning and taunting him. The closer he got, the further away she seemed. His feet pounded the wooden planks after her.

Duval Street was a jumble of two and three-story saloons, their patios and upper decks intertwining to form a veritable tree house city. If Duval was the vespertine heart of Key West, then these wooden walkways in the treetops were its arteries, and siren-like, Piper led him deeper and deeper into the tangled system until he lost all sense of direction. Still new to the city, Kelly knew he could get turned around just venturing to another club or even a bathroom if he was not careful, and though he was not drunk, whirling around the bends and branches made him feel like it. Catching blurred glimpses of Piper disoriented him further.

Suddenly, he reached a dead end. Out of breath, he leaned against the handrail. His heart felt fit to burst. She was nowhere in sight.

"Marco," he said.

"Polo."

Perched like a panther on the thick branch of a banyan tree three feet from his deck, most of her body was obscured by leaves and shadow. Her eyes sparkled with mischief. She was as wild and beautiful as anything he had ever seen.

"I guess this proves it," said Kelly.

"What?"

He wiped his brow with his forearm. "You're the devil."

He leaned over the railing and she stretched out to meet him with a hungry kiss. He felt her mouth shiver and she began to laugh and nibble his lip at the same time. She eased back, tugging his lip with her, and he chanced a look at the ground, twenty feet below.

"You're certifiable."

"It's too hot to dance. I have a better idea."

"And this is it?"

"Follow me. I'll make it worth your while."

"Why don't I just meet you down there."

"I'll be long gone by then."

Kelly looked down again. "I hate you, you know."

"Sure you do," she said. "Now get a move on."

Before Kelly could protest, Piper was halfway down the tree. He climbed onto the handrail, trying to steady himself and not look at the ground. It wasn't a far leap to the tree, but as high as he was, he decided to leave nothing to chance. He jumped, hard enough to nearly bounce off the banyan upon impact. Still, his eyes never left the hefty limb that was his goal, and he threw both arms around it as if it was a life-ring in the sky. His legs flailed for sure footing. When he found purchase on a lower branch, he caught his breath and began his descent. As he clambered down the trunk, he remembered something the Chaplain had said: when all else fails, have a trapdoor. If a picture was worth a thousand words, he thought, then this exercise was worth countless more. He looked above him to the deck. The city was small, it's escape routes limited, and these walkways might prove beneficial one day. He promised to memorize this maze of decks, to stick to a high vantage whenever possible, and failing that, to know every ledge, railing, branch and knot on the way down.

When Kelly swung to the ground, he was calm. He straightened and looked around. He was in someone's backyard, alone. A light came on in the house behind him and he moved through the yard and vaulted over a small fence into an adjacent alley. The alley emptied into a side street where Piper had hailed a cab. With one leg on the running board and her arm draped over the open door, she looked as casual as the first day they met.

"What took you so long?"

Fifteen minutes later, Kelly was staring at his reflection in the placid waters beside *Lady Joanna*. A yellow dock lantern gave the water a green tint and revealed two needlefish hovering off the bow. From the foot of the dock, Kelly could hear the reggae and the rowdy crowd at Turtle Kraals.

Piper walked up to him and gave him a kiss. When he moved to put his arms around her, she wriggled free. "Let's go swimming."

Kelly ran his fingers through his hair and looked into the greenish water.

"I'd rather not."

"You'd rather not?"

"I'd rather not."

"You can't swim, can you?"

"Believe me, I can swim."

"Well, that's too bad." She stuck her thumbs into her pants and shimmied out of them, revealing a pair of emerald panties. She turned around and pulled her top over her head, giving him a full view of her arched back. Before he could protest, she dove over the gunwale. He heard the splash, then laughter. A moment later, something wet slapped the deck by his feet. Kelly bent over and picked up her bra.

He walked over to the gunwale. She had pulled her hair free and slicked it back with dark water, wavelets rolling out around her in an ever-expanding circle. Kelly breathed in the mangroves and closed his eyes. A blast of water hit him in the face.

"What do you have to say to that?" she asked.

"Geronimo," he said and jumped.

After their swim, Piper found some towels in the cabin, and they lay out on the forecastle to watch the stars. Nestled against him, she asked, "What kind of guy lives in the Keys and doesn't like the water?"

"Oh, I like the water just fine. It's just not that fond of me."

"As if it plays favorites."

Kelly propped himself up on one arm. "That's just it, I think it does. I had this friend who never got seasick. Never. I swear I think he had salt water for blood. One time when he was drunk, he told me that the ocean looked out for him, like a guardian angel or something."

"And you believed him?"

"After a while, yes."

"And what about you?"

"Not so much."

"A big part of seasickness is mental, you know."

"Doesn't feel mental when you're hanging over the side."

She laughed, then sat up and took his head in her lap. She rubbed his temples. "Poor baby. How does that feel?"

"Like a pain in the ass."

"You know you love me."

Even hearing the word in jest filled Kelly with promise and he opened his eyes. Above him, her face was obscured behind the dark tangle of her hair. Beyond her, he saw a sky full of stars in the kind of clear night he never believed he could see from land. Her fingers at his temples and the salt smell of her skin were so soothing that his strength seeped out of him like the water in his clothes. He sighed. She shushed him and cupped his ears in her hands, shutting out all of the night sounds. Her palms were hot on his cool ears, and in an instant his whole body was overwhelmed with sudden warmth. It startled him for a moment and he opened his eyes again, but it was becoming harder to focus and all the stars bled together in a pleasant glow. He had had every intention of agreeing with her, but he heard a rumbling in his head, the rumbling became his heartbeat, and then he was asleep.

At noon, Kelly awoke to a harsh rapping at his door. He was alone. He cast a glance at the window, then slid from his bed without noise and crouched toward the door. He peered through the peephole. It was William. Kelly drew back the chain and let him in. The old man was wearing another nondescript cream ensemble, but he appeared nattier than usual. "Get dressed," he said.

"Good morning to you too."

"Incidentally, what was your plan?"

He jerked his chin toward the window and fumbled with a pair of khakis. "Short drop to the first story roof. Water pipe down to the alley."

"It's nice to be young."

Kelly drove, and William directed him north on Duval, then east onto Front Street. It seemed as if they were retracing last night's steps with Piper, and sure enough, they parked in Land's End Village, unsettling Kelly. Turtle Kraals and *Lady Joanna* were in plain view. Without a word, the Chaplain marched in their direction.

When Kelly reached the dock, William was facing the sea.

"What's wrong?" Kelly asked.

The Chaplain stared beyond the mangrove thickets, concentrating on a smaller Key on the horizon. His eyes squinted against the dazzling blue, and his lips pursed in a frown, signaling to him that any topic would be grave indeed.

"Happy Birthday," said William.

"It's not my birthday."

"Not Kelly Sensor's."

Kelly winced. September 21st. Though he had committed the day to memory two months ago, it held no emotional significance whatsoever. It was a statistic. He pulled his wallet from his khakis and read his Key West driver's license.

"Damn."

"I know you know the date. It just doesn't resonate." The Chaplain looked at him and smiled. "Yet."

He gestured toward the slip in front of them. Moored between two small finger docks was a gleaming white skiff with a matching white canopy over the helm.

"No way," Kelly said.

"You told me on the way to the Everglades that you had always wanted to be skipper of your very own boat. Piper verified it."

Kelly stared at his gift, dumbstruck.

"Well," said William, "climb aboard."

Kelly leapt onto long bow. "This is perfect for fishing!"

"I took that into account, yes."

"William, this is great...but I can't accept this."

"Sure you can, you paid for it. Part of your investment."

"Just a quick shakedown cruise today." He had come aboard without Kelly feeling the slightest rocking. "We have to get back for your party."

"Party?"

The Chaplain patted Kelly's shoulder as he turned the ignition.

"Welcome to my world, son."

Chapter 40

Aregood sat on the back deck of Turtle Kraals and surveyed the liveliness of Lands End Village, the comings and goings of the tourists and trolleys and the hustle of the shrimp boat crews, turning the night before over in his mind.

"Captain?"

Aregood stirred. "Pardon?"

The waitress shook an imaginary glass. "Another rum and Coke?"

Aregood nodded and the waitress was gone as quickly as she had appeared. He had told Evelyn he was looking for work. He could not bring himself to say job. His crew had jobs. He had had a career. A calling even. If what he had seen was true, he would have one again.

He sipped his rum, blunt yet sweet, sucking at the drink while the carbonation tingled his upper lip. He closed his eyes. If what he had seen last night were true, the gods were at work.

The night before, a haze had draped over Duval Street like silk. It was too hot to be out on the town, but that had not stopped Hurricane Evelyn, as Aregood had taken to calling her, from club-hopping, insisting her man take her dancing. The two of them were arm-in-arm and marching south on Duval, enroute to another disco, when a young woman dressed in black alighted from a cab across the street in front of Rick's. The girl's figure was lean and perfect and he admired it as Evelyn rambled about the next club. He glanced next at her companion out of curiosity, but for a reason he could not deduce, Aregood stopped on the sidewalk and continued to stare at the man. Evelyn, still walking, was jerked back.

"Hey," she laughed. "What?"

Aregood ignored her and studied the man across the street, trying to pierce the mist between them.

Evelyn followed his gaze toward Rick's, where an abundance of young women stood outside. "Need I remind you that you're with me?" She tugged on Aregood's arm, but he was anchored to the spot.

The man then turned around to pay the taxi driver, and Aregood jerked his arm from hers as if it were electrified. The air in his lungs burned. He broke into a run, mindless of the traffic. He hit a puddle and went down in the middle of the street, opening a gash in his forearm and the knee of his pants. A pink taxi slammed its breaks and blared its horn, raising Aregood enough from his stupor to shake his head. He looked up. Through the passing cars in the other lane, he could see the man look in his direction then turn into Rick's. He tried to shout, but no words came. In a flash, he was up and running again, across the street, onto the sidewalk, and charging the club's entrance when he slammed into a brick wall that sent him sprawling on the sidewalk. Flat on his back, Aregood blinked. There was no wall. The entrance was empty except for a huge hand spread in the air. He followed the hand up a rippled arm to its owner, a massive black man leaning against the building's façade. He looked back at the hand. It gave him a little wave.

"Whoa, cowboy."

Aregood got to his feet and pointed into the club. He was out of breath. "That couple…who were they?"

"No, no, no," the bouncer said, speaking as one would to a petulant child. Aregood sized the towering man up, but there was no comparison. "Proper introductions first," he continued. "Who are you, little man?"

"Please. I don't have time for this."

"My name is James."

Aregood was stunned. This man was barring him access. And smiling. Someone in line snickered. Unsure of his next move, he peered past James into the dark entrance.

"Now, this is where you say, 'Hello, James. Pleased to meet you. I'm the rude asshole who's not getting into this club.'"

Another patron laughed, and Aregood whirled and lunged toward the line. He heard himself hiss. The nearest couples backed a step. He squared up to James again, and having bled off some of his frustration, regained his composure. The bouncer was contemplating Aregood's torn trousers, his bleeding arm, and his wild eyes. It must have been unnerving. Aregood smiled.

"James, was it?"

James nodded.

"I certainly appreciate your duties and apologize for trying to barge in, but I'm an old friend of that couple and I didn't know they were going to be here tonight." He reached for his wallet and wished it were his marlinspike instead.

James looked him up and down. "You're friends with Lady Piper?"

Aregood smiled. "Lady Piper," he repeated.

Evelyn reached their side of the street, frantic. She jumped between the two men, and started pushing Aregood away from the entrance. She hurled expletives over her shoulder at James, at the same time trying to calm Aregood, though he no longer needed it. He put up no fight and allowed her to drag him away, locking eyes with the bouncer. Finally, Aregood smiled and said, "Thank you, James."

At the corner, Evelyn slowed.

He looked over her shoulder. "Is there another way into that club?"

She shoved him square in the chest, catching him off-guard and knocking him into a few pedestrians. He bounced off one of them and caught his balance, ready to spring forward until he realized she was on the verge of tears.

"What the hell was that all about?" she said.

"Darling, it's okay. Everything is fine."

"Are you insane? I'm not taking another step until you tell me what's going on."

"I thought I saw someone I knew."

"So you take off like a lunatic and nearly get into a fight with a bouncer out of the blue? Talk to me, Kevin!"

He was not accustomed to justifying his actions. And it had been a humiliating experience at the door. He filled his lungs and blew out a great breath. She was his only ally in Key West.

"It's ridiculous."

"Try me."

"It was like I saw a ghost."

Evelyn looked surprised for a moment, then her face softened. "One of your crew."

Aregood looked away.

"One of my officers. My protégé, you might say."

Her eyes welled with tears.

"I'm sorry I scared you," he said.

"It wasn't your fault. You have to let them go, Kevin. All of them. All of it," she said. "You'll never be happy otherwise."

"I'm happy with you."

She wrapped her arms around his neck and kissed his cheek. "Why don't we just go home? Let's me take care of those cuts."

"You go ahead. I'm going to walk. Clear my head."

"I'm not leaving you like this."

She took a deep breath and looked down the street. "Stay away from there."

Aregood laughed. "It was a trick of the mind. I don't know what got into me."

He hailed a green taxi and deposited her in it. He leaned in to kiss her.

"Don't scare me like that again, Kevin. Please come home soon."

He gave her a winning smile and patted the taxi's roof. The driver pulled away and the smile slid off his face. He waited until the taxi had turned the corner before he crossed the street to Sloppy Joe's. He offered a couple by the window a round of drinks to commandeer their table and ordered a rum and Coke for drinking and for cupping the sweating glass to cool the scrape on his palm. He watched the front of Rick's.

An hour passed, then another with no sign. At last call, several drinks later, Aregood settled his tab and watched the last patrons file out of Rick's. James still stood sentry; getting near the club was not an option. It did not matter. The bouncer had given him something to work with.

He returned to Rick's in the afternoon, confident he would not run into the bouncer, and discovered Piper was well known at Rick's, a popular regular. With a story about a lost wallet and a naïve waitress, he learned that this Piper worked as a mate on a shrimper at Land's End Village. Aregood had difficulty reconciling such a beautiful woman with such a dirty job, but the world was already upside down and it was his only lead. He asked the waitress about Kelly. She said she thought his name was Jack or something.

Aregood had been waiting at Turtle Kraals ever since. He stood and stretched and headed for the bathroom. Just the act of standing and urinating seemed to rouse him from his afternoon's daze. He looked at his watch. Sixteen hundred hours and no sign of the girl. Maybe she had the day off, he thought.

"Or maybe you're a fool," he said to himself. He flushed and wondered whether he, in fact, had pissed his afternoon away as well. He splashed some water on his face and shook his head at his dripping reflection. What would Evelyn say? he wondered. She would be home from work soon, so what was he doing here? He exhaled a long, shaky breath, and when the air was gone from his lungs, he began to laugh at himself. Maybe he was seeing ghosts.

He returned to his table and hailed the waitress for his check. He was pulling money out of his wallet, when he noticed a sharp white skiff rocking at one of the finger docks, telltale traces of fresh wake fanning out behind it. Aregood admired its gold trim and smooth lines. His lazy gaze followed it to the men disembarking and walking down the planks, a white-haired old man in khakis and a pressed white shirt, and dressed identically, Ensign Kelly Sensor.

The night before, he had darted into traffic at the possibility of seeing Kelly, but now, even after dwelling on it all night and preparing himself all day, his chest burned as if he truly was seeing a ghost or some other unholy creature that returned from the dead to torment the living. Aregood kicked his chair back. The sound it made was like a gunshot to him and he ducked behind a pillar. But Aregood was at the opposite end of the deck and the two men were heading away from Turtle Kraals now, toward the parking lot in front of Half Shell Raw Bar across the street. When he felt it was safe to move, Aregood stormed inside the main bar and peered through the windows. He was set to follow them, when the waitress came up behind him.

"Excuse me, sir? Sir?"

"What?"

She pointed to the front door, a few feet away. He was moving toward it.

"Your tab."

He fumbled with his wallet, dropped it on the floor. He could feel the other customers' eyes on him. He was making a scene, but he did not care. He needed to be outside, following them. He pressed a wad of bills into the woman's hand and fled.

He bolted through the door and stopped, skidding on the shell fragments and white rocks like a careening vehicle. When the white dust settled, Aregood found they were gone. He was stunned; in the moments it had taken him to pay, they had vanished. He ran along the outside of Turtle Kraals until he was next to the deck. Two men were sitting at a table by the railing.

"Did you see two men just now? One young, one old?"

"Pardon me?" one of them answered.

"The younger one, kind of dirty blond. Didn't you see them? Just now?"

Aregood could tell he was making them uncomfortable, but he wanted verification.

"Buddy...I don't know," one man said, and his friend gave a nervous laugh. "I guess."

"They walked right by!"

"Please. We're trying to eat here."

"Never mind. Forget it."

Aregood spun around and ran his fingers through his buzzed hair. Suddenly, he remembered the boat. He walked toward it in a rush, trying not to run or bring any more attention to himself. At the skiff, he reached for the tip of the bow with his hand. The cool fiberglass kissed his palm, still raw from the night before, and it steadied him. He gripped the boat and let out a deep breath. If the boat was real, then they had to be too. He looked around; there were enough fishermen milling around on the docks and too many people at Turtle Kraals watching for him to just hop aboard and look around. He would come back tonight or return to Turtle Kraals tomorrow. There was no rush now. If there was one thing Aregood had in Key West, it was time.

Chapter 41

Aregood would have never thought of taking *Sentinel* into uncharted waters, and that is how he viewed The Wayfarer. Further inquiries at Rick's and reconnaissance of the boat had led him to the tavern, and he had spent the days of the last two weeks sweating in his car, parked on Amelia Street, watching the bar without so much as a glance at Sensor. He had seen the old man come and go, and the girl, but he had not seen so much as a glimpse of the ensign since the afternoon at Turtle Kraals. He theorized Sensor emerged at night, while Aregood was with Evelyn, lying to her about the job search and playing house in her condo on Petronia.

The day before yesterday, he approached from the alley that ran behind the bar. He even listened to the sounds of the kitchen from the screened backdoor. There was a heavier storm door, but it stood open. And yesterday, he had entered the courtyard and looked around. He found several heavy, iron tables for outside diners, of which there were none. One night, he walked past with Evelyn under the pretense of an evening stroll, and the courtyard was packed with queers. But during the day, The Wayfarer lay mostly fallow.

Today, he entered the empty courtyard once more and peered inside the door. Empty. Not even a bartender was in sight. He grasped the knob, took a breath, and pushed the door open.

Wind chimes jangled in his ear. Their shrill sound startled him and the change in light disoriented him. Set off the street, the structure itself was shaded by a cluster of banana trees and palms, tropical sentries against the sun, and the dark, grainy woods of the tabletops seemed to soak up any ambient light that made it through. He scanned the tavern and was surprised to see the décor was a mariner's paradise with nets, spears, and billfish adorning the walls. There were deep red bookshelves and cases for fine cigars.

"How may I help you, sir?"

Aregood backed a step. The old man, the one he had seen with Kelly, was standing across the tavern's hardwood floor. He had not noticed the man emerge from the dark hallway.

"I'm sorry," the man said. "I didn't mean to frighten you."

"No…I'm fine. I was just wondering if you were open."

"We are, but apparently it's a closely guarded secret."

Aregood cocked his head and studied the man. The confused look on his own face must have been similar to a smile in the lack of light because the old man laughed.

"We're open, but you'll just have to settle for me this afternoon. Have a seat." He moved toward the bar, and Aregood, cautious, mimicked him from across the tavern, moving in the same direction. Again the old man wore pressed khakis, with walnut loafers and matching belt, a dress shirt pressed crisp and gleaming white. Aregood looked at his own clothes, khakis considerably more rumpled and an old blue polo. He longed for his uniform.

The old man smiled from behind the bar. "What's your pleasure?"

"Rum and Coke."

"Very well then. May I see some identification, young man?"

Aregood opened into a wide smile and he laughed a bit, but the old man waited.

"You're not joking."

"Please. Take it as a compliment."

Aregood patted his back pocket and felt the bulge of his wallet. "This is embarrassing, I seemed to have left my wallet at home." He patted his front pockets for effect and looked into his lap. He pulled his billfold from his pocket. "I remembered this though."

"Well, youngster," the old man said, folding his arms, "I suppose this time we can let you slide."

"Much obliged. Kevin, by the way." He extended his hand.

"Call me Bill."

"I must say, Bill...I'm a bit bewildered."

The man dropped some ice into a tumbler. "Bewildered?"

"This place. The theme."

"What were you expecting?"

"Well, for the area, I expected the place to be a little more...you know."

The old man offered a polite smile. "Looks can be deceiving."

"It's just that I've spent some time in the service, and this has the feel of a real waterfront saloon. It's a pleasant surprise." He twirled his hand, conjuring up the neighborhood beyond their immediate surroundings. "In the midst of all of it."

"Not a member of the community, I take it."

"It's unnatural."

"It's a live and let live island. I'm just trying to keep up."

"If you say so."

They talked for more than an hour without interruption. No other patrons came. They traded stories and views on sailing, the island, women, and when Aregood tried to glean personal information from his engaging host, all of his inquiries were redirected. Gently. Expertly. Bill was quite charming, economical in his words and movement, and he met Aregood's looks square in the eye, and despite himself, Aregood felt welcome. He rarely met such gentlemen, and even though he regarded this stranger as an enemy, he savored their time together.

"You're holding out on me." Aregood said. He was up to his third drink.

"How so?"

"These fish." Aregood wagged his finger. "Someone in this bar must be a hell of a fisherman. You?"

"I dabble. Mostly the fish are from associates. Even donations. Some people are very grateful to find a place that welcomes them as they are."

"That so?"

"You had mentioned you were in the service, Kevin?"

"Yes, sir. Shipping out later today as a matter of fact." He rattled the ice in his glass. "One for the road and all that."

"You must be a little down then."

Aregood was astonished. "Why would you say that?"

"To leave your family behind for such long stretches."

"There's no place I'd rather be than out there."

"A true sailor then. The isolation though, it doesn't bother you at all?"

Aregood swirled his drink. "That's the juice."

"How long have you been in?"

Aregood straightened in his chair. "*All me bloomin' life, sir. Me father was King Neptune, me mother was a mermaid. I was born on de crest of a wave and rocked in de cradle of de deep. Me eyes is stars, my teeth is spars, me hair is hemp and seaweed, and when I spits, I spits tar. I's tough, I is, I am, I are.*"

Bill's eyes widened, and then he stepped back and clapped his hands. "Bravo!"

Aregood gave a tiny bow from his stool. The rum had set in some and he felt good. Both he and his audience were smiling.

"That's marvelous. Where did you pick that up?"

"Tradition. Academy indoctrination."

"I didn't realize I was in the presence of an officer as well." Bill stepped back and offered a salute. His smile was charming and genuine, and for a moment, Aregood felt sad.

"Well, it's almost time for us to part company, Bill."

"That, sir, is a shame. But I am curious about one thing though."

"What's that?"

"It's funny, I hadn't heard about any Navy ship movements today."

Aregood stifled a laugh. This man is good, he thought. He had waited over an hour to ask that single question. He looked at the old man for a few silent moments. The man stared back, smiling, but concern had seeped into the corners of his eyes.

"Everything all right, son?" asked Bill.

Aregood cocked his head and fit his mouth into a smile, but even to him it didn't feel like one. He wondered what it must look like. "Did I say Navy?"

"I don't recall. I assumed it was the Navy."

"Actually, Bill, I'm in the Coast Guard."

"Coastie, eh?" He sounded cheerful, but Aregood was pleased to see him pour himself a glass of water. "Noble missions."

"You might say I'm on a bit of a mission myself, search and rescue. I'm looking for a friend of mine."

The old man straightened cocktail napkins on the bar, stacked tumblers. He cleared his throat. When Bill went for another drink of water, Aregood slid the glass out of reach. "I was hoping you might help me find him."

The old man stared at the glass, at Aregood's hand cupped around its base. He did not look well. For a moment, Bill's arm remained outstretched for it, and Aregood watched the man's eyes as they traveled up Aregood's arm. Bill withdrew his arm and straightened, and when his gaze finally met Aregood's, he was the consummate host once more. Bill lifted his chin and smiled.

"I live to serve, Kevin."

"Funny. Me too, Bill."

"How do you know this person?"

"I was his captain."

"Was."

"Are you asking me or telling me?"

"My apologies. Continue."

"Tell me, Bill, ever served a single day yourself?"

"You'd be surprised."

"And?"

The man's complexion was gray, Aregood noted, but Bill still leaned into their conversation. You have to give the old fellow credit, he thought. Bill pressed his tongue to the tip of his lip in contemplation. Suddenly, his eyes flashed. "If you can't join them, beat them."

"No. No. No." Aregood slapped the bar three times, one for each no, harder each time. "I actually thought you might understand."

"Why don't you enlighten me?"

"That's a terrible way to think. It's just not productive. It's undermining, chaotic."

"People need a little chaos. That's life, Kevin."

"Life is chain. And people are the links."

"Come back in a few hours and I'm sure there will be someone who's happy to talk to you about chains," he smiled. "Seriously, about your friend…" Aregood was surprised to see Bill spin on his heel and walk toward the other end of the bar. But the man's fluid grace congealed as he made his way down the bar, his gait stiffening into shuffle. Aregood noticed one knee buckle for a moment, then resume its syrupy progress. The old man's visible discomfort at Aregood's presence, mixed with the sweet rum swirling in his own blood was a buzz Aregood had never felt before. Aregood's chest swelled. Such was his reverie with Dill's reaction that the man was halfway down the path before Aregood realized what he was doing. At the corner of the bar sat a phone.

"…I could make a call or two…for you…"

Aregood reached him at the phone. Bill reached for the receiver and Aregood seized the old man's hand. His fingers met around the man's warm wrist.

Bill raised an eyebrow. "Asking me to dance?"

"My name is Captain Kevin Aregood," he said, "commanding officer of the Coast Guard Cutter *Sentinel*."

The last veneer of pretense dissolved. The old man grabbed his own forearm as if his hand was caught in a bear trap and threw himself backward, trying to jerk it loose. The receiver rattled against its cradle. His eyes darted from his hand there to Aregood's face and back again. Aregood held fast to his wrist. Bill gritted his teeth.

Aregood reared his head back and looked down his nose at the trapped man. "I'm here for Sensor. He belongs to me."

The old man thrashed. With his left hand, he tried to pry Aregood's fingers off of his clamped hand, scratched it until he drew blood. Aregood let him. The man had the strength of desperation, but Aregood was younger and stronger and he flared his powerful forearm. The rattling of the phone ceased.

Aregood watched as Bill's focus began to fray. His free arm flailed now and again, trying to swing at Aregood's face, but there was no strength in it. Aregood batted his hand away and caught a glimpse of himself in the mirror behind the bar, the chest muscles like to two plates grating underneath his shirt, his rounded bicep, the taut chords in his neck and forearm standing up. Aregood was brought back around by Bill's breathing. Something was wrong. It was quicker now and ascending from grunts to wheezes. The weak and frantic man clawed and clutched at his own shirt. Suddenly, he collapsed from Aregood's sight.

Aregood peered over the bar. The old man dangled by his wrist with one leg folded beneath him. It looked undignified. Aregood released him. Bill slumped into a sitting position, still clutching the phone. Aregood ducked underneath the hatch and crouched in front of him behind the bar.

The heat coming off the man shocked him. He placed his hand over the man's heart. It was racing, arrhythmic. Bill panted without making a sound. It reminded Aregood of a grouper he had hooked during his last fishcall on *Sentinel*, a massive fish from the Gulf Stream, shiny and gasping for air on his deck. But unlike the vague eyes of the dying fish, Aregood saw that Bill's eyes were fixed on him alone. A hiss escaped from Bill's mouth, a sibilant whisper. Aregood realized the old man was trying to tell him something. He leaned in.

"Cedarbird."

Aregood frowned. "I don't understand."

Bill's top lip was stuck over his dry teeth. To Aregood, it seemed as if his face were already revealing its skull. Perspiration ringed the man's underarm. Aregood poked his nose closer, sniffed the tang of sweat and deodorant. Bill turned away.

Aregood cupped his chin, and as gently as he could, moved the old man's face back around.

He fixed Aregood with a final, baleful glare and shut them down tight. Aregood still held the man's chin and gave it a tiny shake. The moment had passed. Two fingertips beneath the jaw told him the old man had slipped his cable.

Aregood released the man and he slumped to his side. He stood and washed the glass he had been drinking in the sink, then found a damp dishrag and wiped down the countertop and brass railing near his barstool. He inspected the dead man's wrist, wiped that down too. In the event of bruising, he clasped the dead man's other hand around it, pleased that his mind was as open and even. He raised his own hands in front of him—still as the horizon at sea. Surveying the bar and the crumpled man a final time, Aregood grabbed the doorknob with the tail of his shirt and strolled outside.

The burst of light after the shade of The Wayfarer made his eyes water. He cupped his hand over his brow and looked up. The sun was at its zenith. As expected, no one was in the courtyard. Though unexpected, he was satisfied with the events of the day. Sensor would not be so easy. Aregood needed him alive. It had been Sensor all along, and when he returned with him, Stokes would see. They all would. He would need a gun.

Suddenly, he remembered the Cuban. Aregood smiled. He was always finding ways to be useful, that one. Aregood walked two blocks west, then north, then east, careful to avoid looking passersby in the face, until he emerged onto Duval Street, where he smiled at everyone.

Chapter 42

Fritz had found William when he came in for the dinner crowd. Kelly awoke in his room to the bartender's yells for help, but it was too late. Now Fritz sat holding his head in his hands giving his statement to two police officers as two paramedics worked behind the bar. Kelly was in shock, but watching Fritz with the policemen, he could not afford to get lost in grief. It felt like a final test from William.

With an explosion of chimes, Tim bounded in. "I got the message."

Kelly led him to one of the empty tables, the one with the open bottle of rye on it. "Looks like a heart attack," he said. "It was quick."

Fritz looked up then. He glared at Tim, his mouth hanging open in shock.

"Quick," Tim repeated. "Quick is good, considering."

The bartender jumped to his feet and stormed down the hall. A moment later, Kelly heard the door to the alley slam shut. The police moved on.

Kelly and Tim both stared at the bar, watched the paramedics appear and reappear as they ducked below the bar to do their work. In the corner of Kelly's vision, he noticed Tim's hand shaking.

"You knew him a long time."

"Came down here together, you know."

"After Korea."

Tim looked at Kelly, raised an eyebrow. "Not many folks know about that."

"I didn't mean to be presumptuous."

Tim dismissed Kelly's concern with a wave. "He liked you."

Kelly stared at the wooden tabletop. His concentration was broken then as the gurney crashed and rattled behind them as the paramedics tried to navigate it from behind the narrow bar. Tim winced.

"Will and I came down here with nothing," said Tim. "I came down for a vacation and stayed forty years. I sure as hell didn't have a plan. But Will did." He gestured toward the walls and glass cases. "Look at those fish. The booze, cigars. He made this place so I could feel at home."

Kelly thought of his new boat docked at Land's End Village. "That sounds like him."

Tim faced Kelly, firming his expression and his voice. "He built a kingdom down here. Out of coral and shell. Out of nothing. He gave you a key. What you plan to do with it?"

"I'm not going anywhere."

"That so?"

"I owe him. And I love her."

"A toast then." Tim grabbed the bottle and filled up his shot glass and the glass Fritz had left behind. "To Will. My best friend. And the craziest, kindest, sharpest son of a bitch I ever met."

"To the Chaplain."

They touched glasses and down their shots. It burned Kelly's throat and his eyes watered "Have you found her," asked Tim.

"Piper!" said Kelly as the burning faded. "Does she know?"

Kelly shook his head. "I can't find her. I was hoping she was with you."

"Time to go," someone said. Kelly turned. The paramedics stood ready, their burden sheathed. Tim made a rough swipe of his eyes with the heel of his hand. Both men rose from the table.

Tim followed the gurney to the door.

"I'll take care of Piper," Kelly called after him. "I'll find her."

Tim nodded. "I think I'll take one more trip with my friend," he said.

Kelly watched the paramedics negotiate the door, one in front of their bundle, the other behind, and they rolled it through with no resistance. Tim followed. The door closed behind them with a tinkling, then quiet. Kelly was alone.

He walked behind the bar to look around. Nothing was out of the ordinary; it looked like it had every other night he was behind it. He tried Piper's number for the tenth time that hour, and as it rang he looked around the dark tavern and its shadows stretching across the bright floor. He thought of the Chaplain's death, his grandfather's, his parents', and wondered if he was bad luck. He turned on all of the lights, then left to find Piper.

Piper kept a one-bedroom apartment on Stock Island, the island just east of Key West. For someone who gave Kelly such hell for not being born a conch, he always thought it strange of Piper not to live on the island herself. As he headed east on his Sportster, he wondered how badly she would take the news.

When he could not find her at the apartment, he drove to Land's End Village. *Lady Joanna* was moored, but empty. It was dark now, and he took care as he stepped around the nets and sundry equipment that littered the shrimper's deck. Overhead, thunder rumbled and the still air preceding a storm drew smells of shrimp and fish from the wooden decks of the boat. Kelly disembarked the boat and stopped by his own. It glowed against the drab tones and rusted hulls of the shrimpers and other fishing boats in the harbor.

Three hours later, he returned to The Wayfarer. Someone had been here to clean up. The lights had been turned off and the silhouettes of the chairs stacked on the tables looked like toy soldiers in formation. As he made his way across the dark bar toward his room, he felt another presence nearby and froze. One table by the window had not been stacked. Kelly crouched, lowering his center of gravity, and his hands floated up as if to touch the darkness around him.

"Relax, cowboy."

"Fritz, are you trying to give me a heart attack?"

"That's not funny."

"It wasn't meant to be. Why are you sitting in the dark?"

"Why are you soaking wet?"

"It's raining and I've been in and out of every bar along Duval trying to find Piper."

"You tried her apartment? The boat?"

Kelly took a seat across from Fritz. "Yeah," he said. "I told Tim I'd handle it and I couldn't even manage that. Did she come by here?"

Fritz shook his head.

"Can I get you anything?"

Again the bartender shook his head.

"Why are you even here?"

"I live here."

"Exactly! Why? Why are you even in Key West?" He spat the last word at Kelly. Kelly sat back in his chair, stunned. He pushed himself off his thighs and left the table. After a moment, he returned with a bottle of rum and two glasses. He poured one for Fritz, and as he poured one for himself, Fritz pushed his back. "I don't want this."

Kelly downed his rum. "You think I have no idea what you're going through right now, but I do. My parents died when I was seven. Rainy night, car wreck.

"After that, I went to live with my grandfather. It was just the two of us. It's funny, you call me All-Star and Boy Scout, implying that I come from this idyllic background, and you're right. I couldn't have asked for a kinder man to raise me."

Kelly poured another shot.

"He died this year. Long story short, I wasn't there when he passed. And the organization I worked for would not allow me to bury him."

"The Coast Guard?"

Kelly took a deep breath, paused in thought, then left it out, his shoulders softening. "That's unfair, I suppose. It was really just one man. But at the time, that distinction was lost on me. So, that's why I came here. I stayed because of William." He tilted his glass toward Fritz. "And his family."

The bartender propped his elbows on the table, massaged his scalp. "I should have been here."

"You've been here all night. Take your shot and go home."

Fritz complied, then stood and stretched. His knuckles brushed the ceiling. "What are you going to do?"

"Wait for Piper. If you hear from her…."

"I'll let you know, Jack."

They put up their chairs and said goodnight. Kelly took the glasses to the sink behind the bar and headed for his room. He found the light switch for the stairwell and flicked it on. He took another step and stopped. His door was open. Shadow spilled onto the landing. He took a deep breath and climbed the rest of the stairs. He stepped into the room, closed the door behind him, and found the light switch.

In that instant of brightness, he surmised she had been there for hours, since he had been out searching for her. She sat cross-legged on his bed, the sheets nested around her. Her arms were wrapped around a pillow and mascara tipped the edge of its white case. Her shoes were kicked off. She was wearing his jeans. When he saw her wince at the flood of light, he immediately turned it off.

"Thank you," she said.

He closed the door behind him and in a second was around her. "I'm so sorry."

She wrapped her arms around him and held on. She took a breath and he felt her jaw tighten by his cheek. Her chest heaved. After a while, he asked, "Who told you?" he asked.

"It's a small island."

"How did you get up here?"

She rapped her knuckle against the window.

"I heard you and Fritz," she said.

Kelly froze.

"I wanted to tell you."

"I'm not mad. No, I am mad, but we'll deal with it." She sighed. "I just want to know you."

Kelly put his arms around her again. "I promise, I'll tell you everything."

"Tell me now."

"Tonight?"

"Please. Just...distract me."

"Where do I start?" he muttered.

"With your real name," she said.

He let her go and sat on the bed, suddenly exhausted himself. "Kelly. Kelly Sensor."

Beginning with childhood, he omitted nothing. He told her about his parents and the real Jack, about his struggles with Jorge against Aregood, and how her own father offered him a second chance. Hearing all of it, she burst into tears now and then. It took more than an hour.

"Your father helped me. He helped a lot of people. It's what he did."

Piper sat against the headboard. Kelly rubbed her feet. "He never told me about Korea," she said. "I mean, I knew he was there...it helps explain why he was so against my joining the military."

"I'm sorry. I know it's a lot of information."

"No, it's good to hear it."

"I'm sorry I lied to you. I wanted to tell you, but the longer I waited, the harder it was and I was afraid I'd lose you...."

"Jack. I mean, Kelly, whatever your name is. I don't care. What your name is, where you come from. I don't care," she said. She closed her eyes and her head lazed against the headboard. "Just be nice to me."

He reached out and touched her cheek. It was wet. She nodded in his hand, then took the hand in her own and kissed his wrist. She pulled him closer. Her lips quivered and her face was sticky with tears, but she kissed him in great gulps. She rose to her knees. Stunned, he followed. She pressed her body against his and peeled his shirt, still damp with rain, over his head.

"Please," she cried.

"Are you sure?"

He leaned her back down onto the bed. With one hand, he cradled her neck and slid pillows underneath. He unbuttoned her jeans and slid them off in a sibilant rush. With one hand he tugged at his own belt and ran the other along the smooth of her thigh, the skin behind her knee, tracing a supple calf. He hooked his fingers into the thin straps at her hips and slid her panties off as well, already catching the cloudy scent of her in the still air of the small room—that same quality of air preceding the storm he had breathed earlier, a heavy scent, with a tang of sweetness in the back of his throat. Lime, he thought. He wanted to be gentle and warm, but the smell of her activated something inside him and he felt himself swell, unbearably. He ripped them off and plunged his fingers into her hair as she grasped and guided him, and in an instant he was welcomed with the warmest wetness he had ever known. The blinds were drawn, the darkness in the room total, but light exploded behind his eyelids.

She bucked against him, not making love as much as vying to occupy the same space. She pulled him down to her and rolled him onto his back. The tips of his fingers traced her breasts, sought the curve of her spine as she raged above him, storm-tossed. She threatened to overwhelm each of his senses until, with her in control astride him, she calmed finally. They settled into a rhythm and he felt a year's worth of sin and pain and loss roll away for a blissful moment on an outgoing tide. Soon her pace quickened again, and he clasped her thighs, thrusting upward to stay with her momentum. She whimpered and thrashed until she came with a howl, and hearing the sound of her primal cry, the pressure inside him was all at once too much to endure—his legs stiffened and his back arched in a release as hard and jagged as it was exquisite.

After, Kelly brought her a glass of water. She took it with both hands.

"Well, don't go now."

"I couldn't if I wanted to."

He pulled the sheets back and with his hand on the small of her back, gently guided her beneath them. He slipped in behind her. He kissed the nape of her neck. She grabbed his hand and cupped it around her breast, pulling him against her and he held her tightly as her body went rigid again, dissolving into a shudder, then a rhythm of small, quiet torments that led finally to sleep.

Wearied and wrapped around her, Kelly wanted nothing more than to fall asleep with her, but his brain would not rest. Careful not to wake her, he slid out of the bed and went into the bathroom. Without turning on the light, he found the screwdriver in the cabinet below the sink. From there, he bent toward the ankle-high vent by the toilet. Without the slightest rattle of the screen, he removed enough screws to reach his hand inside and withdraw his copy of the Chaplain's log. Kelly returned to the main room. Through the blinds, the soft, slatted glow from the street lamp dappled Piper's back, and the rain against the windowpane was magnified and projected onto her, rolling ample drops down the sheets around her body like a makeshift screen.

After William's own succinct fashion, Kelly logged the man's own death, then turned back to the first page. Eager to lose himself in the ledger, he pulled the room's sole chair to the window and started reading from the beginning, forty years prior, but he could not concentrate. Piper now owned part of The Wayfarer. And so did Kelly. It was all too much. He wondered about Jorge. He wondered if Jorge wondered about him. With so much death, he wondered about remedying that.

He watched the alley as if he was watching it through the window of the bridge. It was no different than the dogwatch, he told himself. While Piper and the rest of his world slept, he would hold the conn. Blinking hard, he straightened in his chair and watched the incoming squall.

Chapter 43

Jorge heard the growl of the Mustang as he fed it gas, then felt it surge forward. Nancy, her head lolling against the headrest, opened her eyes.

"Speed," said Nancy.

"Sorry."

The newlyweds had flown into Miami that morning, picked up their rental car, and set out for their honeymoon. Jorge relished the fact that while the north continued its slide toward winter, they were migrating south, where the Florida Keys enjoyed perpetual summer. Nancy shifted in the passenger seat and her shorts allowed him a glimpse of her inner thigh. He raised his eyebrows.

"I feel like hell," she said.

Nancy had battled the flu for the last week, through the final days of wedding preparation and the ceremony itself, but she finally seemed to be ready to emerge from it in time to enjoy their honeymoon.

"Do you want me to put the top up?"

"No, the sun is nice. Warm."

"Well, I'll tuck you in when we get to the hotel. I'll make you warm."

"You can try, Mr. Vargas."

She flashed him a weak grin then closed her eyes again, leaving Jorge to the tropical scenery and his own thoughts. The waters of the Atlantic and the Gulf trying to burst forth from behind the palms rushing past along Route 1.

Approaching Key West, the traffic had thickened and Jorge had to slow the Mustang. As he did, the breeze veered from blasting through the convertible from the road in front of them to washing over them from the Atlantic side. The air was light and salt-tipped, that same clean taste of what had come over the gunwales of *Sentinel*. He breathed it deeply. Just as quickly, the exhaust from the line of cars in front reached him.

Nancy sat up. "Fantasy Fest," she said.

Jorge nodded. "The island is going to be packed," he muttered.

"It'll be fun." Her grin told him she was starting to come around. "Like Mardi Gras or Carnival. Parades and dancing all day and night, everyone in crazy costumes, people throwing beads..."

"Sounds like one giant freak show to me."

"Just give me one more good night of sleep and we'll be showing the freaks a

thing or two."

Twenty minutes later, the Mustang crossed the short causeway into Key West and Jorge turned left onto South Roosevelt Road. Nancy sat up now, beaming at the topaz waters before them, blocked intermittently by a royal palm or a stand of mangroves.

They took Roosevelt around the southern perimeter of the island until it emptied onto Atlantic. From there, they crisscrossed northwest, taking the smaller avenues until they reached South Street. The Southernmost on the Beach Hotel stood within paces of the foot of Duval Street. At the lobby counter, a young Cuban man in a pressed white shirt with colorful epaulets gave them their key and when they let themselves into their suite, Jorge was immediately taken with its size and airiness. The sliding glass door to their private balcony was open, allowing a full view of Key West's southern beach and the blue Atlantic beyond. The colors in the room blended seamlessly with the colors outside the window: the Bahamian blue of the walls was the same shade as the sky, the golden lamps and fixtures melted into the sunlight filling the room, and the gleaming white trim and the balcony were indistinguishable from the sailboats that bobbed past their room. In fact, the blue and the white, and the gold shining between them, made the roses that much brighter. Nancy walked straight for them.

Nancy read the card and spun around into her husband as he approached. She threw her arms around his neck and squeezed. "Thank you, baby," she whispered. "That's so romantic." Before Jorge could answer, her mouth was on his. Startled by her sudden burst of energy, he opened his eyes. Over her shoulder, he spied the red roses on the table in the center of the room. Their color burned against the lighter tropical tones. The sight of them and the heat of her reminded him that, thanks to the flu, they had not made love on their wedding night, his body blared that they were behind schedule. She pushed him toward the bed. He dropped their luggage where he stood.

The afternoon left her spent. Jorge stood on their private balcony with a towel wrapped around him, staring at the sea, letting the ocean breeze lick the perspiration away. From his vantage, he could not see the sun. It had begun its descent on the Gulf side, behind their hotel. Jorge turned back toward the room and was surprised how quickly the light had faded inside.

"Do you want to go out for dinner?" he asked.

"For feeling so good, suddenly I don't feel very well."

"Room service it is."

"I'm sorry."

Jorge laughed. "Don't be sorry. Just rest."

Nancy lay sprawled on the comforter, letting the breeze cool her body. From her pillow, she nodded. "Deal."

"How about I draw you a bath in that big Jacuzzi tub?" he asked.

"Do that and I'll marry you."

"That's not going to work anymore."

"I'll give you a male heir."

Jorge whistled. "Let's not get ahead of ourselves, Mrs. Vargas."

Nancy laughed and Jorge left to run the bath. When it was ready, he went back out to the suite and scooped up his bride. She tried to protest at first, but finally laid her head against his chest and let Jorge carry her. He placed her in the tub and she sighed. He turned to leave.

"Where are you going?"

"I just want to make sure I didn't leave anything in the car. Be right back."

He switched on the lamp by the couch and walked over to the roses. His fingers brushed over the embossed "Thank you" on its front. He opened the card. "...for coming full circle with me," it read.

Jorge put on a tee shirt and a pair of shorts and sandals and left the room. As he rode the elevator to the lobby, he mused that the flowers and the note were a stroke of genius. The only problem was they were not from him.

The young Cuban man with the epaulets was still behind the counter. When Jorge approached the man cocked his head and offered a generous, toothy smile.

"Hello," Jorge said, glancing at the man's nametag, "Frederick. I'm in Suite 1209 with my wife."

"Congratulations. What can I do for you today, Mr. Vargas?"

"Some flowers were delivered to our room today."

"I remember. The roses. Very nice. Is there a problem?"

Jorge looked over his shoulder, "Only that I didn't order them and my wife thinks I did."

"Oh. Was there a card?"

"Not signed."

Frederick smiled and leaned in. "Very cloak and dagger."

"Do you know who delivered them?"

"Blossoms Florist on Duval."

"Thanks. Maybe I'll check. It's probably my brother or someone busting my balls. Even so, could we keep this between us?" He slid a twenty dollar bill across the front desk.

"Not necessary. I love a good mystery. Do keep me posted, Mr. Vargas."

Jorge thanked him and turned to walk away. "Oh," Frederick called after him. "You have something else."

Frederick walked over to the rows of empty slots and stopped at the nameplate for Suite 1209. A note leaned against the wall of his slot, the only piece of correspondence left in the rows of the hollow mail slots.

"That's funny," said Frederick, "mail was already delivered."

He plucked the note out and handed it to Jorge. When Jorge saw it, his face fell. It was a postcard. The same crowd stood along the water, lined and illuminated golden, awaiting the same sunset.

Chapter 44

Winsome Days, Wicked Nights. As Aregood strolled Duval Street at six a.m. he thought this year's Fantasy Fest theme was only half right. He scanned the debris floundering in the low tide of the previous evening's high, the dank fraternity house smell of Duval, sticky gutters putrid with stale beer congealing in the morning heat, scattershot blasts of vomit on the sidewalk. Winsome Days, my ass.

Chaos reigned and he was only six days through the festival.

Aregood still wore his costume from the night before. A simple hooded black cloak and a white papier-mâché mask with a severe grin, devilish mustache and pointed Vandyke beard, and two circles of rouge for cheeks as its only concession to color. Evelyn hated it. It gave her the creeps, she said. He told her it was perfect for the theme. And it was. The mask concealed his face. The cloak, black as midnight, allowed him to stay in the shadows if necessary and could conceal a variety of instruments. And best of all, like any good uniform, it struck fear into anyone who looked at it.

He passed under a storefront awning and nearly tripped over a dozing man in a tie-dyed tee shirt and ripped jean shorts. Aregood bent down for a closer look. Long dreadlocks, unkempt beard, but young. A dog and a guitar case with loose change and scattered bills by his side. A breed of street urchin specific to Key West, the dropout.

The man's dog, a golden retriever whose coat smelled thick and looked shiny with grease, growled. The boy stirred.

"Easy, Jake…God!"

Aregood had wandered through those first few nights of Fantasy Fest in his costume, but last night he had performed a test. The crowds were so thick and chaotic at night that if you lost sight of your people for an instant, they were gone. Evelyn had found a bar with a relatively short line to the ladies room, and as soon as she was out of eyesight, Aregood, who had been rooted to his spot in the street, put on his mask and let himself go. He allowed himself to be jostled and shoved by the thick and chaotic crowd, and instantly he was down the street, swept up in a roaring tide of vampires and Martians and ghosts, bobbing along Duval as just another anonymous piece of human flotsam, and this morning the tide had deposited him here.

The dropout winced. "What the hell are you?"

"Ghost of Christmas Future."

The retriever's ears were pinned back and the dog emitted a low growl.

"Go on, man. Move on before I turn him loose."

Aregood kicked over his guitar case and strolled away, ignoring the curses and the barking. He continued south along Duval until he reached Angela Street, which brought him to the Key West Cemetery, across from which was Petronia and the cool, shaded comforts of Evelyn's condo. He decided to cut through the graveyard to save time. This was a tiny, infuriating island with not one, but two bodies of water to rattle a marooned sea captain. But this place was quiet. It was always quiet. He was bone tired now, but he stopped at the monument to the lost sailors of the USS Maine. He looked around to see if he was alone, then up at the

Maine sailor atop his pedestal. He scanned the horizon, solemn as ever.

"A few more days," said Aregood.

He exited the cemetery onto Petronia and in moments, he was under the trees. He slipped off the cloak before he entered the house. The polo shirt underneath was pitted with stains of perspiration and the light wind through the trees now cooled him.

The front door swung open before he grasped the doorknob. Evelyn, in her bathrobe, blocked his path. She looked drawn and tired.

"Where the hell have you been?"

"I got turned around."

"That was seven hours ago! You don't call? You don't try to find me?"

"You're the conch. You want me to be worried about you?"

"Don't fucking turn this around, Kevin! I was worried about you."

Aregood laughed.

"It's not funny!"

"You're blocking the door, Evelyn."

"And you've been out all night."

"Then throw me out or get out of my way. Choose one or the other, but choose now."

She scanned every inch of his face. After a moment, he turned around and headed back down the walkway.

"Wait!" She chased after him and spun him around. She raised her arms to bring them down on his chest, but his look of menace froze her fists in mid-air. Her arms fell to her side helplessly and she burst into tears. "I just want you to fucking talk to me!" she yelled, and it seemed as if her last bit of strength fled her body.

He led her inside. She fell into a chair at the kitchen table and wept into her hands. Aregood stood in front of her, watching her cry. He had never seen her cry before.

"I'm sorry," he said.

"You don't even know why I'm crying."

"No."

"That's why I'm upset. You have no fucking idea. What's worse, you don't even care to know."

"I care. Of course I care."

"Then why do you say it with that look on your face?"

Aregood looked away.

"Baby, I know it's too much chaos for you here. I know none of this is normal to you, but I'm trying to do whatever it takes to make it normal for you. I took off work today to tell you—."

"Ah, the crux of the matter. Work."

"Yes, Kevin, I want you to work!" She raised her hands as if pleading. "Is that so wrong? I want my man to work. I don't care what kind of job you have, I just want you to distract yourself from all the shit that's floating around in there about the ship! Shit you never share with me!"

She rose from the table and walked over to him. "Yes, I want you to work, so you can come home tired instead of miserable. To have a normal life where I can take care of you. God damn it, do you have any idea how humiliating it is for me to even say that out loud?"

Aregood's adrenaline had long since faded. Tears reminded him of Lisa. Yet with her, he was surprised to find he was not disgusted. He put his arms around her.

"You could watch reruns of *McHale's Navy* all day for all I care, I just want you to open up to me. Jesus, Kevin, I have a feeling that if you don't something terrible is going to happen to us."

"All the bad stuff has already happened."

"I'm serious."

"Me too. I'll swear that things will be…as they should. Very soon."

"How can you swear that?"

"Everything will be normal again after this damned festival. You just have to trust me. But please, let's go to bed. Please, I have nothing left in the tank right now."

They stumbled into the bedroom. The vents of the kitchen had pumped chilled air against his sticky clothes, and when he stripped, they were dry and stiff. The bedroom was as cool and silent as a crypt and Evelyn slipped out of her robe and slid under the covers. Drained as he was, he stood over the bed and looked at her, waiting for him, and wondered what could be more normal than this. Gooseflesh spread on his skin and he realized he was standing over a vent. He slid into bed next to her. She pressed her naked body against his. He felt both warm breasts against his chest as she rolled into him. She wrapped a leg around him, and her inner thigh burned against his waist. His eyelids fluttered as he plunged toward sleep.

Every year, the ten-day Fantasy Fest culminated on the Saturday before Halloween, and by that morning, when the revelers were at a fever pitch. Earlier in the morning, the street cleaners gave Duval a hasty makeover in anticipation of the parade. Heavy storm clouds threatened, but the crowds were undaunted. By late morning, the inhabitants of the bars had already spilled out into the streets, the side streets were barricaded with saw horses and police tape, and the local entrepreneurs were out en masse to catch the overflow funneled onto Duval. Every few feet a fifty-five gallon drum was filled with ice and beer, and carts popped popcorn, crackled fried dough, and sizzled hot sausages, and their sharp smells wafted into the air. In tents, women had their breasts airbrushed. Everyone was in high spirits. There was jostling but no shoving, shouting but no fighting and even Aregood, after three restful days with Evelyn, saw for a moment the promise of anonymity and camaraderie in a brightly-colored congregation of strange and happy people in paradise.

Evelyn had spent the last three days at work, leaving him to sleep, but instead he chose to shadow Vargas and his new bride.

The Cuban made no move toward The Wayfarer though. He had to be in league with Sensor, he thought, both of them in Key West was too much for him to accept. Regardless, it meant no difference. Aregood had planned for that.

Tonight was the night. He had planned on slipping free of Evelyn as he had before to venture inside The Wayfarer once again. With the crowds at their peak, every available bartender and waiter would be on hand, and if Sensor did work there, as he believed, he would have to be there. He could not perceive a time when conditions would be more ideal for surveillance; at the height of the Fantasy Fest no one would think twice about a costumed man in the midst of a bar. Yet with the last three days, his resolve had wavered, and now, he lounged against a street lamp at Duval and Greene. He carried their costumes in a backpack, so intent was Evelyn to get to the center of everything early enough to not miss the floats or a moment of the day's festivities. He had not anticipated her enthusiasm, and had to leave his other tools at home.

Evelyn walked toward him. "Hot date?"

"Huh?"

"Your watch."

"Sorry. Force of habit. How'd the scouting mission go."

"Captain Tony's has space. We'll hang there for a while."

"You have this all mapped out, don't you?"

"Claim your real estate early."

"Spoken like a true conch. I have to admit, seeing you planning every little detail turns me on."

"Spoken like a true obsessive-compulsive."

"Come here." He pulled her into a bear hug and nuzzled her neck. She shrieked and struggled against him. "That tickles! What are you doing?"

"Just enjoying my girl."

She pulled back and touched his face. "I love you, you know."

Aregood stared at her for a moment. "I love you too." He meant it.

"Good," she said. "Now come buy me a drink." She grabbed his arm and pulled him along.

Inside Captain Tony's, Aregood drank into the early evening. The small bar soon became packed and people had to shout above the blaring reggae and rock and roll. He drank and danced and threw himself into the proceedings. He kissed her passionately on the dance floor and the crowd cheered. At first, it was to distract himself from his mission later that night, to burn off nervous energy. Soon the alcohol kicked in and he discovered he was having fun.

They took a break. Aregood leaned against the wall, waiting for Evelyn to return with drinks. He laid his head against it and watched the room sway, as much from his alcohol as the dancing people. She was in costume now, hers as vibrant as his was dark, a crimson bodysuit stretched taut with a neck that plunged deep into her tanned cleavage. She twirled a plastic red trident and in her other hand she brandished a thin red staff with a devil's half-mask attached, complete with slanted eyelets and horns. She looked back from the bar and saw him staring. She aligned the eyelets to her eyes, and her face was hidden except for her smirking, ruby lips. She dragged her matching ruby fingernails across her behind and burst into laughter that Aregood could not hear over the din of the bar. He smiled.

Aregood closed his eyes and took a deep breath. Did he have to move from this spot? When he opened his eyes, he spotted an advertisement on the wall, charter cruises that made day trips to the Dry Tortugas. He could take Evelyn tomorrow instead of what he had planned. They could pack a lunch and sun themselves on the deck of a giant catamaran. There was a national park there that he remembered too, with an old fort surrounded by bleached coral reefs teeming with thick clouds of tropical fish. They could spend the day snorkeling around its stone walls, walking around the stone fort, and identifying all of the different sea birds. And by the time they returned, most of the tourists will have begun their retreat back up Route 1, leaving the island to piece itself back together. It would be bearable again. Perhaps he could work on one of those catamarans. He smiled at the simplicity of it.

Why hadn't he thought of it before? There were so many boats in Key West. Surely, there was room on one for him. He could captain one of them or save up enough to buy his very own boat, a sportfisher or a trawler. He could spend his days plying the crystal waters off Key West and his nights returning to the docks where Evelyn would be waiting. She would take him home and cook for him, then take him to bed. And early in the morning, she would rise and put on the coffee and sit with him at the kitchen table because she understood him and his sailor's need for camaraderie in darkness while the rest of the world slumbered. Finally, he would kiss her goodbye and make his way to the boat for another day's work. Their routine. He would spend his days sailing and wishing for his woman and his nights dreaming of the open sea. The circuit would continue on forever, and it would be a good life.

He looked at his watch. He could still have that. That and more. When he watched her return to his spot with the drinks, it was from the street. He let the surging crowd bear him quickly away as the sea would carry him away if he were a man overboard.

Where Greene met Duval, he picked up his pace. It was already dark and the streets had not yet been cleared for the parade floats. Even drunk, he realized there was no way she could spot him in the throng, let alone follow him, but he found himself hurrying anyway. Instead of flowing with the crowd as he had learned to do, he panicked and fought the grip and drift of the crowd and was quickly knocked to the ground. Stunned, he tried to get to his feet, but he was assaulted with garish images. Every other man he saw was in drag, a battalion of hairy-chested men in platinum blonde and cherry red wigs, faggots in chaps with their asses hanging out. From his vantage, he saw two men, dressed as the Tin Man and

Dorothy, kissing and fondling each other as a crowd watched and cheered. He struggled to his feet and shoved back, but it did no good. Instead, he closed his eyes, submitting to the deviant crowd just to get clear of it. His arms were pinned to his sides, but in a few moments, he was pushed past the horde and far away enough to raise his arms again.

Finally, he found a break in the crowd and began running, knocking over several revelers, until he found a side street. The people thinned there on the side street, which intersected Simonton, the avenue that ran parallel to Duval, and he broke into a sprint. A few tourists watched him run and stepped aside, but it was hardly the strangest sight to be seen on the island during Fantasy Fest. Still, he ran until the next side street and crossed over onto Elizabeth, then to the next side street, and crossed over onto Williams, crisscrossing and zigzagging at top speed. He ran until his heart pounded in his chest and salty perspiration ran into his eyes, burning and blurring the gray headstones of the cemetery now looming into his view. Above them, the dark skies looked ready to open up. He burst into the graveyard and pigeons and seagulls took to the air in a cacophony of shrill cries. He did not stop to acknowledge the monument this time and seconds later, he was bolting up Petronia, up the walkway to Evelyn's condo, bursting through the front door and into the bedroom.

He upended his seabag, and among the sundry items that thumped to the floor was a set of each of his old Coast Guard uniforms. He decided on tropical blue long; the trops were certainly the least elegant, but they would be far cooler beneath his cloak. He stripped off his shorts, tee shirts and sandals, and wiped away the sweat. He fastened his epaulets and pinned his ribbon bars and command pins to his chest. He removed his shoes from paper bags that had protected their shine all summer. Calmer now, he strode into the closet and removed his lockbox. He dialed the combination and retrieved his new black holster and wove his web belt through it. Then he removed the nine-millimeter he had purchased after his afternoon in The Wayfarer. The holster made a snug fit for the pistol, which he snapped into place before surveying himself in the bedroom's full-length mirror. He wiped a thumbprint from his brass belt buckle and smiled at his reflection.

Let her see me, he thought. Let them all see me.

He emptied the backpack onto the bed. He grabbed the cloak and slipped it over his shoulders. He pulled the hood over his head and put on his leering mask. Once more, he looked at himself in the mirror, then around the bedroom.

He could have everything. He could have Evelyn and be exonerated. She liked their life now. But how much better would it be when he marched those two onto the base at Trumbo Point, a hero again? Restored. She would understand in the morning. The Tortugas could wait one more day. He turned off the light, grabbed a bottle of rum from the kitchen and left the house.

Chapter 45

A part of Jorge itched to be down among the throng as he watched the festive thunder along Duval Street from the balcony of Crabby Dick's. He had never seen anything like it. The sheer volume of people flooding the street truly was staggering. His gaze traveled to another balcony across the street. A woman there noticed him and hoisted her drink. Jorge nodded. Suddenly, she lifted her shirt and shook two enormous breasts at him. When a fount of beads and cheers flew up from the street below, she forgot about Jorge and leaned over the railing to dangle her pendulous breasts for the crowd.

"Eyes front, Ensign Vargas."

"I was just admiring the architecture. The, um, gingersnaps."

"Gingerbread."

"Right. Feeling any better?"

Nancy put down her fork and sighed.

She had insisted on a snorkeling trip that morning. The prospect of seeing the coral fingers and schools of tropical fish had reinvigorated her, just as the flu relented, it was replaced by good old-fashioned seasickness thanks to the chop. She had not even bothered to get into the water when they reached the diving grounds. He reached across the table now and massaged her hand.

"I'm sorry," she said. "This isn't how I pictured our honeymoon."

"Don't be sorry. I just want my wife to get some rest and feel better."

Nancy nodded toward the other side of the street. "So I can flop my tits over the side?"

"Only if you feel up to it."

After lunch, Jorge led Nancy to Whitehead Street, where taxis were running to circumvent the crowds. The people were still thick there, and it took the cab ten minutes to travel the few blocks back to the hotel. Nancy lounged against him as the car lurched through the throng. Back at the Southernmost, they passed through the lobby and Jorge noticed Frederick make an unsuccessful attempt to flag him down without attracting Nancy's attention. Nancy looked at Jorge.

"Your best friend wants you."

"Funny."

Nancy waved to Frederick. "What an odd little guy."

They approached the front desk and he offered them both a wide smile. "How is the lady feeling today?"

"Not too swift, I'm afraid. Jorge, I'm going to head up to the room. You boys have fun. Bye, Frederick."

"Ma'am."

The two men watched her get into the elevator. Once the doors closed, Frederick deflated himself with a huge breath. "That was close."

"Nice work, Double-oh-seven."

"Do you think she suspects anything?"

"She suspects you're weird, whereas I know you're weird. Thanks for the tip about the restaurant though. Great view."

"Never mind that, Mr Vargas. There's been another note!"

"What?"

304

Frederick handed him a folded sheet of loose-leaf this time. "Not terribly elegant this time."

"The Wayfarer, 2300. Alone." Jorge looked at the concierge. "Did you see who delivered it?"

"It came before my shift started. Either last night or early this morning."

"Damn. What's The Wayfarer?"

"It's a bar on Amelia, a cross street just a couple of blocks up Duval."

Jorge looked at the note again. His brow tensed. He stared as if another message might materialize on the page.

"Is 2300 military time?" asked Frederick.

Jorge nodded, still absorbed in the note. "Eleven o'clock," he mumbled.

"I knew it! Will you need backup?"

The offer was so genuine it made Jorge laugh. Frederick frowned.

"I don't think so." Jorge did not know what to think, but the note, though not very illuminating, was clear on one point: he was to come unaccompanied. Jorge forced a smile. "Just another practical joke, I'm sure. Still, could we keep this to ourselves too? Nancy doesn't know this friend is in town, and I don't think she'd be too pleased to have our time together interrupted."

"I understand completely."

"You're a good guy, Frederick." Jorge extended his hand.

The concierge beamed as he shook it. "Thank you, Mr. Vargas! If there's anything else, please don't hesitate to ask."

"I won't." Jorge waved and started across the lobby.

Frederick began to chuckle. "Oh. I get it now."

Jorge turned around.

"It makes sense. The Wayfarer. I mean, if it's a practical joke and all." He laughed again, louder this time.

"What about it?"

"Let's just say it's my kind of place."

Jorge raised an eyebrow.

"Watch your back," laughed Frederick.

Jorge and Nancy spent the day by the pool despite the thunderclouds rolling in. It was quiet, and despite being just steps from Duval, secluded by comparison. Nancy lounged and dozed and read a paperback, while Jorge sat coiled like a spring. He swam laps in the pool or stalked the narrow beach alone while Nancy slept. The wait was maddening, and he racked his brain for a way to explain to his new bride that he wanted to spend a night alone. On their honeymoon. He returned to their chaise lounges. Nancy had a ball cap pulled low to cover her eyes.

"Sit down, Jorge. You're making me nervous."

"Sorry."

"Why are you so agitated today?"

"I'm not agitated."

"Please." Nancy lolled her head toward Jorge and lifted the bill of her ball cap.

"You want to go play with Frederick."

"Quiet."

"B.F.F." she said. "Best friends forever."

"I will throw your ass in this pool."

"You should go out tonight. Have some fun."

Jorge was taken aback. "What?"

"I pride myself on being one of the coolest, most perceptive women on the planet," said Nancy, "and you have been a dutiful, doting husband...mostly. You've earned a pass."

"Is this one of those tests where you say you're not mad but you really are and then you hold it against me for years?"

"Actually, you're driving me fucking crazy."

At ten o'clock, Jorge sat in the dark with his back against the headboard. Nancy's head was in his lap and he stroked her hair while she slept. He slid from beneath her and pulled the covers up to her neck. Jorge pulled on a pair of shorts and a tee shirt from the room's dresser then grabbed his tennis shoes.

He grabbed his wallet from the nightstand, and casting a final glance at his sleeping wife, made his way for the lobby. Frederick was gone. The night concierge nodded.

Jorge nodded back, took a deep breath, then stepped outside and into the vespertine madness of Fantasy Fest. It was like his first dive into the waters of the barrier reef earlier that morning. The tumult pushed him this way and that. The crowd was an undulating, colorful mass of darting images. Strings of iridescent beads shot past his head like darting yellow jacks and blue parrotfish.

On Duval Street, the parade floats loomed above the swaying crowd like billowing coral heads as they made their way north toward Mallory Square. Jorge elbowed his way through the crowd of lavish costumes, yelling drunks, drag queens, and painted breasts. Even crossing over Duval to Whitehead and travelling the side streets, it took nearly an hour to transit the few blocks to Amelia Street.

Amelia was barricaded and the crowd was much thinner than on Duval, but there was no sign for The Wayfarer, and he passed by the courtyard entrance twice before a passerby told him where it was. When he passed under the lattice archway and stepped into the courtyard, the scene came alive again. He walked among the wrought iron tables and scanned the faces of the patrons as best he could despite the large number of masks. Finally, he approached the front door and with a greeting of door chimes, entered the tavern.

At first, he was relieved to see the inside of the bar looked normal enough, but he soon realized that most of the women in the place were actually men dressed as women, and the number of real women was scant. The juxtaposition of the clientele and the nautical surroundings surprised and confused him. The thump of the house music was offset by lanterns that bathed the whole bar in a crimson glow, reminiscent of his stateroom and the corridors of *Sentinel* at night. He scanned the crowd again and they scanned him back. Not wearing an outrageous costume, he felt utterly conspicuous.

Just then, he felt a hand on his shoulder. Jorge spun around.

A Lone Ranger, complete with black mask, a bandoleer over each shoulder, and holsters for two toy pistols held his hands up. "Easy, cowboy!"

"You scared the hell out of me, Frederick." Despite himself, Jorge laughed. In fact, he had never been happier to see a familiar face.

"Did you honestly think I wasn't going to be here at twenty-three thousand?"

"Twenty-three hundred."

"Whatever. So," he said, rubbing his gloved hands together, "who are we looking for then?"

Jorge shrugged. "I have no idea."

"Regardless, you clearly need to relax. What are you drinking?"

"The most masculine drink available."

"One bahamarita coming up."

"Hurry back. I don't like the way that Marilyn Monroe with the five o'clock shadow is eyeballing me."

Jorge leaned against the wall and watched Frederick navigate the crowd, greeting people he knew on the way, tossing salutations over his shoulder. The throng of people at the long bar parted long enough for Frederick to wedge himself in to greet the bartender, an enormous bald man dressed as a pirate. They seemed to know each other, but Frederick seemed to know everyone in the bar. The pirate wore a ribbed black and white striped shirt with a stuffed parrot perched on his shoulder. Pulled to side of his shiny pate was an apparently more stylish than functional eye patch. The pirate bellowed to the other bartender, a man of normal human proportions dressed as Zorro. Zorro nodded then moved on. Before Jorge could get a closer look, a stacked drag queen dressed in a cheetah suit sidled up to him

"You look lost."

He tried to look past her to the bar, but Zorro was gone. Jorge looked at the cheetah again. She was a woman. A real woman and powerfully attractive.

"So how's that ring treating you?"

Puzzled, he looked down at his hand, then back up at her. "I'm married," he blurted.

Piper laughed. "I remember. Follow me."

"I'm...waiting for someone."

"Frederick's played his part. Come on."

"Where are we going?"

She smiled. "Behind the curtain."

"Wait," Jorge said, but she was already on the move. This is insane, he thought as he struggled to keep up with her and not to stare at the striped tail that danced just above her behind. He failed, and when he looked up again, they were on the other side of the bar and walking down a darkened hallway, past the bathrooms and the kitchen. It was nearly pitch black until she opened the door to a small office. The room was lit only by a small lamp, but it cast enough light to see Zorro leaning against the desk and smiling an incongruous smile.

"Hello, Jorge."

'I don't think that's regulation use of your officer's sword," said Jorge.

Chapter 46

They were alone in the spare office. The din of The Wayfarer sounded far away as Jorge scanned the framed aerial photographs of Old Town decorating the walls. In the middle of the room, Kelly leaned against the front of the desk. Behind him sat his Zorro's gaucho hat and mask, and a cooler.

"I think I'll need one of those," said Jorge.

Kelly handed him a bottle.

Jorge cracked it and the hiss of escaping air filled the quiet room.

Kelly raised his bottle. "A toast to the crew."

"Is that supposed to be funny?"

"No. I had friends there too. At least I was starting to. I was in Georgia when I saw it in the paper." Kelly kept his bottle raised. "To them."

Jorge relented and hoisted his. "You have a lot of explaining to do."

Kelly whistled. "Where to begin?"

Jorge allowed himself a half smile. "Start with the cheetah."

"Girlfriend."

"Oh thank God."

Kelly looked at Jorge, puzzled.

"Come on. This place."

"Oh."

"Yeah. Oh."

Kelly gestured toward the bar beyond the office. "It was weird at first, but I don't even notice anymore. They're just living their lives. Would it really matter if I was?"

Jorge squirmed.

"Relax. I'm just fucking with you."

"Really?"

Kelly held up a hand. "Who lives here reveres honor, honors duty."

"Don't quote me Academy indoctrination."

Kelly drank his beer. "Wow. You're making this tougher than I thought."

"What did you expect, I'd throw you a fucking parade? I went to your funeral. So did Nancy. Your classmates were there. Bud gave the eulogy, for Christ's sake."

"I would have liked to see it."

Jorge lunged forward and pulled Kelly off the desk by his black shirt. "You made my wife cry and you're glib? I should break your fucking neck."

"I'm already dead."

Jorge looked in Kelly's cold, dark eyes. He released him and sank into a chair in front of the desk and tried to digest the presence of his friend. "You're crazy."

"That would be a cop out." Kelly walked around behind the desk and took a seat. "I'd planned it for months. That night, I went over the side. I swam to the bay bridge tunnel then made my way back to my apartment."

"We never passed through the tunnel. We evaded in the bay."

Kelly offered a bitter smile.

Jorge made some quick calculations in his head. "Jesus."

"Yeah." Kelly sat down. Inside the small nimbus of light cast by the desk lamp, Jorge thought his friend looked worn out. "Remember the first time we were here, when my grandfather had the heart attack?"

"I remember."

"I was pretty torn up that night and I wandered into this bar. I was drunk and got into a fight. The owner followed me. He died last month, but he was an old vet. He could tell I was unhappy with my 'employer,' so long story short, he offered to help me if I ever decided to move on."

"Call it what it is. Go AWOL, you mean."

"Fine. Go AWOL, yes."

"So then what?"

"So man overboard. I left my car at the base so no one would ask any questions. I bought a Sportster, and made my way down here, then bought into the bar with the money from the house in Ocean City."

"Back up," Jorge said, laughing for the first time, "A Harley? You?"

"Anyway...it was supposed to look like an accident. Or sleepwalking. Suicide, even, I didn't care at the time. That my tracks would be covered this completely was...unexpected. Were you on watch when it happened?

"It never would have happened if I was on watch."

"I figured. In the rack then?"

"Yeah."

"Were you scared?"

"I didn't have time."

"So you didn't find the postcard?"

"I found it."

"So you had to suspect."

"Why would I? Who could even conceive of such a thing?"

"You didn't seem too surprised to see me."

Jorge looked into his beer. "I didn't know what to think."

"Well, you found me."

"You practically gave me directions. You're taking a big chance. Telling me."

"You won't rat on me now."

"And why's that?"

"You're my best friend."

Jorge pointed a finger at his chest. "I was Kelly Sensor's best friend. I don't know who you are. Jack."

"I started over. It happens a lot more than you think."

"So that makes it right?"

Kelly leaned forward and put his hands on the desk. "Don't lecture me, Jorge. You have your parents. Grandparents, a brother. A wife I'd kill for and aunts and uncles and cousins. And you used to bitch around the holidays about all of the people up your ass."

Jorge looked away.

"He was all I had. And all I needed was three days, three days off that ship to bury him. Proper. And that fuck denied me that. Just because he could."

Kelly sank back in his chair and sneered. "You don't get to judge me, Jorge."

Jorge remained quiet. He drank his beer and tried to see his friend, but Kelly sat in the shadow just beyond the lamp's glow.

Finally, Jorge said, "You had me, you fucking idiot."

Kelly opened another beer. He drummed his fingers on the desk. "Did Nancy get the flowers?"

Jorge chuckled, relieved at the tack in subject. "Nice touch."

Kelly lifted his beer and grinned.

"So now what?" asked Jorge.

"So tonight, two old friends enjoy each other's company. Tomorrow, you'll wake up with your new bride, you'll leave Key West, and you'll remember that your friend Kelly Sensor is dead, and this was all just a pleasant, albeit weird dream."

Jorge shook his head.

"No good can come from telling anyone. You know I'm right."

Jorge did, as much as hated to admit it. Everyone had already grieved. Made peace with it. No one would understand.

"All right," said Jorge.

"Let's forget this mess for a while and go outside and get fucked up like two civilized people."

"Do we have to?"

"They won't bite. Unless you ask, of course."

By the time they emerged from the office, it was late. It was raining outside, the streets were clearing, and most of the crowd had left. Kelly joined Fritz behind the bar and poured drinks for Jorge and the few remaining patrons. Jorge filled Kelly in about their shipmates and Bud and the wedding. Kelly listened and smiled, and told him about Key West. After a few more drinks, they finally loosened up enough to make fun of one another in front of Fritz. They reminisced about better times because for one night they knew they could.

Despite his misgivings, Jorge could not help but notice the change in Kelly's manner. Kelly's brow was no longer set in a perpetual furrow. When he spoke of Piper he beamed. Jorge had forgotten what Kelly's laughter sounded like long before he believed him drowned, so if he had any doubts about keeping his secret, seeing his friend slap the bar and howl and wipe away happy tears erased them for good.

Jorge looked at his watch. It was almost four. He looked around. Fritz was in the office counting the evening's take and it was just the two of them left in the bar. They were both drunk.

"So where'd your lady run off to anyway?"

"When I saw you come in, I told her I'd need some space tonight. Honestly, I think I was more surprised to see you than you were to see me. I hadn't really made up my mind."

"You left me a note."

"No, I sent you a postcard. With nothing on it."

"Whatever. Someone told me to be here tonight." He shoved off his barstool and started for the bathroom. "It was probably your girlfriend. I think she likes me."

"If you see Fritz back there, tell him to go home."

"You know, Sensor, there wasn't a soul on this planet more in need of getting laid than you—."

Jorge stopped short. There was a figure in the darkened hallway, but Jorge could not discern its features. "Here he is now," he called over his shoulder, then realized the silhouette was considerably smaller than the bartender's. A bizarre theater mask loomed out of the darkness, and Jorge stepped back, startled.

"We're closed," said Kelly.

It was just a costumed straggler, but something about the red light against the eerie mask at such a late hour made the hairs on Jorge's neck stand on end. Instead of moving past him toward the bathroom, Jorge remained there, motionless. So did the straggler. From over his shoulder, he heard Kelly put down the glass he was washing and flip the bar top over.

"I said we're closed," said Kelly.

Jorge noticed a small, hypnotic ruffle in the cloak. Against the midnight black of the garment and with the alcohol fogging his head, it took him a moment to realize he was staring at a nine-millimeter pointed at his belly.

"Kelly," he said.

"What is your problem—," his friend began, then froze when he reached Jorge.

"Look," said Jorge.

"I see it. It's all right. He just wants money. That's no problem," he said. Then to the gunman: "You'll get no problems here, man."

The ghoul waved them back with the gun. They complied. When the gunman came forward, Jorge heard the sharp reports of hard soles on the hardwood floor. He looked at Kelly, but his friend's face had gone slack.

"Two for the price of one," said the man with the gun.

Chapter 47

For one night, Kelly had believed it safe to pretend they were not in Key West at all, but somewhere else, a tavern at the Jersey shore maybe, the kind of place he and Jorge had patronized during summers on their few breaks from the Academy. Worse, he had believed that he could leave his old life behind free and clear. When the shock faded and he caught his breath, there was only the numb resignation that it was all over.

But now there was Jorge. He was in the middle of this now. And Piper. Kelly grabbed Jorge's arm and backed up. The man was rambling now, drunk.

"And in every ancient civilization," Aregood was saying, "whether it was the Egyptians or the Romans or the Greeks or the Norse, every function had its own god. It was very organized. Just like the divisions of a ship. The Romans had Apollo for the sun, Mars for war, Neptune for the sea. Orderly systems. Clean."

"What do you want?" asked Kelly.

Aregood dismissed the question with a shake of his head and waved them back with the gun. He looked annoyed.

"I'm trying to explain about Neptune. As ensigns, you answer to me. As a sea captain, I answer to him. Neptune to Jupiter, and so on and so on."

Aregood seemed to wait for an answer, but the only sound was the downpour outside. "It's a chain of command," he continued. "And if it's good enough for the gods, it's damn sure good enough for us."

"So you're going to kill me," said Kelly.

"Kill you?" Aregood laughed. "I'm here to bring you back to life."

"I'm not going back."

"Oh, you are. When I come back with you, they'll realize it was all a quest, an odyssey. Like Jason and the Argonauts. You're my ticket back to the land of the living, Sensor. You're the fleece."

"I thought you were only temporarily insane when you sacked XO," said Jorge. "But it's the kind that sticks."

Aregood swiveled the pistol toward Jorge.

"Wait!" Kelly held up his hands. "I'll make you a deal."

"You're in no position to bargain, son."

"I'll go quietly if you let him go. He was never here."

"No fucking way," said Jorge. "He's nuts."

Aregood continued to stare at Kelly, his grin as thin and cold as a crescent moon. "In all fairness, it was never about you, Vargas. All you ever really did was muddy the waters. Go. Before I change my mind."

"I'm not going anywhere.

"You should listen to your friend. I'm prepared to leave you out of this. Why get yourself into trouble?"

"Because I'm not leaving him alone with an armed lunatic."

Kelly noticed movement in the darkened corridor behind Aregood and wondered if Jorge saw it too. "Jorge," Kelly shouted, "isn't it bad enough you led him here?" He shoved Jorge hard, knocking him off his feet. "Just fucking go!"

Fritz charged from the hallway then and drove his shoulder into the base of Aregood's spine. The captain went down, and Fritz folded him up like a lawn chair. The gun skittered away toward the front door. Kelly registered the alarm in Jorge's eyes at the free gun, but Kelly was on his feet and Jorge was not.

Chapter 48

In that instant, if there was one thing Jorge imagined both he and Aregood dreaded, it was for Kelly to reach the gun first, but he did. And no sooner was it in his hand than Kelly spun on his heel. His own black cape swept behind him like a dark wind, and with a purpose that made Jorge shudder, he strode across the room to the struggling men and kicked Aregood in the face. His scabbard rattled. Aregood crumpled. Fritz leaped back.

"Jack!" yelled Fritz. A blue welt swelled on his head. "I had him."

"Back," Kelly said to bartender without looking. Fritz edged toward Jorge.

Kelly leveled the nine-millimeter at Aregood's head.

"Up," he said.

Aregood rolled over. He tried to get to his feet, but sank back to one knee. His lip was split and bleeding. Aregood wiped it with his cloak. "Dress it up however you like, Mutiny on the Bounty or whatever, but I am your commanding officer and you are AWOL, boy. You're the criminal here." He spat crimson.

Kelly cocked the hammer.

"For God's sake, Aregood," Jorge yelled, "shut the fuck up!" He did not like the look in Kelly's eyes. He would have rather have found tears or rage or fear. Something he understood. Get everyone talking, he thought. "Fritz, what happened?"

"Bastard cold-cocked me from behind. Who is he?"

"Our old captain," said Jorge.

"Oh shit," said Fritz.

Kelly settled the muzzle on Aregood's forehead as gently as a kiss.

"Okay wait," Aregood said. "You didn't remember who you were. Amnesia. We both go back to a heroes' welcome. Together."

"Aregood," Jorge said, "do yourself a favor and shut up."

"Son," Aregood continued, "everything I did was to make you a better sailor."

Kelly's eyes grew keen.

"Call me son again."

"Kelly!" yelled Jorge. He stepped forward and Kelly raised his free hand.

"Not one step closer."

"He's not worth it."

"Twenty dead sailors are worth it, Jorge."

"He has to live with that. They're all on him."

Jorge watched his friend's finger. It continued to take slack out of the trigger. Kelly looked up and Jorge recognized a smile, barely held together.

"And my three days?" asked Kelly.

Jorge shook his head.

Wind and rain rattled the windows. Jorge held his breath, thinking of what to do next.

Kelly lowered the gun.

The anxious captain met Jorge's gaze. On his forehead, a small pink circle remained.

Jorge sighed. White light flickered throughout the tavern. A moment later, the sky over Key West growled and the tumblers clattered in their stacked pyramids behind the bar.

"Now what?" asked Kelly.

Chapter 49

Crouched as he was, Aregood's cloak spilled around him, concealing his hands. He reached gingerly for his belt. His body ached, his head hurt. It was hard to think, but he waited. He would brook no more indignities.

Sensor lowered the gun. Aregood watched him remove his finger from the trigger guard.

When the thunder rumbled, Aregood unfolded the marlinspike and gathered his legs under him.

"Now what?" asked Sensor.

Aregood sprung.

Chapter 50

The folds of Aregood's cloak flowed into the folds of Kelly's own, and the captain drove him against the wall, pinning his arm. A searing coldness split his side then, followed by a rising sound like a pup baying at the moon. The howl was his, he realized, then lost all thought as his brain exploded in a cacophony of pain.

He felt the quick breaths on his face and opened his eyes.

Aregood's face, empurpled with rage, was close enough to kiss. The agony was exquisite, encompassing every breath, every instant so totally there was no escaping it, and Kelly felt each shard of every moment so acutely that time all but stopped. Over Aregood's shoulder, Jorge and Fritz dashed toward them, but they may as well have been mired in chest-deep mud. Aregood twisted his arm to regain Kelly's attention.

Reason shattered.

The captain was whispering, but Kelly could not hear anything over his own bleating. Sounds came to him as if through water. Then a single word jolted him from his pain-drenched reverie like an electric current and gave him the strength to jerk his arm free.

"Cedarbird," said Aregood, and Kelly understood.

He punched the gun into the captain's chest and squeezed the trigger. The hammer slammed home. The slide rode the wave of impact, the muzzle flashed. A shattering roar. Heat. When the slide returned to rest, Aregood was no longer there, but several feet away, on his back and no longer flinging deadly words, but mouthing them now and gasping for air as smoke curled from his chest, the very same smoke rising from the nine-millimeter in his hand. The acrid smell of the gunpowder burned Kelly's nose and he dropped the gun. His legs deserted him then, and because Aregood was no longer there to prop him up, he slid down the wall.

Kelly felt his side, found something foreign. He looked down and saw the handle of a marlinspike. "Cedarbird," he muttered. Suddenly, he felt embarrassed. He tried to conceal the handle with his fingers. He looked up and saw Aregood staring back.

The captain grinned.

Kelly fell to his side. The hardwood floor was a cool kiss on his cheek. The pain grew remote. Still, Kelly watched the other man, transfixed by his struggles for air.

Aregood stared back. Then his eyes went gray, his head lolled, and the captain was dead. Kelly looked on, and felt the same undertow begin to drag him down too, but then Jorge was sliding across the hardwood floor on his knees, upon him finally.

Chapter 51

They had been locked together like two prizefighters in a corner, grunting and elbows jutting, when Jorge heard a scream like nothing he had ever heard before. Next came the awful thunder and lightning that filled the room and froze Jorge in his tracks. Aregood exploded backward. For a moment, he watched the captain flail on the floor as the spent and pungent gunpowder bit his nostrils. A few breaths later, the man stopped sputtering and Kelly was down, on his side, his eyes closed. Jorge ran to him, dropped to his knees.

"What!" he yelled. He grabbed the front of Kelly's shirt. "What did you do?"

Kelly screamed. Jorge dropped him.

"Look," said Kelly. The word was like a tiny punch at the air. He lifted his cape.

Jorge saw the handle. "Oh, God."

The shirt was black and the lights were red. Just like the ship. When he pulled his hand back, it was sticky.

"Turn on the lights!"

Fritz complied, and the room flooded with brightness. Jorge had been kneeling in blood and had not even realized it. The small puddle around him was connected to small rivulets Jorge traced back to the black of Kelly's shirt. It looked bad, but he had no experience. Jesus, he thought, I'm a sailor.

"We need a doctor," he said.

Kelly shook his head then looked at Fritz. Fritz nodded and shot for the phone on the bar. When Jorge heard Fritz talking in a low voice, he turned back to his friend. Should he pull it out, he wondered? No, he had read somewhere that you should leave knives in. Leave it in, apply pressure. He grabbed the free end of Kelly's cape and balled it around his hands. He placed his covered hands around the sides of the marlinspike handle and pressed on Kelly's abdomen. Kelly winced, made a whistling sound.

"I'm so sorry," said Kelly. "I've made…such a mess."

Jorge looked over his shoulder at the body of his former captain.

"Jesus, Kelly. Please, just don't talk."

When Fritz returned, he said, "Tim will be here in two minutes," then to Jorge, "He said to apply pressure…"

"And?"

Fritz looked at Kelly. "Can you hold out?"

"Yeah."

"Hold out?" asked Jorge. "Wait. Is this Tim guy a doctor?"

"He takes care of things," said Fritz.

Jorge jutted his finger at the marlinspike.

"Well, a hospital can take care of that!"

"Can't," said Kelly.

Jorge turned back to his friend. "Can't?"

His friend was still eye level with his old captain on the floor. "Just sit me up."

As Jorge helped Kelly into a sitting position, Fritz came closer. "Jack," he said, "Tim said something about a trapdoor…."

Kelly stared at the bartender for a moment, then glanced at Aregood's body. Jorge had no idea what Fritz meant, but from the look on Kelly's face, it clearly meant something to him.

Jorge knelt in front of him. "It's okay, buddy. I'm calling an ambulance."

Kelly shook his head.

"Come on, man," he begged, "it's over. My head feels like it's going to explode here."

"Jack," said Fritz.

"His fucking name is Kelly!" Jorge yelled. He spun on Fritz and swung a haymaker into his stomach. It bent the mighty bartender over and for a moment they were the same height, but as Jorge tried to dash past for the phone on the bar, Fritz closed an enormous hand around his wrist and flung him backward. Jorge spiraled into a table. The stacked chairs on top tumbled onto him. Amidst the melee, there was a bang from the alley door, and both men froze. A moment later, a raw-boned old man with a large Adam's apple emerged from the same hallway Aregood had appeared from. The man surveyed the scene: the sprawled corpse in the middle of the room; Kelly in the chair, pallid and bleeding; the wheezing giant; then Jorge, the panicked newcomer, buried under an avalanche of furniture. He scratched his chin.

"Jesus H. Christ."

The old man approached Kelly and moved his friend's hand aside. He made a sound like air escaping from a tire, then looked at Aregood's body again. "You knew each other? From before?"

Kelly nodded.

The old man sighed. "Turn off those damn lights unless you want every straggler out there knocking on the door for a drink." Fritz straightened up and limped over to the lights. The room plunged into darkness again except for a few swaths of crimson from the lanterns. Jorge climbed out from under the chairs.

"Well?" the old man asked Kelly.

Kelly pointed his chin at Jorge. "He needs to go."

"Hey, wait," said Jorge. Everyone ignored him.

"I can't be here." Each word was a labor Jorge could read on Kelly's face. "You'll have to dump me."

"I suppose you have a plan for Sleeping Beauty over here?"

"*Joanna*," he grunted.

"You owe me."

"Hold on," said Jorge. "This is crazy."

Tim, still inspecting the wound, didn't bother to look at Jorge. "Considering he's

the one with the marlinspike in his gut, I'd say it's his call."

"We can't just dump him. He needs a doctor."

Tim turned to Jorge. "Friend or foe?"

Looking at the man's bobbing Adam's apple was like looking at a hypnotist's swaying watch. "He'll get a doctor," the old man said, "but if you're really his friend, then you know he'd rather get dead than get caught."

Jorge tried to stammer a response, but his adrenaline was shot and he found himself wavering. He wanted to be in bed with his wife—not to sleep, he didn't think that would ever be possible again—but to just be in bed with her again.

Tim did not wait for an answer. He gave orders to Fritz, then turned back to Jorge. "Follow us," he said. Then he and Fritz each grabbed an end of his late captain, and without a hint of fanfare or ceremony, hauled him down the dark hallway, into the alley behind The Wayfarer, and the waiting cars and driving rain beyond.

"I don't think I can walk," said Kelly.

Jorge fit his arm under Kelly and began to lift. From the edge of his vision, he could see Kelly grit his teeth, and was close enough to feel his friend's breaths, short and quick and sweet with rum on his cheek. Jorge shuffled them toward the dark hallway. "Can you see?" he asked.

"I can see."

"Then we'll make it."

Chapter 52

Desperate for a silver lining in the *Sentinel* affair, Coast Guard officials had poured over the ship's official logs and documents, the evaluations of every sailor onboard, and the transcripts of crew interviews, and in every instance their investigations revealed that Lieutenant Junior Grade Vargas had served his boat with distinction. Six months after his honeymoon, he was transferred from his interim desk job in Portsmouth to an executive officer billet on a patrol boat out of Miami, a fast track position. He knew the decision had as much to do with politics as it did with merit, but it did not bother Jorge. He believed the ocean was as much his as anyone else's. More so even. He never told Nancy what had transpired his last night in Key West. Not wanting to burden his new bride, and unsure of what to tell her even if he had wanted to, he simply packed up and drove out of Key West the morning after and did not look back.

Jack Richardson knew all of this about Jorge Vargas and more because it paid to know. Even in Key West, *Semper Paratus*, Always Ready, at least was still valid. And Jack felt better knowing he was out there, doing his duty and doing it well, in sync with the wind and the waves, at home among the birds and the fishes, and with his shell out of his pocket and brandished around his neck.

But he was out there too.

Jack tried not to think about Aregood, well past the reefs, wrapped in canvas and undulating in the dark currents. Perhaps he might have felt better had he been the one to leave him, a sense of closure maybe, or at least the absence of doubt, but timing and his injuries had not permitted it. He sat at the corner of the bar now, engrossed in his work. Every so often, his hand dropped to his side and fingered the jagged reminder of their last night together.

In the hospital, there had been police, questions. In the end, they had informed him that the final night of Fantasy Fest, with everyone drunk and in costume, in the pouring rain no less, was the perfect environment for criminals. His case was far from unique. They told him he should just be happy to be alive. He was, he had told them. He would not press it. They seemed relieved to let the matter fade.

Piper had not been as easy to placate as the police, at least not at first, but for the same reasons as Jorge, Jack never wavered from his story. To tell her the entire truth meant the possibility of losing her, and right or wrong, he could not bear that. In bed however, in the silence after making love, she too would trace her fingers across his scar.

The soft clink of glasses and boisterous laughter at the other end of the bar reminded Jack that his friend Fritz was on duty, and his darkness passed. He heard wind chimes and glanced up. A boy with a crew cut and khaki shorts stood at the door, straining to see inside the shaded tavern.

It was a nice, bright day, so Piper and Tim would be on the water. He didn't like her out there on the water, on that boat, anywhere near a place Aregood had once occupied, but how did you reason with Piper? It was like trying to argue with a hurricane. She was always home for dinner and that was enough. They still had their quiet nights together, and in the mornings, he was always up before her, ensuring she was never sent off without coffee or conversation, a pocket of light and warmth she could carry with her throughout her day.

The boy with the crew cut slumped at the bar. Fritz said something and a moment later, the boy produced a green ID card.

"Navy, huh?" asked the bartender. He glanced over at Jack.

Jack nodded.

"Hey, what's the difference between a sailor and a bucket of shit?"

The sailor shrugged.

"The bucket," said Fritz.

Despite himself, the sullen sailor joined in Fritz's laughter. "Good one," he said. "I needed that."

It seemed there were more of them coming all the time. He would need to focus in the days ahead, remain vigilant. Jack had ideas. For The Wayfarer and the island.

"Hey, another day, another kick in the peaches," said Fritz.

Jack returned to his ledger, diverting his smile.

ABOUT THE AUTHOR

Bill Schweigart is a former Coast Guard officer who currently works for the Department of Homeland Security. He lives in Arlington, VA with his wife Kate and their daughter Sidney, who provide him with all the adventure he needs. He is hard at work on his second novel.

Made in the USA
Charleston, SC
21 October 2012